THE STONE MAIDEN

The ground shook unexpectedly. Buck sprang around with a sharp exclamation. 'Get up! For heaven's sake, girl, don't be so slow!' I heard a series of bangs and bumps, a slither and jolting that grew steadily nearer. I couldn't move. He bent down and jerked me to my feet, then flung us both sideways to fall on the stony ground. Something crashed close to my head, then went bounding and tearing down the steep hillside. I shuddered, then became aware of the hard pressure of his body against me, the banging of his heart against my breast. His head moved slowly. I could sense his eyes searching my face. Then his mouth covered mine and the whole meaning of the Midsummer Festival became known to me.

The Stone Maiden

Alexandra Manners

CORONET BOOKS
Hodder and Stoughton

To Harrogate writers without whom *The Stone Maiden* might never have been written

Copyright © by Alexandra Manners

First published 1974 by Millington Ltd.,

Coronet Edition 1978

Printed and bound in Great Britain for Hodder and Stoughton Paperbacks, a division of Hodder and Stoughton Ltd., Mill Road, Dunton Green, Sevenoaks, Kent (Editorial Office: 47 Bedford Square, London, WC1 3DP) by Hunt Barnard Printing Ltd., Aylesbury, Bucks.

ISBN 0 340 22320 0

I

I stood by the window and stared out at the bright May sunlight as it lay on the red-tiled roofs and old gray stonework. The curtains flapped in a warm breeze. It brought with it the scent of wallflowers and lilac. I could hear the sleepy clucking of hens from the bottom of the garden and another sound that aroused a feeling of joy and excitement. It was my birthday, which always coincided with the town fair. Above the drowsy cackling of my grandfather's Rhode Island reds came wild snatches of fairground music. Only a short distance away there was a colorful huddle of merry-go-rounds and whirling swings. There were strange, dark faces, an alien flavor of barbaric rhythm, painted caravans.

I wondered if I would recognize any of those closed, brown faces from last year. Then I had been seventeen, only a child. Now I was a young woman, intoxicated by the intermittent blare of the hurdy-gurdies, the promise of something new and strange. Somewhere a piper played a stirring strathspey.

The fair was never the same. I could never decide if I liked it better by day or in the secret garishness of dusk. Then there were dark places between the stalls and caravans and yellow pools that lit the laughing faces of the crowds. The noise and brilliance made the elm trees in the churchyard retreat. The gravestones seem quieter in contrast. It was a funny place to have the fair, just outside the church wall.

I danced a few steps in time to the music and curtsied deeply in front of the dressing table. My face almost touched the mirror. My breath clouded it, making my reflection dim and unreal, oddly frightening. A stranger's face, in keeping with the curious atmosphere of the house in which I lived. Three hundred years old. How many people had lived, loved and died in this old dwelling? Sometimes I could feel them pressing around me as though they waited to tell me some secret that had died with them. Occasionally I seemed to see some shadow not

5

connected with the living inhabitants of the house. The dusk was worst, when the gas lighter walked the darkening streets with the long pole over his shoulder, touching the gas mantles, leaving soft pools of radiance. Then the crouching buildings took on grotesque shapes. The chimneys turned into people who waited. I could never quite decide what they waited for – or whom.

I shivered. The mist was clearing from the mirror, showing me a pale, big-eyed face splashed with small freckles, a rope of dark hair. There was a darkness behind me that was like the outline of someone else. But the house was empty but for myself. Grandfather was at his work at the railway station and my aunt was out visiting. I was waiting for Jenny, for I couldn't go to the fair without being accompanied.

I swung around, my heart hammering, but there was nothing there but the clothespress and the shadows cast by the moving curtains, curious greenish reflections shifting like the surface of the sea. I smoothed down the fresh white blouse nervously and felt the cameo brooch at my throat to make sure it was properly fastened. I put on my flat straw hat with the black band that matched my long skirt, inspected my buttoned boots, and went up the step from the bedroom and into the low-ceilinged living room. The big heavy furniture was suddenly oppressive. The clock ticked, the brasses glinted and I knew with an uneasy certainty that nothing would ever be the same.

I looked at all the familiar things that seemed subtly altered, the clipped rugs on the floor, the photographs on the chiffonier, the orange luster jug, the chenille tablecloth with the crimson bobbles.

I tried to blame it on my imagination. Nothing was ever how it seemed to other people. There were always undertones or overtones. But deep inside myself there was the conviction I wasn't alone, that Grandfather's rocking chair had moved ever so slightly. I wished Jenny would come. Her brother James was going to take us to the fair. Her parents would insist that he went too. Girls of our age must never go by ourselves however much we might prefer it. I made myself think to shut out apprehension.

Someone was walking down the flagged passage under the house. Their heel taps echoed in the confined space. I waited, holding my breath. The visitor could be for one of the other tenants of the yard. The door knocker banged once. I ran down the steep narrow staircase.

James stood on the whitened step. He raised his tall hat politely. A chill struck my heart. Jenny wasn't coming. That seemed obvious. The sunlight polished the rounded cobbles. Out of the corner of my eye I could see the shawled figure of Mrs. Rafferty crossing over to tap on Mrs. Fenton's door. The old women were great friends.

'I'm sorry, Margaret. Poor Jenny's not well. Something she's eaten, Mother thinks. I'm just off to Doctor Tait's to ask him to call. I hope you aren't too disappointed?' His cold greenish eyes were like those reflections on the bedroom wall. James never called me Maggie like everyone else. Always Margaret, prim and starched, shut up inside a hedge of convention. He hoped stiffly that I wasn't disappointed when all the time my inside churned with frustration and regret.

'It can't be helped,' I forced myself to say with a semblance of calmness. I wished I hadn't put on the straw hat. It showed eagerness and I didn't want James to sense my despair. All year I'd looked forward to today, and now the delicious expectation was turned to dust and ashes! My better feelings prevailed. 'Poor Jenny. I hope she isn't in too much pain.'

James's face warmed slightly. 'I think she'll be better in a day or two.'

'I won't keep you,' I said. 'You'll be wanting to get to the doctor's. Thank you for telling me.' Thank you for spoiling my life, for jumping on my dreams!

He hesitated for a moment as though there were something else he must say. Chill intuition touched me. James was not so cold as he always appeared. There was something in his eyes that I didn't want him to put into words. Like all other girls, I imagined the man I would meet someday, suitably chaperoned, of course, and he in no way resembled Jenny's brother. My secret love had a wild, dark face like one of the gypsies on the fairground. The distant music washed over me in a dim, regretful tide, leaving me pale and shaken with longing.

'Goodbye, James,' I whispered. 'Give Jenny my regards.' I closed the door and leaned against the carved panels. The stairs creaked as though someone crept to meet me. I shut my eyes. The day stretched ahead, infinitely long. The smells of the house encompassed me. Sparerib soup simmering, furniture polish, camphor, black lead, cabbage. There was lavender too, but it was almost submerged under those other stronger odors.

'Damnation!' I pronounced unexpectedly. The echo of the dreadful word bounded and rebounded in the enclosed place, filling me with a secret, fearful joy. I said it again, half-expecting to be blasted where I stood, but nothing happened. The music, muted behind the closed door, took on a macabre distortion.

I began to walk upstairs slowly. The tap was dripping in the scullery, and the sly sound added to my previous uneasiness. My aunt wouldn't be back for a long time. The picture on the landing looked larger than ever. It was a painting of Red Ridinghood in the forest with the wolf skulking behind a tree. She had on a blue dress and there were flowers in her plump pink hand. Her hair was impossibly gold, her cheeks round and red as apples. No one bothered to paint pictures of people like me, pale, ordinary girls with abundant and rather untidy hair. My eyes were better than hers, though, large and gray-blue, changing color with what I wore. I remembered James and the look he had given me, and my heart gave an odd twist that was half excitement and half distaste. At least I'd always have the knowledge that one person had found me worthy of his – love? – desire? – interest? Whatever it was, I would have none of it. What I wanted was a dark gypsy like Emily Brontë's Heathcliff, and if I never met him, I'd stay unwed like Aunt Sarah. Not that she really wanted to remain a spinster –

I bit my lip and thought of Josh Davidson. He'd been courting my aunt for some months, very correctly. He always came when Grandfather and I were at home, invariably at the same time, never deviating from the moment of departure by a minute. My gypsy would spend his time surprising me, always doing the unexpected! Josh didn't really like me. I could feel it in my bones. He brought us sweets every Saturday night, and though he always proferred mine politely, I could sense that he didn't altogether want to give them to me. Perhaps he resented the fact that Aunt Sarah was fond of me, that I'd live here until I was married. He made me feel like an encumbrance. I was conscious of a horrid little stab of resentment. I was here first. It wasn't my fault I was an orphan. My father had been a soldier, and after he'd been killed in the Boer War, my mother had seemed to have no will to live. It was as though she had nothing to live for. But she had me! Wasn't I worth the effort? I had a deep-rooted sense of failure for a long time after she died. It was never my mother's ghost I felt in this house, but other older shades, more vital, more interested in me.

I'd never known Father's family. He'd cut himself off from them. Whether it was his own wish or theirs, I'd never discovered. He seemed inexplicably close to me here in the dark well of the stairs. I drew a deep, uncomfortable breath at this suggestion of contact. His face was almost forgotten, but I could sense his physical presence with all of my being. The clock upstairs still ticked and the sound seemed as loud as hammer beats. The hens still clamored, and the fair music went on rising and falling like giants' breathing. I ran back to the foot of the stairs without quite knowing why.

I opened the door and almost fell out into the sunlight. A beam of light played over the brass letter box, the keyhole, the polished footscraper. James had left the imprint of his boots on the whitened step. They were large footprints, alarmingly masculine. My heart moved in piston rods of disturbance. I'd come out without my gloves, but nothing would make me go back for them. The flat, painted housefronts watched my progress up the street. Lace curtains moved and I knew that I was noticed by neighbors. I held my head high and went on my way. Something continued to direct my steps.

I was nearly at the top of Church Street when I saw a man who stared at me. Dark eyes, a brown face, black rumpled hair under a tall hat, a strong vigorous body. A white shirtfront contrasted with all the other darkness of skin and hair, cravat and clothing. He was my wild gypsy to the life, a Heathcliff poured into the garments of a gentleman and losing nothing by the transformation. How tall he was!

Our glances met for a long considering moment, and in his eyes I saw hostility. Why should he dislike me? My face flushed deeply. That one disparaging look had hurt me more than all of Josh Davidson's veiled disapproval. I turned my face away from the dark stranger, who still glowered from the other side of the street in a typically Brontë fashion. The music still played, but the magic of it was soured.

I turned the corner into the square. The fairground wasn't too busy as yet. It was early afternoon. The trees in the churchyard were covered with a film of tender green. There was lilac and the yellow cascades of laburnum. Caravans were drawn up opposite the barrack gates. My heartbeats quickened. How beautiful and mysterious it all was. Scarlet and gold paint, thin black chimneys, windows draped with lace, geraniums in pots, little rickety steps where swarthy children played and old women in shawls sat, their gold earrings flashing. And yet, for all my excitement there was a flatness over my spirits. I couldn't put that young man from my mind. His frown was a cloud that shut out brightness. He'd seemed to know me, though I knew I'd never seen him before outside my imaginings.

I began to walk through the crowd, trying to look as though I were first with this group, then with another. How different it would have been if James and Jenny had been with me. There wouldn't have been this feeling of guilt. I would have been able to hold my head proudly and laugh, enjoying myself. I didn't care for this heavy secrecy, yet something unidentifiable kept me here almost against my will.

I stopped walking abruptly. At the other side of a stall my Brontë gentleman still watched me covertly. The dark eyes held curiosity and a kind of acceptance that puzzled me. He moved forward and I fancied he meant to accost me. Hurrying sideways, I came to the merry-go-round and ran, stumbling up the steps, striking my shin as I went. Pain ran through me and my eyes filled with water. The white horses and swans looked strange in the blurred sparkle of tears. They swam, undulating like sea creatures in a cloud of whiteness and shadow. I saw the wet gleam of gold.

I pushed my hand across my eyes. The pain was lessening. The music slowed and stopped. I climbed onto one of the smooth, painted backs and grasped the long gilt pole. Out of the corner of my eye I could see the Heathcliff man at the front of the crowd. The other faces were merely blurs, meaning nothing. The merry-go-round began to revolve again, slowly to begin with. A youth with dark-golden skin and bacchanalian hair was moving in my direction. I was conscious of shock. He was coming to collect the money for the ride, and not only had I forgotten to put on my gloves but I'd left my purse behind!

The white horse was whirling around by this time, its gilded mane shivering. All the smells of the fairground were suddenly accentuated, filled with danger. Shame was added to my sense of shock. How could I explain my presence here?

I began to fumble uselessly in my pockets. The dark face that looked up at me from the crowd came and went with a smooth regularity. I fancied he smiled a little unpleasantly as though aware of my unfortunate predicament. My face burned, then turned pale. It seemed worse that he knew of my stupid absentmindedness.

The curly-haired youth was beside me now, his eyes inquiring.

'You must let me off,' I muttered. 'I've no money – '

The brown eyes flashed, the burnt-golden face changed. 'I

can't stop now. You shouldn't have got on, should you? Haven't you any friends who'll pay?'

I stared down at the Heathcliff man, although I was unable to tell him of the situation I found myself in. But it seemed that he understood. He dipped one suntanned hand into his breeches pocket and took out a coin. 'I'll pay!' he said, and threw the piece of silver to the bacchanalian youth, who caught it dexterously, flashed white teeth at me, and moved mercifully on.

Trembling, I recalled the gypsy's angry expression when he had learned that I had not my fare. What would have happened if the Brontë man had not noticed my discomfiture? I didn't care to think about it. My eyes sought out the black ones pleadingly. The brief laughter was gone from his face and the contemplating scorn returned. He seemed pleased that I was in his debt. Who was he? Why did he feel so strongly about me?

Someone was shouting. I became aware of my Aunt Sarah's voice crying, 'Maggie! Maggie! Come down, please. It's Grandfather!'

The eyes of the world seemed focused on me alone. I held onto the gilt pole as it rose and fell, wishing that the earth would open and swallow me up.

'Grandfather!' Aunt Sarah was calling with a dreadful, wild note in her voice. 'He's dead, Maggie. Dead –'

A gray blanket seemed to envelop my head and shoulders. My mind struggled in this confining mist. How could my grandfather be dead? I'd go home to find him sitting in his rocking chair, the gaslight outlining his white curls, his eyes busy with some favorite book. I thought I said, 'No! I could feel my fingers relaxing their hold on the jerking pole. The dark man's face stared up at me, the black gaze registering a warning I couldn't at first comprehend.

Then the earth, a kaleidoscope of bright color, rushed up to meet me.

I opened my eyes reluctantly. I felt very sick, and the elm trees inside the church wall were blurred and wobbly. There were faces all around me. Aunt Sarah's was nearest and I had never seen it so pale and distraught. It was usually calm and closed, revealing nothing of her thoughts. Now everyone could see her fear and pain. She had said dreadful things, but I could no longer remember what they were.

My head was hurting and I raised my hands to press at my temples. The fairground scene seemed to change, becoming shadowy and indistinct. It was as though this moment had happened to someone else a long time ago. There were shrieks and cries of pleasure more abandoned than those I had heard when I first arrived at the square. The houses around the perimeter looked oddly different. If it hadn't been for the church and the elms, I would hardly have recognized the place. And the people! What had happened to them? Their clothes were so strange. Aunt Sarah had withdrawn, for I no longer saw her. The world spun around and righted itself.

'We must get her home,' Aunt Sarah was saying, and the faces, no longer those of strangers, acquiesced and made sympathetic noises I understood.

I was supported and directed into a trap and a rug placed over my knees. Dr. Mackenzie had been returning from a call in the Walkergate, to a baby with croup, and had been summoned to the fairground. My fresh white blouse was torn and stained and I had lost my straw boater. There was dried mud on the folds of my skirt. My head still ached abominably.

It was only a short journey to Grandfather's house. Our footsteps made hollow reverberations in the passage. The polished brass of the keyhole and letter box dazzled my eyes. I managed to walk up the stairs and across the living room. The remnants of the fire glowed. The tick of the clock was remorselessly loud. The shadows pressed about us like living things, reminding me of the moment when the square had seemed to become another place, another time than this. My stomach shifted queasily.

I remembered little of being undressed and put into the high brass bedstead, clad now in a starched nightgown, long-sleeved and virginal, the patchwork quilt pulled up to my chin and the smell of lavender in my nostrils. The curtains still cast their green reflections. The door closed with a click of the latch that shut me away in uneasy quiet.

There were only snatches of recollection after that. Children running through the flagged passage, shouting 'Tallyho!' their boots clattering over the cobbles, the window glass black and shining, reflecting the ragged candle flame. There was no gas fitting in the bedroom. That was a luxury reserved only for the living room and stairs, the musty splendor of the parlor with its gilt-framed pictures, the linen valances that concealed the chair legs, the horsehair sofa that pricked my thighs when I sat

12

on it, the glass dome that covered the arrangement of branches, grasses and stuffed birds.

I woke to the sound of voices in the next room and a bar of soft light proceeding from the gap in the doorway. The door was almost closed. My stomach muscles tightened as I recognized Josh Davidson's voice, quiet, controlled but filled with a kind of urgency. 'No, Sarah. That I can't do. I want to marry you, especially now. But she's in the way, love. I want children of my own. I could love them but not someone else's bairn. She doesn't like me, Sarah. I can feel it. I'd not be fair to her. You see, I'm trying to be honest, for both our sakes. You wouldn't be happy watching bad feeling grow between Maggie and me, now would you! And she couldn't help but see how different my attitude would be to my own flesh and blood. She'd resent that and no one could blame her. The truth of the matter is that I'm not big enough to accept another man's child. It's wrong of me and I'm the first to admit it. Why can't she go to her dad's folk? You've had the burden of her long enough – '

'Never a burden,' Aunt Sarah said with a soft desperation that hurt me far more than what Josh had said. 'She's never been that.'

'But with your father gone you need someone to take care of you. I want to do that – '

'Only you can't find it in your heart to take care of Maggie.'

'I wish I could. But I'd not want our marriage based on lies.'

There was a silence in which I was aware of a gathering of fear within myself. Her father gone. That was Grandfather. Gone. That one little word had all the impact of a stone striking me above the heart. A dark world opened around me into which I was afraid I would fall. The scene at the merry-go-round returned with a horrible clarity. I'd managed to push it away until now. Grandfather was dead. The shock had led to my fall and that head injury. My aunt wanted to marry Josh Davidson and have his children, only I was in the way. Part of me admired his honesty, but the other experienced all the pain of rejection. He was right of course. We would never be compatible. Ours would be a sour relationship. Poor Aunt Sarah, who must choose between us. And being Aunt Sarah, she would put my well-being before her own. I couldn't accept her sacrifice. Somehow I must set her free to do what she so obviously wanted. Josh wasn't perfect, no one was ever that, but he was genuinely fond of her and would make her a good husband. She deserved some happiness. She had done her duty by Grandfather and by me. She'd been far kinder than my own mother, who had loved only a ghost and followed it out of life without a struggle.

'Well, Sarah?' Josh said in a heavy voice.

My body stiffened. I listened intently for her reply.

'You must let me think about it. I have to be fair to the child. Please, Josh.'

'She should be working to keep herself. She can't stay at that fancy convent now – '

'Her father left money for her education.'

'Don't tell me you used it for her keep, though, for I wouldn't believe it. There wouldn't be enough for both.'

'No.'

'Lots of girls are wed at eighteen,' Josh growled.

'Not Maggie. She's always been young for her age.'

Not anymore, I thought, my gaze fixed on that yellow gap. I thought I'd never feel young again. Marriage meant someone like James, cold green eyes like spoonsful of seawater, stiffness and lack of ease, footprints on a whitened step, strangeness. But it needn't, it needn't. It could mean someone like my glowering benefactor with his timely silver, his white smile, his dark derisive eyes. Only one rarely met anyone like the Brontë man. Where was he now and why had he singled me out for his disapproval?

'I'll be going now, Sarah. You know where to find me when your mind's made up.' Josh's footsteps moved across the room, shaking the floorboards.

'Good night,' Aunt Sarah said in a tone that could have meant 'goodbye'. She made no move to go downstairs to see him off at the door. The echoes of his tread rang out long after he was gone.

My aunt sighed heavily and came into the bedroom. 'Maggie?' she whispered softly. I lay still, not answering. She moved over to the bed and straightened the coverings, then laid a hand on my brow. Her touch was gentle. I wanted to cry out that I was awake, but I could never hide the fact that I'd heard what Josh had to say. She'd been hurt enough for one day. She stood there for a while, staring down at me. Even with my eyes closed, I was conscious of that gaze. Then she stretched out her hand again and smoothed a strand of my hair across the counterpane. I lay awake for a long time after she went to her own room, watching the sky through the uncurtained

14

windows and the black outline of the roof opposite.

Dr. Mackenzie came back to see me in the morning and seemed pleased with my progress. The hammers in my head beat less hurtfully and my sickness and dizziness had abated. 'Another day or two in bed and plenty of rest,' he told Aunt Sarah. 'Keep her quiet.'

This suited me, especially as the house was now filled with friends and relations who called with their condolences. I became used to seeing silent figures silhouetted in the doorway who stared quietly and went away again. I should have found speech impossible. Even the conversations with my aunt were an ordeal, for I was afraid she would realize what I'd overheard. My future plans depended on her thinking that my desire to contact my father's people was quite unconnected with Josh Davidson.

I was not able to go to Grandfather's funeral. I was very relieved about this. The sight of a coffin disappearing into a hole in the ground, the rattle of earth on the lid must be a traumatic experience. I preferred my own memories of the old man who had been very dear to me. I would always have this picture of him in my mind and heart. Grandfather rocking gently in his painted chair, his white hair curling, his blue eyes moving along the printed lines of a book. I would see the glass jar in which his favourite striped candies were kept on the sideboard. It was still half full, but I knew that neither my aunt nor myself would ever finish them.

I got up, thinner, rather white of face. Aunt Sarah had said nothing about my having gone to the fair unaccompanied, like the wild, young misses from Walkergate or Crawford's Alley. I don't think she had even noticed the fact in her acute distress. And Jenny, when she came to see me, kept a discreet and loyal silence. She had asked me why when we were alone, but how could I tell her that ghosts had barred my way upstairs after James's visit? That I had experienced some foreknowledge of my grandfather's death? I'd told Jenny, rather flippantly, that it was a whim but sensed that she was unsatisfied by this explanation. It was completely out of character.

It was the day after her visit that I asked Aunt Sarah about my other relatives. 'Don't you think, Aunt Sarah, that it's high time I knew something about my father's folk? I've meant to ask for ages, but lying in bed made me think much more than I've done before. It seems all wrong that I've never seen them. I think I'd like to write to them. Whatever it was that prevented Father from visiting them shouldn't make any difference now, should it? I haven't done anything wrong. Shadows don't stretch that far, do they?'

She stared at me, her face paling, her eyes suddenly alive. 'But – Why now?'

'I didn't like to say anything before. But I'm growing up and I'd feel as if I'd lost something important if I made no effort to contact them at all. I do have a right. Don't I?'

There was a silence. The fire whispered and the clock ticked. Rain beat against the windowpane and I realized the sky was dark. I held my breath and waited.

'You do have a right, Maggie. If that's what you want –'

'It is what I want.' I pleated the folds of the black skirt and fingered the cameo brooch that had been my mother's. I wore it because Father had bought it for her and I liked the thought of wearing something he had touched. We evaded each other's eyes, but I sensed my aunt's excitement, an impression of relief she tried to hide.

'There's an address in amongst your parents' papers. They live at Maidenstane. Your Grandfather Stewart was still alive the last time your father heard, but that was a long time ago. Several years. We dropped them a line when your mother died, but Mrs Drummond answered. She's your aunt.'

'Was she . . . friendly?'

'It was hard to tell. It was a formal letter. No family news was exchanged.'

'You don't know why Father quarreled with them?'

'He didn't tell me. Neither did your mother. I think your grandfather knew.'

Grandfather. He hadn't told anyone the secret and now he never would. Tears pricked the backs of my eyes. I realized for the first time how irrevocable death was. The rain made soft, weeping noises on the dim panes. I noticed the new lines around Aunt Sarah's eyes and felt a fresh pang of pity. The future held nothing of certainty for either of us. All I knew for sure was that I was going to write to the Stewarts of Maidenstane, and soon.

The rain stopped and the sun shone and it semed like an omen. Then it darkened again and the sky was the color of bad plums. There was going to be a storm. Perhaps that was the truer omen. Only time would tell.

16

2

The station was quiet. I knew the parting was going to be difficult. We stood uncomfortably beside the Gladstone bag and hatbox that held my possessions. There weren't many. Some essential changes of clothing, a new dress in a mulberry shade I hadn't worn before, one or two favorite books, some trinkets that had been Mother's, my father's photograph and his silver watch.

'You're to come straight back if you aren't happy,' Aunt Sarah said for the fourth time and began twisting a handkerchief with gloved fingers.

'I will,' I assured her. 'You mustn't worry.' But a cloud of butterflies rose up in my stomach at the thought of the coming journey. I took a last look at the familiar sights. It was easier than conversation and I'd never been very good at small talk. Two fingers of crumbling stone pointed toward the sky, remnants of the castle wall. The railway ran through what had once been the banqueting hall. Robert the Bruce had once dined here. That was before he had laid siege to the town. The rest of the ruin plunged down a steep, knobbly hillside and came to rest on the riverbank. The water wound in a great silver loop, and where it finally curved out of sight there was a cloud of purple and gray and blue that always reminded me of a lost city. I knew it was only woods and fields, but that made no difference to my conviction that if only I went there at the right time I should see the spires and towers and palaces. There was a little cottage beyond the fingers of stone. I'd often been in it, for my uncle lived there with his family. I wondered when I would see it again or my relations.

My new boots had begun to pinch a little. I felt constricted in the bottle-green dress trimmed with black braid, the short mantle and the small bonnet with the green feather, the tight black gloves. I hated to be overdressed, but Aunt Sarah had wanted me to make a good impression. I'd have preferred wearing my blouse and skirt and the straw hat, but I'd given in to her wishes. Once the journey was over I could change.

Maidenstane was in the country. Surely there would be no need to be permanently uncomfortable? The butterflies seethed and fluttered inside me. Only another minute before the express came.

I stared down at the river a little desperately. The swans were there now, floating toward the sea in a pearly chain. Would there be swans where I was going? I hoped so.

The air began to tremble with the sound of the oncoming train. Even the platform shook. The guard walked forward importantly and shouted 'Berwick!' for the benefit of those travelers who had started off at King's Cross or York.

The third-class carriages looked like the interior of an immigrant ship and were crowded to the very last place. A bench ran down the center of each compartment, a sort of frontier between the English passengers and the Scots. Folded rugs were placed on the hard wooden seats and over the unyielding edges of benches and armrests. A heated argument arose between a stout woman demanding fresh air and a thin, vinegary lady who complained of being blown away by the strong draft. 'Wouldn't take nothing to blow *you* away!' the fat matron commented.

I looked at Aunt Sarah with the beginnings of panic. The guard had been requested to find me a seat beside a respectable family, but I had lost sight of him in the sudden hurry and bustle. Out of the corner of my eye I could see the swans floating peacefully, their white feathers shadowed. When I had written to the Stewarts, I hadn't envisaged the mechanics of getting to Scotland. But there was a hard core of excitement in me now that counteracted the seeming impossibility of the journey. The train wouldn't leave until the guard gave his permission. Uncle Robert would meet me in Edinburgh. He wasn't a Stewart. He was the husband of Mrs. Drummond who had acknowledged Aunt Sarah's letter. Still, he was my uncle by marriage and that was almost the same.

'Maggie! Maggie!'

I turned my head. Jenny and James were hurrying along the platform. My already-churning insides shifted again. It was bad enough saying goodbye to Aunt Sarah. It would be worse parting from Jenny. But why had she brought James? The thought of him since that disturbing encounter on the doorstep always made me feel uncomfortable. Perhaps I was running away from James as much as I wanted to help my aunt marry Josh Davidson.

'We'd have been here sooner,' Jenny apologized, her cheeks flushed with exertion, 'but James was held up with a client.' James worked in a solicitor's office and would be a partner one day. He was good at his job. I eyed him warily. He still had that bemused look of one who had discovered something just too late and couldn't put the disappointment into words.

'It's lovely to see you,' I said to Jenny. 'Both of you.' That was an afterthought!

'You'll write, Maggie, won't you?'

'Of course.'

James stood clutching his tall hat and looking regretful as well as aloof. One couldn't warm to him however much one tried. He would always have the effect of constraining me.

'Miss Stewart!' The guard beckoned imperiously. The noise was beginning to subside in the third-class carriages. Just opposite us, a woman traveler began to suckle an infant. I saw James's face flush. He bent to pick up my portmanteau and the hatbox. I murmured my thanks and we all moved off toward the guard. Aunt Sarah looked terribly sad, but behind the sadness I detected an incipient anticipation. What if my Scots relations didn't like me once I got there? It was too late for such thoughts. They *had* to approve of me for Aunt Sarah's sake.

I was ushered into a carriage beside a gimlet-eyed lady with a very straight back and tight lips that spoke of self-will. She was accompanied by another middle-aged woman who was quite different. There was a gentleness about her brown eyes and indecisive mouth that made me feel sorry for her, for I was sure she must be a companion. Why else would she be with the severe traveler?

'You'll be quite comfortable here with Mrs. Leitch and Miss McNab,' the guard told me with a meaning look at Aunt Sarah, who was compelled to tip him. Mrs. Leitch didn't look at all pleased that I was to be inflicted upon her, but Miss McNab smiled and made room for me beside her. James put my luggage inside and stood back. There was a great deal of slamming of doors and a fierce hissing from the engine. A bell rang. The breath tightened in my throat. I remember trying to smile. I saw Jenny's face crumple and Aunt Sarah's eyes all blurred and blind. They waved and called parting admonitions, James still stiff and wooden like some toy soldier. Then the train was moving and I felt my old life draining away in little waves of poignancy. My aunt and uncle were waving vigorously from the little green in front of their cottage. A gull swooped over the roof of the train, screeching loudly, reminding me of the pier and the beaches, the cliffs and the caves. The swans were gone from sight, but I still saw them in my mind's eye, infinitely beautiful.

I didn't look at anyone for quite a long time, only clutched my bag and stared out the window. The sea was violently blue and the clifftops covered with the greenest of grass. The cliffs were red and deeply fissured. Farms and barns and scattered houses, the clean grazing cattle, all looked like toys that could be picked up and put down somewhere else. Far away, ships sailed.

The pangs of homesickness were extraordinarily strong. But this was my own choice. I must remember that. I must push away the memories of the house I had left, the steps up and down when one didn't expect them, the clipped rugs, the high bed with the patchwork quilt. Tonight I would sleep in Edinburgh. Heaven only knew where I would find myself tomorrow. My stomach muscles knotted with fresh excitement.

The fields were very beautiful. Great trees spread their shade in blue pools. Pale drifts of Queen Anne's lace overlaid the grass like a lace petticoat. The country seemed painted in prodigal richness by an uninhibited artist. A swirling tide of wild flowers swept up to whitewashed stables. I saw a pink bridge above olive-shadowed water, a pink house on the edge of a forest. There were poppies, turbulent greenery, glimpses of red soil, a blue-brown wilderness pushing aside glass bubbles of distance. Berwick seemed so far away that I could scarcely remember it.

Mrs. Leitch asked me grudgingly if I were all right, and Miss McNab smiled at me to soften the harshness of that query. I didn't mind that they seemed disinclined to indulge in conversation. Poor Miss McNab might have wished to speak to me, but it was obvious that she was supposed to defer to her employer's wishes and remain quiet unless Mrs. Leitch decreed otherwise.

I stared out at the flying countryside. There were big white daisies on a bank. They whirled past like a train of stars. I was conscious of some queer, lovely magic. Shooting stars that would carry me to what? The spirit of adventure took over from my former homesickness. Some of my tenseness disappeared.

After a while I began to feel hungry, but one sidelong look

at Mrs. Leitch's basilisk eyes stopped me from taking out the delicious spelder sandwich my aunt had thoughtfully provided me with before leaving for the station. I thought longingly of the fresh herring split up the middle, dipped in oatmeal and fried to a crisp golden brown, peppered and salted and placed between thin slices of bread and butter. I wished Aunt Sarah had not been so fussy about my chaperone for the journey. Something told me I'd have enjoyed the third-class carriage much more with its crowded humanity and warmth. I wondered how the feud between the fat woman and the thin one was progressing. It might have been amusing to have heard more of that verbal battle. Regretfully, I left my lunch unopened.

I passed the time looking covertly at the different plaid rugs and trying to decide which one the Stewarts would be entitled to wear. Queen Victoria had popularized tartan greatly. She even used it as wallpaper at Balmoral. Was Maidenstane near the Queen's Highland home? It might be very exciting living near the royal family. Maidenstane. 'Stane' meant stone. Maiden stone. Stone maiden. A little thrill of discovery crept up my spine and made me shiver in spite of my overwarm clothing.

The railway turned west, following a coastline I knew must be the Firth of Forth. I began to see valleys and parks in the sunshine, cobbled highways and bridges, houses, traffic and people. A great blue hill rose lionlike out of mist and smoke, seeming to hang over the city.

I stared entranced. How different this was from Berwick, so quiet and sedate apart from market days and the fair, the March Hirings and the Tweedmouth Feast. Even the fair lost some of its remembered luster in all this colorful activity that took place on an ordinary day. The fair. My mind went back to the scowling man and his piece of silver. I saw again his proud gypsy face, the broad shoulders and slim waist, his shining boots and elegant coat. Where had he come from? Where had he gone? Why hadn't he liked me? I would never see him again. He had obviously been passing through the town and had an hour or two to while away. And yet he seemed to recognize me.

I stopped thinking about the dark stranger when the train began to slow down. The knotted stomach muscles tightened up again as I realized I must soon meet Robert Drummond. How would he know me? All he knew was that I was to wear green. I knew nothing at all about him. What if he never came?

Mrs. Leitch began to fuss as soon as the express ground to a halt. I helped Miss McNab assemble the numerous portmanteaus and valises and deposit them onto the platform while her mistress bawled for a porter. Then I went back for my own luggage. Mrs. Leitch was all ready for departure when I returned to the busy platform. 'I hope you don't expect me to hang about here, Miss Stewart!' she said loudly. 'I haven't the time. I'm a busy woman.' I found myself reflecting dryly that it must be tiring to watch two women scurry about with one's luggage. How dreadful to be forced to summon the porter oneself!

'It's quite immaterial, Mrs. Leitch,' I told her. 'I'd rather wait for my uncle alone as it happens. I don't think I'll be kidnapped and sent to a sheikh's harem. Not in broad daylight and with so many witnesses. Thank you for looking after me.' I looked very pointedly at Miss McNab as I made my last remark. Mrs. Leitch, at a loss for words, stared at me angrily, then turned her back to follow the laden porter, her shoulders disapprovingly stiff. Miss McNab's eyes gleamed for a moment. She smiled, not the gentle deprecating smile I had noted up to now, but a full-bodied grin.

'McNab!'

She broke into a smart trot, clutching two hatboxes that swung about as she scurried in Mrs. Leitch's wake. I watched her until she had disappeared from sight. Poor, poor Miss McNab who was so much more a lady than her mistress had ever been. Maiden ladies never had a fair deal from life. I made a mental vow not to remain a spinster all my days. Even James would be preferable to Mrs. Leitch. Or would he? A companion would have some time alone in the solitude of her room. One shared one's husband's chamber.

No one had so far spoken to me. I picked up my things and began to walk slowly toward the ticket barrier. The crowd of passengers was already thinning out. None of the persons on the other side of the rail seemed to be interested in me. I showed my ticket and passed through the gate. There were a number of men of all shapes and sizes, old, young, shifty, benevolent, handsome, ugly, saintly, lecherous. I stood patiently, watching them approach other travelers, drifting toward exits, gradually dispersing.

A clock boomed out the hour. A chill swept over me. Uncle Robert had not come.

22

I waited. Perhaps he had mistaken my time of arrival? Or even the day! Common sense reasserted itself. Unless he were very absentminded, either event seemed unlikely. There had been some breakdown. He would come eventually. And even if he didn't, it wouldn't be the end of the world. I would inquire at the office as to the best way to travel the rest of the way to Maidenstane. There was always a way out. Always . . .

It was a quarter of an hour later that I noticed the man in the plaid suit. The checks were large and aggressive. His rather full paunch strained against the fancy waistcoat, across which stretched the opulent gold links of a watch chain. The tipped bowler concealed much of his face. Only the eyes were alive above the sensual red of his lips. I wished he would remove his intent gaze. There was something about him that repelled me. My flippant remarks to Mrs. Leitch seemed not so amusing now. He went on leaning against one of the station pillars until I went some distance away. Then, when I had just put down my Gladstone bag, he was there, only a yard from where I stood. He couldn't be my uncle. Robert Drummond was a Scottish country gentleman. This man was obviously a town dweller, one of the 'heavy swells' I had heard about from Jenny, who was surprisingly sophisticated for being a sister of James. It was Jenny who had read Ouida and was full of entrancing, wicked, romantic stories as a result, all about cold, handsome, dashing men in riding boots who whipped their lady friends and gave them scent bottles with silver stoppers.

The man in the plaid suit smiled. I frowned and looked the other way.

'Hasn't he turned up, then?' I hated his voice. There was a hoarse, insinuating undertone to it that grated on my nerve ends. I pretended not to hear, but I had a panicky feeling that I'd find it hard to rid myself of him. I wished Mrs. Leitch had stayed until Uncle Robert came. How late he was!

A shadow fell over my arm and a little shock of fear stabbed me. The man was leaning toward me with a confidential air. 'I know a place where we could eat. Somewhere nice and private. Coming, dear?'

I bent down and picked up my luggage, almost running away from him. There were two railwaymen engaged in conversation near a barrier so I took up my position beside them. Only loose women loitered in public places without an escort or chaperone. My face burned with humiliation. Any other woman but Mrs. Leitch would have had more sense of responsibility. They would have seen me in safe hands before they left the station. Even if I hadn't been rude to her, she wouldn't have stayed.

The man waited at a safe distance like a vulture at the edge of a battlefield. I wouldn't go with him to an eating place if he were the last man on earth! I remembered my spelder sandwich nostalgically. I was quite hungry, I discovered.

Just as I was about to accost one of the railwaymen whose conversation showed signs of finishing, I saw a tall man striding toward me, a pretty girl at his side. The man wore a kilt and tartan stockings and a tweed jacket that strained over immense shoulders. His hair was thick, what I could see of it under the Highland bonnet, and his brown beard curled. His skin was brown too. He was a splendid sight, a Rob Roy of a man.

The girl was tall and slender. She wore a cool, pale dress, much more suited to the weather than my green and black outfit. I had an impression of lazy grace, of peat-colored eyes that gleamed in the fugitive sunlight that found its way to this spot alone, eyes that seemed to conceal amusement.

'Miss Margaret Stewart?' the big man asked. His voice was deep and pleasant.

'Yes. Are you Robert Drummond?'

'Oh, thank heavens you had the sense to wait. We couldn't get here in time. Shiona was unwell on the way to Waverley –' He went on talking. Shiona. It suited her, a beautiful name for a lovely girl. She must be the loveliest girl I had ever seen.

'I'm so sorry,' she said with charming compunction. 'You must have been very worried. Were you?'

I nodded. The man in the plaid suit was still there. He made a small, regretful moue I found inexpressibly repugnant and began to move away slowly. I found that I was trembling with reaction.

'Poor – Maggie, isn't it?' Even her voice was infused with a delightful mockery. She didn't look like someone who had been ill on the way to the station. I wondered what had been wrong with her. Still more, I wondered just who she was.

'Shiona, of course, is your cousin.' Uncle Robert was evidently a mind reader. I saw his eyes for the first time, dark and curiously penetrating, watching me closely.

She was older than I, I thought. Or was it only because she was so superbly self-possessed? 'How do you do?' I said conventionally.

'I'm better now,' Shiona replied, smiling. Her dress was the

24

color of tea roses, and the beam of sunlight edged the tawny
hair she wore braided Greek fashion. She had no hat and I
fancied she eyed mine a little satirically. More then ever I felt
overdressed and awkward, wishing I had insisted on the white
blouse and comfortable skirt.

'Are you hungry, Maggie?' my uncle asked, picking up my
portmanteau.

'Oh, yes. I am rather.'

'I think there was real feeling there,' he commented. 'We'll
take a cab to the hotel. And afterward you must see something
of the city.'

'Aren't we going straight to Maidenstane?' I tried, unsuccess-
fully, to keep up with his long strides. Shiona seemed to flow
along the ground but I had almost to run. My boots were pinch-
ing again. I had tantalizing thoughts of a bath, of long, cool
drinks. Every now and again I felt Shiona's eyes on my profile,
studying my hat and the overwarm mantle.

Outside the station, Uncle Robert signaled to the driver of a
passing 'growler', and we climbed into the rather stuffy interior.
I was definitely relieved to be on my way to food, water and
the prospect of a comfortable bed. The streets were crowded
with other vehicles. I wondered how it would feel to travel by
hansom, but as there were three of us and hansom cabs only
seated two, I didn't think I would ever find out. The gray,
majestic shapes of ten-story houses rose against the skyline. A
wide, pleasant street stretched into the distance, and at the very
end of it a castle glowered on a crag. I thought it theatrical.

'This is Princes Street,' my uncle told me, noting my fascinated gaze. 'They say if one stands here for any length of
time, one sees the rest of the world pass by.'

'Don't take that too literally, though,' Shiona said softly, the
corners of her lovely mouth amused. I thought she found her
young cousin vastly entertaining. Staring out at the hundreds
of walkers who crowded the pavements, my heart gave a sudden, disconcerting plunge. A man was coming in the direction
of the station, a large young man with a country tan, his face
shaded by a tall hat, his strong body encased in a well-cut coat
and tight fashionable trousers. There was a gypsy darkness
about him. Surely his profile was that of the man at the fair? I
was almost certain I was right. But people walking in the other
direction obscured my view and the 'growler' turned up a side
street just beyond a monument that appeared to be made of
black lace, hiding him from view most decisively. To my sur-

25

prise, Shiona had stopped smiling and was now quite pale. I remembered that the reason for their lateness had been her indisposition. Fortunately, the cab had stopped in a pleasant square in the center of which was a little railed park, where nannies sat with infants in perambulators and watched toddlers playing in the sunshine with their hoops and whipping tops and balls.

Uncle Robert paid the cabdriver and picked up my luggage. We followed him up the steps of an imposing building with a pillared porch and dimly lit hall. A woman in black handed him a key, and a small boy in a page's uniform scuttled ahead of us with the portmanteau and hatbox. The hotel was filled with threadbare floral carpets and damask curtains with faded tassels. I saw a quite bewildering number of doors. How should I ever find my way around this place?

Our rooms all were in the same corridor, I was thankful to note. My bedchamber seemed to belong more rightly to some old castle in which generations of lords and ladies had passed away. The bed was a sinister-looking four-poster with curtains of rusty red. A smell of fat pervaded the room, obviously rising from the kitchens. Shiona wrinkled her nose and departed for her own bedroom. Uncle Robert hesitated. It seemed he had something private to say to me.

'Your aunt and I were impressed by your letter, Maggie.'

'Oh?' I looked at him blankly. I'd considered it a poor letter, hesitant and difficult to compose. A trifle ink-stained, too, if I remembered rightly.

'It was kind of you to be so concerned for your Aunt Sarah's well-being. You were perfectly right to be completely honest about your reasons for coming to Maidenstane at long last. To be quite truthful, we'd given up hope of ever seeing any of Alex's family. Your Aunt Margaret and I never agreed with the quarrel between Alex and his father being kept up for so long. He's a very obstinate old man, your Grandfather Stewart. Your father was too. They were alike. Too alike –'

'It – it wasn't only because I wanted Aunt Sarah to get married to Josh. I – I always wondered what you were all like – and to see Maidenstane.'

'And so you shall, child. You don't mind being buried?' His gaze pierced me.

'Buried?' My eyes grew wider still. A draft made the blood-red curtains sway. They were the color of old blood – very old – I felt a little sick.

'Stuck away in the wilds. It's remote.'

'Oh, no.' The sickness subsided. 'I'm sure I shall like that.'

'Good. Well, I'll leave you to wash and get ready for dinner. Half an hour be long enough?'

'Yes, thank you.' I was very aware of his dark scrutiny. How hypnotic his eyes were! As he closed the door behind him, the curtains rustled and whispered like conspirators. I found them unnerving.

I was washed and engaged in brushing my hair when there was a light tap at the door. 'Who is it?' I called. I was standing at the dressing table in stays and camisole and wasn't dressed to receive callers. The door began to open and I snatched up my nightdress and held it in front of me, half imagining the stealthy advent of the plaid-suited masher I'd seen at Waverly Station.

It was Shiona, beautiful and elegant, her hair smoothed to perfection, all her pallor gone. She began to laugh when she saw me half-concealed, my eyes apprehensive over the barrier of white cambric. 'I can still see your drawers, you goose! Just imagine if it had been a man! Oh, Maggie. It's going to be such fun having you at home. Oh, dear, what gloomy curtains they've given you.' She fingered the rusty folds. 'You'd think they'd been subjected to an endless succession of murders, wouldn't you? That reminds me, have you seen the place where Rizzio was stabbed to death? Fascinating. There's a great splotch on the floorboards just the color of these. Now, what did I come in here for? Oh, yes. You looked so hot, poor sweet. I wondered if you'd like to borrow this? I think we're much of a size, though I'm taller. This happens to be on the short side for me.'

I saw, for the first time, the dress she carried over her arm. It was light-colored, like her own, and the material was a turquoise shade that I'd always liked particularly. I lowered my nightdress a little self-consciously, aware of her smiling mouth. 'It's – it's lovely. Aren't you worried I might spoil it?'

'Not you, Maggie. You don't spoil things. You look a very careful, upright little creature to me. And with such a conscience! Oh, I heard all about your letter from Mother and Father. You quite captivated them before they'd even seen you.' The peat-brown eyes glowed.

'I'd like to borrow the dress very much,' I said awkwardly.

'I'm only sorry I can't give you it, but having another sister, I'm expected to pass on the good ones for her benefit. Not that Fran would look as pretty as you in it.'

27

'Fran?'

'Short for Frances. You'll meet her soon enough so I won't say too much about her. It's best if you form your own impressions. One can be so misled by the opinions of others. She's just your age.'

I took the dress with a feeling of disquiet. Something in Shiona's voice sounded like a warning. I had the strong conviction that she disliked Frances and expected me to do likewise.

'I'll let you finish dressing then.' Shiona bent forward and kissed my brow. 'I think we'll be friends, don't you?' She smelled of some subtle perfume I liked. I imagined it belonging in a cut-glass bottle with a silver stopper like the ones in Ouida's books. All my previous excitement rose to overwhelm me. I could feel my cheeks grow warm.

'We'll be friends, I know,' I murmured.

'Good.' She laughed gently and went out of the room, closing the door so quietly that the bed hangings scarcely moved at all. I held up the dress, hardly believing my luck. I'd never anticipated having a friend like Shiona. She was so attractive, said such unexpected things, was so considerate and such fun.

I was ready when Uncle Robert came for me, looking more magnificent than ever without his bonnet and changed into a black velvet jacket. 'You look nice in that,' he said.

'It's Shiona's,' I told him, pleased.

'Is it? I never notice clothes. It's the general effect I see. The same with everything. Details escape me.' He took my arm in his. I was proud to be seen with him.

We collected Shiona and went to the dining room. It was immensely high, very rococo and filled with scattered tables where people sat eating and talking. There were two Jews in olive-colored waistcoats and dark-blue coats with large buttons. Uncle Robert told me they were Christian Israelites. The other diners were more conventionally dressed, but no one was so arresting as my uncle or my cousin. Several people glanced at them, all with interest. Even I felt prettier than usual, for the pale turquoise suited me, showing off my thick black hair and gray-blue eyes to advantage. I was glad I'd kept on my newer boots, for they were more elegant than the comfortable ones. I didn't feel like myself at all but some complete stranger. The girl at the fair, who had lived in the house in Church Street, no longer existed. The memory of Aunt Sarah and Josh Davidson dimmed and receded. I was in a hotel – my first ever – in a

28

great, exciting city, with colorful, exotic people totally unlike James or even Jenny.

There was roast mutton for dinner. I had expected this after the smell of fat in the upstairs room. Shiona toyed with hers, but I enjoyed mine after the long fast. All she seemed to eat was the barley broth which was served first.

'Shouldn't we tell Maggie about Kate Graham?' my cousin suggested when we had reached the dessert orange and preserved fruit stage.

'Kate Graham?' I stared at them across the table. 'Who's she?'

'Our next-door neighbor,' she said. 'She really ought to know, Father.'

'How could she concern me?' I asked, disturbed by the expression in her eyes. 'I've never been to Maidenstane. She can't possibly know of my existence.'

'She does, though. She knows everything about you and your father and mother.'

'But – how? Why?' The sweetness of the preserved fruit became cloying.

'Shiona's right,' Uncle Robert said slowly, wiping his lips with his napkin. 'It would be better if you were prepared.'

My uneasiness intensified. I had already been prepared to meet Frances, now this unknown woman who apparently spied on what couldn't possibly be her affair.

'You'd better tell me, then, hadn't you?' I suggested. A tightness enclosed my throat.

'Kate Graham – Buchanan as she was then – was once engaged to your father.'

'Oh' was all I could think of as a reply. 'No one said – '

'I don't suppose they told your mother's relations.'

'I believe . . . Grandfather knew.'

'That was the reason for your father's estrangement from his own family. You see he left her at the altar – '

'Oh, he shouldn't have done that!' I said, distressed. 'So late – '

'He'd met your mother in Berwick. He was held up there on a journey from London. Some rail breakdown. He stayed at your grandfather's. Someone recommended them. He was deeply attracted to your mother. When he got to Maidenstane, he couldn't put her out of his mind. Kate went on with her wedding preparations and he found he couldn't tell her his feelings had changed. Kate was a beautiful, headstrong girl in those days. I remember her well as she was then. All the young men for miles around wanted to marry her. Your father was considered fortunate to have won her. He couldn't bear to hurt her feelings, you see. He was essentially a kind man – '

'Yes,' I said abruptly. 'Yes. He was.'

'He thought he could go through with the marriage until the very last day. Then he knew it was impossible. But Kate had already left for the church when he went to the house. I think that was what she couldn't forgive. Waiting in the public eye for someone who never came. Alex's father couldn't forgive him either. He adored Kate – still does. I've never seen him so angry. He and Alex had a dreadful quarrel, then Alex left. Kate was bitter for a long time. She married Johnnie Graham, but it wasn't a happy marriage. And Alex married your mother – '

'They were happy. Mother couldn't bear to live without him when he was killed. She just . . . let herself die – ' My voice broke.

'Kate wouldn't have done that. Kate was always a fighter. Buck takes after her – '

'Buck?'

'Kate's son. She called him Buchanan after her family, but it's rather a mouthful. Anyway, Buck suits him. Doesn't it, Shiona?'

There was a long silence. I raised unhappy eyes to meet Shiona's. She looked like a stranger, all the smiling warmth shut away. Buck Graham meant something to my cousin, of that I was certain. And whatever it was, I didn't like what that emotion did to her. She was much, much too good for Kate Buchanan's son. Hers was not a happy face. He couldn't be good for her.

'It does suit him,' she murmured at last. 'I can't imagine him with any other name.' She smiled now, but it was a pale imitation of her former amusement. Her hands trembled ever so slightly.

I thought I could quite easily hate Buck Graham as much as his mother probably hated me.

3

We didn't go straight to Maidenstane as I had expected. Shiona
had prevailed upon her father to spend one more day in Edinburgh before she was 'buried' again. I thought it would be very
easy for my cousin always to have her own way, for she had a
charming method of overcoming opposition. Her smile and a
look from her golden-brown eyes were enough. There was
a dark side to her imagination as I'd already discovered after
her remarks about Rizzio's bloodstain and the color of my bed
curtains. Sleepless, as I found myself after such an eventful day,
those curtains pressed around me in the dark like a coven of
witches or crows with blood-dappled beaks. If she had known
how active my imagination was, I don't think Shiona would
have said what she did. She probably thought me a very prosaic
miss indeed. But she liked me enough to seek my friendship.
That was good. Very good.

I did sleep eventually, as one always does, and woke to
brilliant sunshine streaming in pools across the windowsill.
Breakfast was a more pleasant meal than dinner last night.
There was wheaten bread, oatcakes and Dundee marmalade. A
waiter brought the visitors' book and I signed my name very
importantly. Margaret Anne Stewart. Shiona's second name
was Margaret, so I felt we had another bond. Uncle Robert confessed that he was always known as Rob and that was what I
was to call him in the future.

Edinburgh was a delight. There were picturesque rock land-
scapes, and the High Street was crammed with interest. It ran
down the spine of a hill dominated at one end by the castle
and dropping at the other to the wide valley where Holyrood
Palace lay in the shadow of Salisbury Crags and the purple
mound of Arthur's Seat. Shiona wanted to go back to Holyrood. She showed me a miserable little building she swore was
Queen Mary's bathhouse. Inside, the palace was much more
inspiring apart from the portrait gallery, which contained one
hundred and ten portraits of Scottish kings, right from Fergus
I, 330 B.C., to Charles Stuart, who needs no introduction. I was

astonished when I saw them. 'But they all look the same! They are the same! They couldn't have looked so alike. It isn't possible.'

Shiona laughed. 'They didn't! A gentleman called Jacob de Witt was commissioned to paint them. The walls must have looked bare or something like that. How much was he paid, Father?'

'Two hundred and forty pounds.'

I stared down the long room. 'They had a good bargain.' This made Shiona laugh harder than ever. 'Oh, Maggie. Life is going to be much more amusing, I can see.'

'But – only two pounds a picture!' I was impressed.

Uncle Rob started to laugh then and I felt a little foolish. It would have been better, of course, if the features had been different, but how was De Witt supposed to know what Fergus and all those Alexanders and Roberts and Jameses *had* looked like when they were already dead?

The queen's apartments were quite eerie – Queen Mary, that was. I had a horrible claustrophobic feeling in the little wood-panelled supper room. 'That's where she stood the night Rizzio, her secretary, was murdered,' Shiona told me. 'Ruthven stuck a pistol in her side. They say that's why James was born with such a mortal terror of firearms. And that's where Rizzio groveled on the floor, hanging onto the Queen's skirts.' Her voice had changed as she spoke. It was filled with a scorn that I knew wasn't entirely for poor Rizzio. 'Come and see where the bloodstain is. See? There you are. They say he was stabbed nearly sixty times. It was Darnley's doing. He was jealous.'

I stared down at the floor where the dull, irregular patch still showed. There was an unpleasant drumming sensation in my head, a queer throbbing that reminded me of the square at Berwick after my fall from the white horse. The whole place was subtly different, the smells, the atmosphere, even the people. The bloodstain was no longer dull and rusty. It was new and fresh and smelled sickeningly of a slaughterhouse.

Someone pulled at my arm urgently. 'Maggie! Are you all right?'

I saw Shiona watching me anxiously. Her tongue crept over her lower lip. 'Are you? All right?'

'Yes. I felt funny for a moment. It's happened before. It only lasts for a moment. It's as if – '

'As if what?' Her voice was curiously hushed.

'As if a little crack opened in the past and I looked into it. Then it closes up again.'

'How very odd.' Her eyes went past me and widened with shock. 'Why, Buck!' All the color drained away from her cheeks, leaving them paper white. Her eyes had darkened and hardened into topaz. She looked suddenly older and more finely drawn. I turned away from the stain on the floor. It was almost inevitable that the person who stood there was the Brontë man. I was almost as shocked as Shiona appeared to be.

Strangely enough, he wasn't looking at her as one would have expected with her extravagant beauty, but at me. There was doubt in his handsome eyes, his lips were set in a disapproving line. Buck Graham. The name rang through my head in almost as unpleasant a fashion as that nasty moment when the palace interior had seemed dark and different and the blood-stain fresh.

Shiona recovered first. She laughed lightly, some of the lovely color restored to her cheeks. 'Well! Talk of the devil!'

'Were you talking about me?' Buck Graham asked. 'Hadn't you anything better to do?'

'Merely filling in our immediate neighborhood for Maggie. She's coming to live with us. Buck, meet Margaret Stewart – from Berwick. This, as you've gathered, is Buchanan Graham.'

'Living with you?' The black eyes flickered, rested on me briefly, passed on.

'Don't make it sound as if the poor child's being thrown into a snake pit!' The peat-brown eyes challenged his. I was glad Shiona wasn't going to allow herself to be intimidated. 'I, for one, am looking forward to having her.'

'I hope you'll enjoy your stay,' he said distantly, without showing any trace of recognition. Could he have forgotten me so quickly? It was only a few weeks since my fall and his eyes looked remarkably observant. Of course, I was still wearing the turquoise dress, which made me look very different. Then I remembered Kate Graham and her apparent obsession with my family and knew that he only pretended we were strangers. He had been sent to spy on me for some reason known only to himself and his strong-minded mother. She would be like Mrs. Leitch, cruel and uncaring.

'I'm sure she will,' Shiona said quickly. 'She's so amusing everyone will love her on sight. As I did.' Her head was held high, exposing the exquisite line of her throat. I saw Buck's gaze fixed on it as on something well remembered. He must have known her all his life. Somehow he had hurt my cousin and I would dislike anyone who wished her harm. She was so defensive that he must have hurt her.

'You always liked to be amused,' Buck replied softly as though I were not there. I had the odd feeling they were fighting a duel with words but would have preferred weapons. Shiona's hands clenched until the knuckles were white.

'Of course. I hate boredom. Some people are naturally dull. I prefer life with a bite in it. What's wrong with that?' Again that strong current of feeling passing between man and girl.

'Twist everything to suit yourself. That's a beautiful woman's privilege, I suppose.'

'Naturally! You mustn't become as stuffy as everyone else, Buck. That's your greatest asset. That dangerous moodiness that gathers about you like mist over the hill and only parts occasionally to show some lowering gulley or rock face. You must never show yourself in the full blaze of the sun. To know all is to destroy illusion.'

'I'd never dream of arguing with you, She-She.' His mouth twisted into the travesty of a smile. 'But I'm sure we're boring Miss Stewart.'

'Not at all,' I answered with surprising self-possession. 'I'm fascinated. Do, please go on. It's better than the theater.'

Shiona laughed delightedly. 'See what I mean? She's alive and unexpected.'

The black eyes were turned on me with heart-stopping effect. He was impossibly attractive, a male equivalent of Shiona. It would be difficult to find anyone better-looking than either of them. Standing there together, they exuded a dangerous alchemy, a kind of poisonous charm that could conceal something very different.

'Didn't know you were in Edinburgh, Buck.' Uncle Rob had returned from his solitary investigation of Lord Darnley's bedchamber. How quietly he had come for such a big man.

'Business, Rob. But I had an hour to spare before my next appointment, and as I was practically at the gates of Holyrood, well –'

'Kate keeping well?'

Buck's eyes slid to meet mine, then returned to their scrutiny of my uncle. 'Quite well.'

'Father keeps asking when she's coming to see him.' That would be Grandfather Stewart.

'I'll pass on the message.'

34

'What about yourself?' Uncle's voice showed curiosity. 'Never see you either.'

'I've been ... busy.'

'Don't think we've seen you since poor Roddy died.'

A heavy silence fell. Buck looked quite pale. Shiona was pretending to study a piece of carving, her small foot tapping all the while.

'Come soon,' Uncle Rob said awkwardly. He was obviously aware of the threatening nature of the silence without understanding the cause for it. I only wished I did. Who was Roddy and how had he met his end? A cold wind seemed to blow down the passages of Holyrood, disturbing the tapestries. Disturbing us too. Shiona's gaiety had evaporated. Uncle Rob's face was set and heavy, all the pleasant liveliness gone. Buck, still gray under the tan, bowed slightly and said, 'I must go now. Excuse me.'

I stared after him until he had gone from sight. I was attracted and repelled at the same time. How was it possible to arouse such differing emotions in a person, I wondered? Uncle Rob had moved away and I prepared to follow. Shiona laid a hand on my arm. 'A word of warning,' she said, a little unwillingly. 'Be careful. Buck uses people. For his own amusement. He lets them think he's fond of them, and then' – she spread out her hands expressively – 'finish!'

How could he have used Shiona so? She made everyone seem dull in comparison, like a piece of gold tissue in a drawer full of rags. I hated Buck Graham violently. The lines of hurt were smoothing out in her face but her eyes were still bruised. Our footsteps echoed on stone. 'Who was Roddy?' I asked since Uncle was out of earshot. 'And how did he die?'

Shiona averted her face to look at an oil painting. 'Roddy? He was a cousin of Buck's.' Her voice was curiously light and childlike. 'He was found drowned in the loch, just beside the Stone Maiden. His body was tangled up in the weeds, poor boy. People thought it very odd. He was such a strong swimmer, you see. Buck too. They were always together.'

I was conscious of a cold chill of disappointment. It was almost as though I hadn't wanted Buck to be mixed up in any unpleasantness. Why, when I disliked him so!

'The Stone Maiden?'

'Aye. It's an island by the loch side. The village is called after it,' Shiona said carelessly.

So, it had been just as I'd thought. Maidenstane had its

origins in legend. Maiden of stone. Stone maiden, and a poor boy caught up in the weeds of her hair. A boy who invariably went swimming with Buck Graham. Who was now dead.

We were in the Canongate before I pushed the thought from my mind. The narrow street was crowded with people walking and the inevitable traffic. Uncle Rob talked interestingly about the twenty-five earls who once had palaces here. 'You'd have found them disappointing,' he told me, seeing my expression. 'They were merely fortresses, plain things of stone with but the necessary apertures for entry, exit and for seeing through. And yonder's John Knox's house.' We were just coming into the High Street again. 'See that doll in the window? It's an effigy of him, supposedly addressing the people.' I secretly considered the brightly colored doll sinister. Its face was sharp and unattractive. Not at all like Buck Graham's. I flushed with annoyance that I still thought about him. We saw the Tron Church and some very dirty hawkers, street preachers exhorting us to practice Christian love. Later we went up to St. Anthony's spring, where poor children were selling tin mugs filled with water taken from it. I bought one, feeling sorry for the tattered urchins who seemed to have nothing. Shiona seemed not to notice them. I fancied she was still brooding about the meeting with Buck. The crags and the great mound of Arthur's Seat were dramatic. The castle at the other end of Princes Street had a kind of imperishable ugliness that left a strong impression upon my senses. A sound of pipes came from far off, small and tantalizingly sad. I wanted to cry for something I could never explain, even to myself.

We went to bed early after our day of sight-seeing, as we had a long day of travel ahead. I lay in the dusk, not tired enough for sleep, very aware of the footsteps in the hotel passage, snatches of muted conversations that never properly began or ended, little bursts of laughter, the thud of closing doors. I would like to have tapped on Shiona's door and been invited into her room for a talk, but it might have seemed like presumption. She did not come to me either. I was very aware of her presence so close and yet so far away. I was conscious, too, of the rusty bed hangings swaying on either side of me and longed in a foolish, childish way for my brass bed and the familiarity of the patchwork quilt. I fell asleep to have a peculiarly horrible dream in which Buck Graham stabbed ceaselessly at a body which was caught in reeds so that the water became discolored and flowed an unpleasant red like old, old blood.

I woke, sweating, to a conviction that my room was not empty. I sat up, the banging of my heart so loud that I thought others could hear it. Pressing my back against the padded tester, I stared into the dimness. There was someone there, a long pale shape that terrified me by its immobility. 'Who's there?' I asked. 'Who is it?'

'It's only me, goose,' Shiona's voice drifted lazily out of the shadows. 'I thought I heard you cry out. What was it, love? A bad dream?'

I nodded, then realized she couldn't see me sitting rigid in the darkness of the four-poster. 'That was it.'

'Want to talk about it?'

I remembered the loch water, brown and rusted, the purposeful arm that thrust and went on thrusting, a blind face caught in distorted moonlight. 'No.' I shivered.

'Very well, Maggie. Be all right, will you?' Shiona, I noticed, sometimes had her father's habit of not starting all her sentences conventionally.

'Fine,' I told her bravely but untruthfully.

'Would you like me to stay?'

The dead face in moonlight still stared at me from the darkness beyond her. 'Only if you want to.'

'Of course I want to. Goose!' She gave her pretty, warm laugh and turned back the covers so that she could get in beside me. I lay tense and wide awake, sensing her vitality and kindness.

'I shouldn't have said what I did about those curtains,' she whispered. 'It was that, wasn't it?'

I was surprised that she should have remembered. It had seemed an idle remark, sandwiched between two more important ones. Shiona had taken the trouble to find out the cause of my fear. I was very grateful.

'Good night, Maggie. Or should I say good morning?' She gave a little conspiratorial giggle and turned to face the other side of the bed.

The night was bearable with her in the room, yet sometime, just before dawn, that little crack into the past seemed to open for a heartbeat of time and the sleeping figure of Shiona became someone quite different.

At breakfast, Uncle Rob told me we would be traveling to Stirling, via Granton, and from there to our eventual destination of Maidenstane. The journey by train to Granton took seven minutes. A stream of people crowded energetically into the open from the station buildings. Quays, basins and wharves met my eyes, all strange and new and chill under a thunderous sky.

'We'll be lucky if the rain keeps off,' Uncle Rob observed. 'You were wise to change back to your warmer outfit. It gets cold on the steamer.' I had discovered this for myself when Grandfather and I had gone once on a boat trip to the Farne Islands. But in any case, I could never have risked spoiling Shiona's turquoise dress on the journey. It was, after all, intended for Frances. A little chill, unconnected with the weather, crept over my spirits at the thought of cousin Fran. How different Shiona's voice had sounded from the way she spoke to me. No warmth, no sisterliness, nothing I could recognize. I had a premonition Fran would prove to be unpleasant, though I was prepared to make a real effort to make her like me. Living with Uncle Rob and Shiona would be easy. They were kindness itself. I enjoyed talking to Uncle. He was so knowledgeable about interesting subjects like history. When I mentioned this to Shiona, she told me he was by way of being a historian and had almost completed a book about old festivals and legends. It had taken all of his adult life and he had traveled extensively in order to obtain the necessary information.

'Good job Grandfather and Charley have always been able to stand in at Maidenstane or else Father wouldn't have been able to be away so much,' Shiona told me.

'Charley?' I queried.

'My brother. Elder brother.' Her voice didn't change as it did for Fran. I was relieved.

'I didn't know you had one.' I was surprised and probably showed it.

'I keep forgetting you know nothing about us.'

I wondered if Charley were like Shiona. I wondered, too, if he called her She-She as Buck Graham did. The dark flavor of my dream returned to haunt me with its bitterness. Buck had something to do with Roddy's death. It seemed obvious. I would probably find out all about it when I knew the Drummonds better.

The steamer puffed and hissed alongside the pier. I could see field stools and benches at the stern of the vessel. Black smoke poured from the funnel, blotting out the distant panorama. A great deal of noise issued from the ship, rattles and

38

snorts mingled with a distant roaring. Feet clattered on gang-planks. Voices rose and fell. People began to seat themselves and spread the inevitable plaids. The sky was almost purple toward the west. I took out my umbrella before we stowed our luggage, not wanting to miss a second of the day's travel, and threw my spelder sandwich to the gulls.

I wanted to go up to the top deck where there were few people, but Uncle Rob and Shiona decided to sit in the stern with the comfort of rugs. 'Come back when you're too cold.' Uncle said, looking up from a rather battered notebook. Shiona smiled and spread out her peach-colored skirts. The cold wind had brought a color to her cheeks. An old fiddler was playing and singing the songs of Robert Burns. There were smells of oyster sauce and port and the sea. My blood sang with antici-pation.

The steamer was moving and there was a queer exhilaration in the pulsing of the engines. I climbed the steps to the upper deck. Only half a dozen figures stood around, leaning over the rails. We were sailing slowly over the Forth, one coastline receding into mist behind us, the other still vague and watery under the plum-colored pall of the sky. From where I stood, I could see the deck below. I couldn't see Shiona or Uncle. They must be at the other end of the ship. I watched the tops of heads idly at first, then with a surge of excitement. I was staring down on black, curly hair, an olive-colored profile, a handsome, rather sullen mouth. Buck Graham had finished his business in Edinburgh and was on his way home. I couldn't take my eyes away from that dangerous face, those broad shoulders that strained against the good cloth of his coat. I was aware of a painful traitorous regret. How could I feel anything but dis-taste for a man who pried into my life on his mother's behalf, who had been cruel to a cousin I loved? I had known Shiona barely two days, but already I admired and felt deeply for her. This regret was foolish and wrong. It should be saved for some more worthy character. I was disturbed by this welling up of excitement and warmth – yes, warmth – for a man who had harmed others and could do the same to me.

The steamer had turned and was proceeding slowly up the leaden reaches of the Forth. Villages and scattered houses lined the banks, all dim and hazy. Somewhere, the sun tried to break through the heavy clouds but only succeeded in showing narrow rims of gold, theatrically beautiful. The church spires began to grow more detailed. There was a rosy house with white lace balconies that reminded me of pictures of flamingos. Dark yews crowded around it like elderly widows. A red Indian fringe of woodland spiked the edges of a nearby hill. Black regiments of firs marched into a valley to merge with a green foam of larch. A gray ghost horse watched while a chestnut foal trotted in a meadow. I was a spectator at a fascinating game of life.

Rain began to fall at last, and the banks grew spectral behind slanting lines of rain. My eyes searched the lower deck again, but there was no sign now of Buck. Nearly everyone had gone under cover. I put up my umbrella and stayed close against the rail, leaning forward so that I missed nothing of the beauty of the sea. It was a hypnotic sight, forever shifting and curling, smoking with white foam, streaked and marbled so that it sometimes seemed solid. It was also very far below. There was no one left on the top deck. I had been fortunate in securing a cozy corner at the top of a staircase and sheltered by the bulk of a lifeboat. I had also been brought up on the harsh east coast and was hardened to the chilly conditions I now encountered.

I leaned forward to study one more effect of the ever-changing water, and horror struck. Hands were pushing me, strong, cruel hands that meant me to fall into that deadly maelstrom. I could not turn around, for I was pinned against the low rails, my own hands taken up with holding the stem of the umbrella. I let it go, watching it fall first against the steamer's side and then whirled out, like some monstrous bat, to land upside down in the waves. Frantically, I tried to gain some purchase on the slippery rail, but the thrusting went on, silently, terrifyingly. The breath was crushed from my body. Great whoops of agony were expelled from my throat. Then, just as I was certain I couldn't hold out any longer, the pressure ceased. I hung against the rail, my wet head hanging forward, the strands of hair obliterating sight. There were footseps, voices.

I turned around slowly. There was no one there. I stepped forward, trembling, and looked down the well of the staircase. Buck Graham was on the stairs, looking down. Uncle Rob was coming up, his face flushed. Or was he coming up? He could have been descending. He was turned sideways. He was a very strong man, I remembered sickly. But I knew Uncle Rob had nothing to do with the attack. It had been a feeble attempt on my part to divert suspicion from Buck. I knew quite well who had tried to push me overboard. But why? Why?

'Oh, there you are, Maggie,' Uncle Rob said, relieved. 'I saw your umbrella and I wondered if you were all right.'

I opened my mouth to explain and closed it again. No one could believe such a story. I hardly believed it myself now. Then I touched my shoulder, and the raw pain under the green and black material told me it was no flight of fancy. My uncle's eyes were very shrewd. Buck said nothing. His eyes were lowered. He seemed to be waiting for my accusation, but I could say nothing against him.

'It – it was a sudden gust of wind,' I lied. 'It's a great pity. It was a favorite umbrella. Still, it was my own fault. I chose to come up here, after all. Fancy seeing you again, Mr. Graham. We do seem to be haunting each other, don't we?'

His eyes seemed to see right through me to some dark place to which I couldn't follow. Then they focused, becoming hard and considering. 'Do we?'

'I have seen you, apart from at Holyrood. From the hansom cab when I arrived, for instance.' For some reason I said nothing about the episode at the fairground at Berwick. He would probably deny that he had ever been there. I must keep that disclosure for when we were alone – if we ever were.

'Oh?' His dark eyebrows lifted. 'And where might that have been?'

'In Princes Street. Near the Scott Monument.'

'I'm surprised you noticed me.' There was rain on his back and shoulders. I noticed that too. But I was left without a retort. I could see he half-expected me to say we had met before yesterday, was waiting with a certain air of enjoyment.

'Come, child,' Uncle Rob said. 'You've got quite wet since you lost your umbrella and there's much of the journey to be completed. I meant it, Buck. I wish you'd come visiting as you used to. Everyone's noticed the lack of your company. Fran said only last week that she missed you, and Charley could do with your advice on the sheep. I'll never understand why you've stayed away.'

'You're more generous than some.' Buck's mouth hardened. 'Not all of our neighbors have been so magnanimous. You do know that I'm suspected of harming Roddy?'

'Gossip, boy. We've no time for that. You'd do better to ignore it. Show you don't care. 'Tisn't easy, I know, but it is best.'

'Aye, Rob.' His voice was softer, almost unbearably so. I realized I wanted to go on listening to it. And yet the remnants of that horror at the rail still clung to me.

'Maybe I'll pay a visit, since you press me.' The dark eyes studied me curiously. 'I've some business in Stirling so I'm going no farther today. It seems I'll be seeing you again, Miss Stewart. Good day, Rob.'

Buck clattered down the steps and was gone. Shiona appeared suddenly at the top of the staircase and swooped down on us like a gorgeous black and golden bird. 'So there you are! I couldn't help seeing that umbrella in the water and remembered you had one like that. I was in the ladies' room. The boat made me feel a bit sick. I'm all right now, though, so don't look so worried, Maggie. I'm quite tough, really.' Shiona was wet, too. I was touched to think she had braved a soaking out of solicitude for me. 'I came up the other stairs and it gave me quite a turn when I saw no one at all on the deck. The sea looks so terribly fierce, doesn't it?' She was wearing a cloak over her dress.

'Actually, it happens to be the river now,' Uncle Rob reminded her, shepherding us into the shelter of the crowded stateroom. 'There's Stirling in the distance. The castle looks remarkably like Edinburgh, doesn't it? Interesting old town.' His cheerful voice restored my shattered morale and drove away the worst of my fears. I must take care not to be alone and I would be all right. I had imagined most of that terrifying episode. Someone had slipped on deck and had been too afraid of being accused of attack to stay for explanations. There was no sense to a purposeful attempt at harming me. I was of no importance to anyone. But my mind remembered that violent, soundless thrusting in spite of all my efforts to repudiate it, to turn it into something more innocent.

The passengers and baggage were transferred near Stirling onto a flat ferryboat. There were cross-benches covered with what looked like pieces of carpet. The old quay rose up ahead of us, dark and antiquated. Vehicles waited for travelers and stores. Although the rain had stopped, the sky was still swollen and heavy with moisture. There was an electrical feel in the air that betokened a thunderstorm.

I saw Buck climb from the ferry and walk purposefully toward one of the narrow alleys that led from the waterfront. He looked very tall, extremely dark, more than intimidating. My eyes were drawn toward his hands. They looked brown and strong. My arms and shoulders ached reminiscently. They *were* strong. I know they were. Didn't I? He had been close by. His mother had hated my father. Perhaps Buck hated me because of his mother's hurt. Perhaps . . .

I turned away to find Shiona watching me with solicitude. 'You do look pale.'

'I was too excited to sleep properly. Not even with you there.'

'You aren't worrying about Buck, are you?'

'What is there to worry about?' I shrugged with seeming indifference.

'He's devoted to Kate. She influences him, not always for the best. She bears grudges, Maggie.'

Just for a moment I wanted to cry out to her to be quiet, that I didn't want to know the worst of people, then I realized that my cousin meant well. Someone in my new life really cared about me. She meant no harm. I needn't be influenced if I didn't want to be.

'We'd better go with Uncle,' I said and smiled.

Uncle Rob took us to a small hotel for late lunch. It was in one of the steep streets that stretched downward to join the cobbled High Street. We ate, surrounded by framed pictures of Queen Victoria and farmers and fishermen very busy with oatcakes, dried meat and whiskey. We were given broth and pigeon pie and the usual oranges and preserved fruit. I found I had little appetite for it. My rib cage was bruised and very sore, and the backs of my arms still ached where thumbs had been pressed into them. My body had begun to stiffen and I thought longingly of a hot bath.

Outside the hotel, passengers gathered for a trip to Loch Katrine. They climbed, laughing, into a conveyance resembling an old-fashioned mail coach with room for four inside and twenty outside. There were four mettlesome horses and a coachman in blue silk jacket and white feather-shag hat. The conductor was resplendent in scarlet. Everyone laughed and sounded gay. I had grown as quiet as they were noisy. I remembered that this evening I would be at Maidenstane. There were new people to face and to impress. Aunt Margaret, Charley, Fran and who knew how many others?

We went on to Callander by coach. The village inn was decorated with a flamboyant picture of Rob Roy MacGregor, and everything possible was draped or covered with the appropriate tartan, even the postal and baggage barrows. A winding road, bordered with trees, followed an impressive river, and the thunder of magnificent falls stayed with us for a long way,

43

roaring like a subterranean monster demanding sacrifices. I saw turf dwellings now and scattered huts of lime and straw, fields of crops and cattle in the blue shade of mountains. There were white birchwoods and rowans, a lake in shadow, gorse blazing on scrubland.

A great, still loch showed under the sapphire bulges of more hills. Smoke rose from the chimneys of cottages that huddled close to the sandy shore. Sheep cropped by this peaceful strand. Men worked in the fields, and women in plaid kirtles and blouses hung out washing. Crops rippled in a warm breeze. The clouds were blowing away to reveal portions of blue sky. There was something in the loch that grew as we approached. A great, reclining shape that took on the semblance of a woman leaning on one elbow. The Stone Maiden, her curves black stone, her green hair trailing in the water. A great shiver ran down my spine. There was an aura around her like the atmosphere in the house in Church Street, as if generations of people had touched that cold stone and left their imprint. The air was filled with the suggestion of muted voices, of movement other than that of the small waves and the flight of birds above the reeds. I seemed to see a face floating there. But that couldn't be. Roddy would have been taken from that dark, gleaming water long ago. He would be buried in the churchyard I could see from here, the cemetery that divided two estates and two great houses that were barely visible in their barriers of trees.

The Maiden dominated the entire scene, the color of the shifting shadows below her taking on the shade of rusted metal. There were swans on the loch, visions of whiteness, beautiful in spite of the fact that they paddled in the semblance of blood.

'Home,' Shiona said close to my ear. 'We're home, Maggie.'

I turned in the direction of her pointing finger.

4

We climbed down from the coach, I very stiffly indeed. My midriff and sides hurt so much that I wondered if I had cracked a bone during that struggle on the steamer.

'Ah, there's Charley to meet us,' Uncle Rob said in a pleased voice and waved his arm to a man in a trap who waited by the roadside. The man looked at me searchingly, and I became very aware of my travel-stained appearance and the locks of hair that had become disarranged during the journey. He was extraordinarily like his father. Uncle Rob must have looked just like this about thirty years ago. His skin was brown as though he spent most of his time out of doors. I remembered what Shiona had said about him taking over the estate duties to allow his father to accumulate his background material for the book.

'Hullo, She-She,' he called out, 'and Father. I came yesterday but realized you must be spending an extra day in the city.' I noticed, chagrined, that he seemed little interested by my arrival while enthusiastic about his own family.

'He's very shy,' Shiona whispered, removing the deeply hooded cloak while her father retrieved our luggage and placed it in the trap. The coach rolled away and Shiona led me over to be introduced to Charley. 'He's really Charles,' she told me while her brother flushed with embarrassment. 'The Stewarts were related to the Bonnie Prince and he stayed here before Culloden. There's always been one Charles at least, ever since. Isn't that so, *mon frère?*'

'You do chatter on, She-She. How do you do, Miss – ' he mumbled awkwardly.

'Maggie! You can't call her Miss, Charley! You'll be seeing a lot of her. You might as well get used to it. Anyway, she's nice. Not what – ' Shiona stopped abruptly, her eyes betraying discomfiture. I knew what she had been going to say: 'Not what we expected.' The Stewart children had discussed the newcomer to the family and I felt a little stab of shock at finding this out so soon. What had Fran said about me?

I ventured another look at Charley. His eyes were kind. Or was he just a good actor? Did that apparent kindness conceal something very different? I held out my hand and he took it carefully as one would hold rare china. Perhaps very large people always feared they might hurt those much smaller and slighter than themselves. I fancied he turned to his father with great relief after we all had entered the little conveyance.

The trap swayed under our combined weights. We were skirting the loch, drawing farther and farther from the village and closer to the Stone Maiden, who kept up her silent pose against the fey blue of the hills. Fran began to loom up in my mind as black and implacable as that stone figure. Soon we would meet. There was no way to avoid that confrontation. She wouldn't like me. She would be difficult. My bones ached afresh with that foreknowledge.

We turned right where the lichened gravestones straggled up the hill. There were pitted gate pillars. The trap went between them and began to ascend a wild, steep drive between rhododendrons and Scotch pines. The Drummonds lived in one of the two big houses I had glimpsed from the coach. It didn't take much imagination to realize that the Grahams lived in the other. Two warring families separated only by a grave-yard! Miss Emily Brontë couldn't have done better. But this country differed from her Wuthering Heights. That had been harsh and bitter. This place was jewel rich with its mountains and the dark pearl of the loch, the ripening cornfields, the pale feathers of the swans that floated past the black boulders of the Stone Maiden. Again I experienced that quiver of super-stitious fear.

Charley and Uncle Rob chatted companionably in the front seat. Shiona showed no inclination to speak now. She stared toward the wall that cut these grounds off from the cemetery, her eyes darkened by thoughts I would never know. 'Remem-ber me,' I wanted to say. 'Don't shut me out!' I could never speak those words. Shiona liked me to be flippant and witty. She had no time for weakness. Again, I heard her voice as she told me how Davey Rizzio had clung to the skirts of Mary, Queen of Scots, on the night of his murder. She would have admired him if he had stood upright, waiting for the blows that couldn't be averted. But I understood his horror, his crav-ing for life. No one wanted to die. I hadn't wanted to be drowned this morning on the steamer. I thought I had fought hard enough to have satisfied even Shiona. It had been no

46

accident. No matter how I tried, I couldn't believe that. I crushed down the dark memory and prepared myself for the meeting with the Drummond womenfolk and my Grandfather Stewart. I was surprised, after finding out more about him, that he had agreed to my coming here.

The shrubbery petered out, and the trap came to a halt outside a house that, while it was large, was nowhere near as big as it had looked from the village. It was built of gray stone and roofed with blue slate. There were turrets and steeples, all similarly slated. The windows were of all shapes and sizes. I stared at it, not quite believing that I was to live here. When I had written to Mrs. Drummond, I had visualized a modest house rather like the one I had been used to. This was a mansion. The sunlight struck one of the larger windows and it gave the impression of being ablaze.

Uncle Rob handed me down from the trap. My feet crunched on the pebbled front. The air was filled with the scent of pine. A warm wind soughed through the trees. Beyond the tangle of woodland that descended the hill, the loch stretched its pewter length, the head and shoulders of the Maiden visible. It seemed to me that the stone woman's gaze was concentrated on the mountain facing her, and as I looked at the mountain, I was conscious of a shape that projected from the upper slopes. It had the semblance of a man, a knight in stone helmet and breastplate, his arms by his sides, his legs shrouded in bracken and bilberry. Perhaps the strong bars of shadow created the illusion.

I pointed it out to Shiona, and she said, 'Ah, that. It's the Warrior. There are legends about him and the Maiden. How they were separated and petrified by witchcraft, how they try, endlessly, to reach each other. Father knows them all. How noticing of you to see him straightaway! The Maiden's obvious, no one could miss her. But not many folk recognize the Warrior. Mother still says there's nothing there but stone and scree. Odd, the difference in people.'

I remembered then that Mrs. Drummond was my father's sister. Would she resemble him? I had a pale picture of him in his soldier's uniform. Darkish hair, blue eyes, features like mine. Everyone said there was a strong likeness between us.

'It's a lovely house,' I told my cousin breathlessly, turning back to look at it again.

'We think so,' Shiona answered, watching her brother and Uncle Rob opening the door to carry the portmanteaus and hatbox inside. 'Come on, then. Let the dogs see the rabbit.' She giggled then when she saw my baffled expression. 'It's just a saying, goose. It means you must gird yourself up to be inspected. Shall I go first?' She entered the house, laughing.

I followed, watching the flow of the pastel-colored skirts. There was a little tear near the hem, I noticed, and some black smears as though booted feet had kicked it. Someone had trodden on it during the journey. How lucky I had decided not to risk wearing the turquoise gown! At least Fran wouldn't be presented with a spoiled garment.

I was in a gloomy hall decorated with animal horns. A great chest lay along one wall, reminding me of the legend of the suffocated bride. Two or three oil portraits, dark and heavy, were hung at strategic positions. The painted eyes seemed to follow my every move. Although I saw no one as yet, I was aware of the same sensations of unseen occupancy as had existed in the old house in Berwick. I stopped involuntarily.

'What is it, Maggie?' Shiona asked. 'Your old complaint?'

'Which complaint?' I pretended not to understand her.

'*Temps perdu*,' she whispered, her eyes mocking.

Temps perdu. It described my odd feelings perfectly. Time lost. How peculiar I must seem to her. I was glad she was diverted by that strangeness, and not repelled. At the same time I didn't want her to tell everyone else about those brief peeps through that crack that led to the past. People have been branded as witches for less, especially in country places where folk tend to live closer to the earth. 'Don't tell,' I whispered back. 'Please, Shiona?'

'I won't. Not if you don't want me to. It's our secret. Would you like to comb your hair before you meet Mother and the others?'

'Yes, please.'

'Come with me then.' She took me up turkey-carpeted stairs that muted the sound of our footsteps. There had been lino-leum on Aunt Sarah's stairs. Aunt Sarah. She was part of some far-off life that had no connection with the present. I found it difficult to recall her face properly. Shiona took me into a room where all the woodwork was painted white and the paper was dark as a thunderstorm in contrast. I was fascinated by the blue, gray and purple background against which shadowy flowers climbed as far as the white plaster frescoes. Even the greenery that pressed close to the window gave an impression of rich, hidden depths from which anything might emerge. It was a secretive room, not what I had expected from my cousin. It had an atmosphere of jungles and buried treasure, things concealed. The subtle perfume I had noticed earlier hung over everything.

'What a lovely scent,' I remarked, laying my hat and mantle on the bed. 'Where did it come from? Was it a present?'

Shiona stood still for a time. 'Yes, it was a present. From Roddy Graham.'

'Oh.' I wished vainly that I hadn't mentioned it. It was obvious she didn't want to be reminded of Roddy. He had been in love with her, of course. What had happened in the loch that last day? Had Buck been jealous? I remembered the way he had studied the line of Shiona's throat when we had talked at Holyrood. It was the kind of look that one gave to something loved and lost, to someone who died, something gone beyond recall. But that didn't fit what she had said about Buck. He took people up, then dropped them when they ceased to amuse him or interest him. One of them wasn't speaking the truth. It would be Buck. Shiona had no need to lie to me.

'Help yourself to the comb and brush,' she offered. 'And use the things on the washstand. You'll feel better freshened up. I'll go down and tell Mother you're here. And, Maggie – it's nice to have you.' She leaned forward and kissed my cheek, her eyes warm with affection. I loved her violently in that moment.

The room seemed to crowd around me when she was gone, reminding me of my ordinariness, making me see Shiona as a beautiful golden cat, only half-tamed. I did as she'd told me and felt better for the washing and brushing. The mirror gave back a satisfactory reflection that was marred only by the suggestion of something just behind me, a vague shape that dogged my footsteps to no real purpose. Roddy Graham's perfume seemed to grow stronger as I moved across the room and opened the door.

The stair carpet drowned the sound of my feet on the stairs. I had always walked quietly. A door stood ajar in the gloom that led from the hall. A woman's voice emerged from it. 'I know all that, Rob, but it doesn't seem fair, not after all this time.' I couldn't move. It was me they were discussing. It must be. My ears burned.

'It's not her fault, my dear.' Uncle Rob's voice. 'Must have been difficult for the child – '

4   49

'I – I feel so inadequate –'

'There's no need, I keep telling you. She's not been used to too much. I did discover some things in the last day or two. Just be your own self and she'll be quite satisfied with that. And as for Charley, you must put that from your mind. After all, we'd have had to contact her ourselves if she hadn't made the first move.'

'Charley deserves more –'

'Margaret. No one is fonder of Charley than I am. But right's right. We've gone over all this before –'

'That was before she arrived. Oh, dear. I hope she doesn't see just what –'

'You must make it your business to make sure she won't.' Uncle's voice was very firm. There was a silence and I knew I couldn't stay outside the room any longer. I tiptoed back to the bottom of the stairs, then returned more noisily, making sure I could be heard. A woman's dress rustled as she stood up. My uncle coughed. I knocked at the door. Uncle Rob pulled it open to reveal a long, comfortable room, not at all like Aunt Sarah's parlor. There were sofas and armchairs, covered in shabby velvet that still contrived to look attractive, vases of greenery and flowers, pictures and photographs, padded footstools and little tables, none of which matched the others. The windows looked out over a wild, sunken garden where greenish statuary stood half-hidden in leafy thickets and where rose-bushes were dragged down under the weight of flowers. No orderly hand had been laid on it for a long time, yet it had a queer, drowned charm I loved at first sight.

I had looked at the room first, putting off the moment when my eyes must meet those of my aunt. It gave me a shock to see how like my father's old photographs she was. It was even more of a shock to realize that I could be taken for her child. The same abundant hair, the large gray-blue eyes, even the light scattering of freckles was the same. I remember being surprised. I had supposed she would be like Shiona, but my cousin resembled neither of her parents. I think Aunt Margaret was equally surprised when she saw me. 'You didn't say, Rob, how like the family she was.' Her voice was different, the complaining note gone, something of warmth taking its place. 'How nice to see you, Maggie. I've heard all about you, except the extraordinary likeness to Alex and me. Fran, I think, is the most like you. Are you very tired?'

'A bit,' I confessed. It could be a convenient way of being

shown to my own room in a little while when the strain became too great.

'Supper's nearly ready. Charley's just cleaning himself up. And She-She's gone to fetch Fran. She'll be sitting with her nose in a book as usual. Are you hungry?'

'Not very. We had a large lunch at Stirling.'

'But that was a long time ago. We planned a special meal, Ness and me, to welcome you.'

'That was kind.' I wondered who Ness was.

'Nonsense,' Uncle Rob said. 'Not kind. Only natural. Ah, She-She. Did you prise Fran from her window seat? I think I must have it removed. She spends so much time on it.' He clicked his tongue, but I suspected he wasn't really annoyed.

'She's coming,' Shiona murmured, seeming to fill the room with her special brand of magnetism. Everything looked brighter and richer for her presence. I wondered, not for the first time, what she could see in me. Even the tawny velvet of the covers seemed not so shabby. The smells of food drifted in through the open door, suddenly inviting.

'We'll go to table, I think,' my aunt said. 'The others can join us there. Ness will never forgive me if her banquet spoils.' She took Uncle Rob's arm as if it were the most natural thing in the world. Shiona and I followed them. She-She. It suited my cousin. I wondered if I'd ever be allowed to call her by this pet name. Buck Graham did, and they were enemies. I, at least, was her friend. I thought of Buck walking the streets of Stirling. Tomorrow night he would be back here, on the other side of the graveyard, back with his mother, Kate, who had been beautiful and wild and engaged to my father.

The dining room was dwarfed by the long table. It was low-ceilinged and small-windowed, and the floorboards glittered with polish. It was lit by silver candelabra that cast wavering lights over the walls and tabletop. There was silver on the sideboard and a variety of glasses and decanters. The light that came in was greenish and mysterious. I realized that it was beginning to get dark. A woman came in with a big tureen of soup. She gave a start when she saw me. 'Oh, Madam! I thought I'd seen a ghost! She's so like yourself as a girl! Like Master Alex too. And the same name. There's always been a Margaret, just as there's always been a Charley. I hope you'll be liking the food, Miss Margaret. Cock-a-leekie, this is.'

'This is Ness, Maggie. She's always looked after us. I can't remember the place without her.'

Ness looked pleased. She was exactly like Queen Victoria without the severity of expression. Like the queen, she wore stark black only relieved by the wide apron she had put on to serve the meal. She put the tureen down carefully and picked up a silver ladle. Charley came in as she ladled out the steaming broth. He nodded to me and sat down in his accustomed place. I was seated next to my uncle. Ness was finished with her task and leaving the room just as Fran entered it. There was something wrong with her walk, I noticed. One foot slid over the polished boards, scraping harshly, the sound loud in the enclosed space. Her body dipped forward as she moved. I was aware of a pang of deepest pity. My cousin Frances was a cripple.

Fran was pale. Of course, her father had said that she spent too much time in her room. I thought it a natural reaction in a deformed girl who couldn't help but see beauty in her sister and brother. She was not even pretty. Her face was longish and sharply clever. Her dark hair was not abundant like her mother's and mine. It hung long and straight and rather dull. Only her eyes were noteworthy, the same large gray-blue eyes that gave Aunt Margaret her attraction.

'Must you always be last?' Uncle Rob asked her, his exasperation obviously feigned.

'I forgot the time.' Fran's voice was as clear and sharp as her angled features. She made no apology.

'This is your cousin, Maggie.'

She stared at me without expression. 'We expected you yesterday.'

My uncle replied for me. 'It was She-She's fault we were delayed. You know how persuasive she can be.'

'I know.' Fran picked up her spoon and applied herself, without enthusiasm, to her soup. I discovered that my cheeks were hot. I had been dismissed very summarily. It annoyed me that I could think of nothing to say. Charley began to talk to his father about rams and ewes. The candlelight made him look extremely handsome. I only wished his conversation were as arresting as his looks. I wondered where Grandfather Stewart was. Was his absence his way of showing his disapproval of Alex's daughter?

'Where is Grandfather?' I was driven to ask when Charley and Uncle Rob stopped talking about farming matters.

Fran stared at me disconcertingly hard. Aunt Margaret said,

'Oh, he stays a lot of the time in his bed. He finds it difficult to get around much. He'll expect to see you when you've finished.'

My heart sank. I seemed to have made no visible impression on Charley or Fran. Would I have any greater success with an old man who harbored grudges? Kate Graham was tarred with that same brush, according to Shiona. Tomorrow night at this time, Kate and Buck would be sitting in another room, on the other side of the graveyard, talking about me. I had a strong unworthy desire to be able to eavesdrop on that inevitable conversation. I remembered the one I had overheard accidentally this very evening. What was it that was unfair to Charley? What possible difference could my presence make?

Ness came back, stout and diminutive, to remove the soup plates and bring the meat course, helped by a tall, gangling ginger-haired girl she addressed as 'You'. 'You do this. You do that,' with never an indication as to the maid's Christian name. 'You' seemed to find everything quite normal, carrying out Ness's orders with a heavy-handed willingness I found touching. She would have to work hard for her small salary and probably help keep a large family of brothers and sisters at her home in the village.

Fran picked at her meat and vegetables in spite of Aunt Margaret's strictures and her father's encouragement. I felt their constant urgings made her even more rebellious. Perhaps a good, healthy ignoring of Fran would be better tactics. I, myself, would be inclined to leave her alone. Ness fussed over her too, like a little black hen with one sickly chick. I thought they were all wrong.

There was a roly-poly pudding with dried fruit in it which everyone enjoyed, the suet pastry was so light and delicious. Even Fran ate that without fuss. Charley and Uncle Rob excused themselves and I braced myself for my interview with Grandfather.

'Don't worry,' Shiona said softly, pressing my hand. 'His bark's worse than his bite.'

'Is it?'

'It is where I'm concerned.'

'But we're very different people. And he knows you – '

'I'll take you to Grandfather's room, shall I?' Fran offered unexpectedly, her voice still sharp. 'I'm going past it.' I had the ungenerous feeling it was the whispered conversation between Shiona and me she wanted to terminate.

'You can show Maggie her own bedroom at the same time.

53

It's next to Fran's,' my aunt explained. I was aware that Aunt Margaret was relieved by her daughter's offer. Like me, she shrank from the confrontation with her intimidating father. 'Shiona. There's something I wish to ask your advice about. Ness, the pudding was very good. You can see how good. There's not a crumb left –'

Her voice died away on an avalanche of housewifely trivia. Fran and I climbed the stairs together. My heart began to pound. I had met too many people today. I wished my senses were blunted like those of poor ginger-headed 'You' who bore all Ness's relentless verbosity with such patience. I still couldn't think of anything to say to Fran. Shiona I could talk to, even the highly dangerous Buck with his fine-boned gypsy face and cruel mouth, but to the creature who cast that painful, dipping shadow on the wall, I could utter no sensible word.

'Why don't you say it?' Fran suggested softly and her eyes slid sideways to study my profile. I missed the next step and stumbled, much to my annoyance.

'Why don't I say what?' We had come to a landing and were turning down a dark corridor.

'I didn't expect my cousin to be crippled and ugly. Not after the other two.'

'Would you like me to?' I asked her with false lightness. 'I will if you do.'

'You were thinking it,' she accused morosely.

'I certainly wasn't! I have other more important things on my mind.'

'Shall I tell you what I was thinking about you?'

'I'd rather not know. Not at this particular moment at least. I need all the self-confidence I can muster.'

'You sound like Marie Antoinette going to the guillotine.' Fran laughed and I was glad to recognize real amusement.

'Do you think I don't feel like that? Worse, if I were truthful.'

'You don't have to. Grandfather can't abide fools, but no one could call you that.'

'Is that intended to be a compliment? If so, thank you very much.'

'It might have been.' Fran sounded surprised at her own magnanimity. 'This is your room, by the way.'

I had hardly noticed where we were going. We were in some sort of corner. The doorway was on a slant and there was a step down to it. I turned the knob and pushed. A candle

54

burned, showing the outline of a narrow white-covered bed.

'It looks like a coffin with a pall over it!' I remarked incautiously. 'Oh, for heaven's sake, don't tell your parents, will you!'

Fran laughed again, and this time there was a note of wildness in it that disturbed me.

'And the room's round!' I exclaimed, going farther inside it. 'It's one of the steeples, isn't it?'

'Yes. We all thought you'd like it.'

'Did you?' My tone was dry in spite of myself. I already knew they had been prepared not to like me. I could see nothing from the window. It was quite dark now.

Fran shrugged and leaned against the jamb, looking like a young and very intent witch. 'I'm next door.'

'Why didn't you want this room?'

Her eyes were suddenly evasive. 'I preferred the larger one. It's got a better view and there's the window seat.'

'Of course. I've forgotten the window seat. Your father threatens to remove it.'

'Just talk. He won't. The bathroom's on the floor below. Just under this one.'

'Thanks.' We stood for a moment like two cats sizing each other up. 'Well, I must see Grandfather now.'

'The more one puts it off, the worse it is, eh?' she suggested.

'That's right.' Looking at Fran in the darkness of the doorway was oddly like seeing a slightly distorted reflection of myself. I shivered, though I was not cold. From the corner of the room came four faint but definite taps. I turned abruptly. 'What's that?'

'What's what?' Fran's voice was devoid of interest.

'Tapping. From . . . that bend to the side of the window.'

She listened. I heard three more taps, faint but unmistakable. Fran appeared to hear nothing. 'There were more,' I said uncertainly. 'Like someone banging.'

'Imagination, Maggie. There couldn't be anyone there. We're upstairs, remember? And this is just a round tower. It's only attached to the house here, where I'm standing. And I didn't hear a thing. I've got awfully good hearing too.'

'I'm sure you have.' Fran had been uncharacteristically helpful. Perhaps she had bribed poor 'You' to hammer on some wall. And yet if this was an adjunct to the main building, how was it possible? Anyway, 'You' would be washing up the supper

55

dishes under Ness's supervision. She wouldn't be free to play tricks.

'Any trees just outside the window?' I asked, seemingly careless.

'No.' Fran was watchful.

'Could have been woodpeckers! Anyway, what does it matter! Show me the lion's den,' I demanded grandly. If Fran wanted things played on a low key, she should be humored. She giggled and moved back the way we had come. She stopped at a door near the staircase and tapped at the painted panel.

'Who is it?' An old man's voice, testy and rasping. My heart jerked hurtfully.

'Fran. I've brought you a visitor.'

'Visitor?' The voice changed, becoming deeper and stronger.

'My cousin Maggie.'

'Oh. She'd better come in.'

Fran pushed the door open. For some ridiculous reason I thought of the picture on the stair head at Aunt Sarah's house, the pretty, highly colored Red Riding hood carrying her basket and her posy of flowers and, behind the tree, the sinister skulking shape of the wolf waiting for his victim. The bedroom wasn't as dark as I'd expected. An oil lamp stood on a little table beside an enormous four-poster bed around which curtains shifted uneasily in the draft from the door. A plaid the size of a small field did service as a coverlet. Grandfather Stewart sat against piled pillows. His face, like Fran's, was pale, with a bristle of white hair around chin and cheeks. He had a beaked, dominant nose and blue, piercing eyes. But, incongruously, he was wearing a blue Highland bonnet with a feather up the side.

I could never decide afterward just how much of my reaction was nervousness, but the sight of the bonnet set me off first giggling and then laughing. I thought I would never be able to stop. Behind me Fran was laughing too. How terrible to be thrown out of his room before I'd had time to say anything.

'So,' he said coolly. 'You find me amusing, do you?' Even the eaglelike glare of his eyes could not prevent a fresh paroxysm of mirth.

'What is it you find particularly funny?' he inquired frostily.

'Your – your bonnet,' I stammered. 'You're wearing it – in bed.'

'I always do.'

It was the wrong thing to say. Pictures of Grandfather wearing his bonnet on every conceivable and unlikely occasion passed in a procession in front of my eyes. I sat down in a chair to continue with my laugh in comfort. My legs had grown strangely weak.

'Send Ness up with some water,' Grandfather demanded. 'Cold water.'

'Oh, don't, Fran!' I said. 'She'll be much too busy. I'll be all right in a minute.'

Aunt Margaret came in, her face anxious. 'What is it? You can hear her all over the house. You haven't upset her, have you?' She stared at Grandfather accusingly.

'Upset her! She's upset me!' But the frosty eyes were twinkling.

'She's had a long, tiring journey –' my aunt said placatingly.

'No doubt. No one's suggested otherwise.'

I had stopped laughing now but only because my ribs hurt. I had to press my hand against my mouth to stifle the undignified remnants of that gigantic amusement.

'She says it's because I wear my bonnet in bed,' Grandfather told Aunt Margaret.

'I've told you myself what a silly habit that is. Many times. Unhygienic, too.'

'Perhaps you should have roared with laughter every time you came into the room. No man likes being laughed at. Takes away his manhood. I might have listened then.'

I ventured another look at him. He appeared surprisingly cheerful for a man whose manhood had been placed in jeopardy.

'Finished?' he asked ironically.

I nodded.

'Good. You can take yourselves off, you two.'

'Come down to say good night, won't you?' my aunt urged.

'I will.' I was aware of the sardonic intelligence in Fran's eyes, then she was gone. I knew what those eyes had said. 'You're clever, Maggie Stewart. You know how to disarm the enemy. How sharp of you to know what to do so instinctively.' And yet it hadn't been like that at all. It had just . . . happened.

Grandfather sat up straighter and pushed his headgear sideways at a more rakish angle. 'No one could say you aren't Alex's daughter,' he said.

'No one has. As far as I know.'

'I'm glad you aren't a simpering miss. I was afraid you would be. And I'm pleased you came before you were sent for.'

'Were you going to send for me?'

'Of course.' The pale eyes sharpened. 'Your father was heir to all this. And you are his only child. Do you mean to say you didn't know?' He couldn't have failed to see my loss of color. So that was what wasn't fair to Charley! I agreed wholeheartedly with the Drummonds. Charley had looked after this estate for years. I had never seen it before today. But inheritances were like that. Disappointing for some, an embarrassment to others.

'It doesn't seem fair. Charley's done all the work – '

'There's nothing to stop him going on doing what he enjoys.'

'But a paid factor isn't the same thing as being owner.'

'Perhaps he won't always be a paid factor,' Grandfather pointed out. 'He's a good-looking lad. And there's no woman in the offing.' His meaning was clear.

I stared at him, my face flushing. 'I haven't been here five minutes and you're suggesting – '

'I suggested nothing,' he disclaimed forcibly. 'I merely said what Charley never would if wild horses were trying to drag it out. It does no harm to mull over the idea. Not that you must feel obliged to take any notice if it doesn't appeal to you. It doesn't do you any good, I've discovered, to place too much reliance on the feelings of the young. You can be disappointed. And it's never fair to build up someone's hopes, then dash them to the ground.' His eyelids were down now and I could no longer see his expression. It was obvious, of course, he meant my father and Kate Graham. There was nothing I could say in Father's defense. He should have been honest. If Kate had to be hurt, he should have seen to it that she suffered with dignity. But to get as far as the altar, all happy and expectant, the toast of the neighborhood, and to be abandoned in the public view. No wonder Kate had been bitter. She must still have loved Father to have made inquiries about him and his family. Was she like Buck? In spite of myself, my blood ran faster. What a fool I was to admit my attraction toward Kate's gypsy son when I knew he had meant to harm or seriously frighten me. It was madness to say the least.

'What of your Aunt Sarah?' he asked when I remained silent. 'Is she going to marry this Josh Davidson?'

'I'm sure she will. After a decent interval.'

'Decent interval! Antediluvian idea,' Grandfather grunted.

58

'What would you have done if we'd refused to have you here?'

'I'd have looked for a living-in post. Being convent-educated would have helped. I did explain about Josh. He's a decent man –'

'Only he couldn't take on another man's child. It's fortunate we don't all suffer from such unwillingness.' Something in his face made me think he had a specific case in mind, someone apart from myself. 'D'you think you'll like it here?' he went on abruptly as though to cover up all trace of his brusque kindness.

'Oh, yes.'

'D'you ride?'

'I haven't had the chance. I'd like to.'

'She-She's good. And so's Buck. Ah! I see you've met him.' Grandfather's gaze penetrated me with a stab of discernment. 'Difficult to tell where the horse ends and Buck begins. He's a centaur, young Graham.'

'We met at Holyrood. And on the boat.' In spite of myself, my voice quivered.

'Cold?' He misunderstood that shiver.

'Just tired.'

'Well. Time for bed, eh? Plenty of other occasions to talk. Good night, Maggie.'

I went around the bed and kissed the cheek nearest me. It was like doing something familiar, something I'd done all my life. The bristles rasped across my lips, but there was a comfort in their roughness. I knew he watched me leave the room.

Fran was waiting for me on the landing, her eyes a little malicious. 'I suppose he's sent instructions for the mess of potage to be prepared and the fatted calf to be killed?'

'What a sharp minx you are! He made it plain, actually, that he still disapproves strongly of what Father did. Oh, and I'm to take riding lessons with Shiona – or Buck.' At the sound of his name shadows seemed to stir in the elbow of the staircase.

'Oh . . . Buck.' Fran's voice was flat. 'You'll wait long enough for him. Mother says you needn't go down if you'd rather just go to bed. I'm to take charge of you.'

'You make me sound like a recalcitrant bull.' There was a smile in my voice.

Fran laughed, some of the flatness gone. 'You aren't as I thought you'd be.'

'That's what Grandfather said. He was expecting a prunes-and-prisms miss. Oddly enough, I was one, until the day I fell from a merry-go-round. It changed me.'

The shadows on the stairs were alive as I spoke, shifting, expanding, shrinking to dark nothings.

Fran looked at me oddly. 'I'll show you the bathroom.'

I found my way upstairs easily enough afterwards. She'd already told me my room was directly above it. She was waiting for me as though she couldn't bear to be parted from her new diversion. I was touched by this, although I realized I'd have preferred to find Shiona in my strange, round bedchamber.

'The moon's out now,' she said dreamily. 'Come and see.'

The moon was out, and I saw, with a little chill, that the steeple window overhung the graveyard. The tombstones leaned in all directions, undersides black, their tops bathed with shining whiteness. Above the trees that lay beyond them the bulk of the Graham house rose against the sky. One window near the roof was lit and somehow that yellow oblong was more threatening than darkness would have been.

I turned around to speak to Fran but she had gone, silently. I was alone. And from that curved bend near the window the ghostly tapping had just started again. Even with the bed-clothes pulled up around my ears, I could hear it.

5

It was a beautiful morning. I woke late, for I'd not found sleep come easily. Even when the muffled banging had stopped, my nerve ends had still quivered expectantly. I still saw the blanched gravestones that tottered and leaned and plunged as far as the loch side. I dreamed of the Stone Maiden, her reedy hair swaying. I dreamed, too, of the Warrior, and he had Buck Graham's face, only it was dead and still as poor Roddy's.

'You' had been sent up with my breakfast, much to my embarrassment. I had come here to be a help, not a hindrance. But Shiona came as I was sitting up, eating it, her peaty eyes alive with that affection I could never quite believe was for me. She had such a warm, lazy voice, such a pleasing personality. It seemed wrong of me to compare her with poor Frances, but I couldn't help it.

Shiona wanted a blow-by-blow account of my meeting with Grandfather. I told her the main details, including his suggestion that I learn to ride. 'He says Buck is marvelous,' I said experimentally. 'Is he as good as Grandfather says?'

The brown eyes held mine, tawny lights shifting in their depths. She was smiling, but oddly enough, she did not seem amused. 'Better. He's like Satan, complete with hooves.'

'Grandfather suggested a centaur.'

'We just see him differently. I can't forget – Roddy, you see. He should have still been alive. You'd have liked him.' The brown eyes were quite dark, completely different.

I got out of bed, disturbed. She hated Buck, that was obvious. I didn't want to listen to the story she wanted to tell of Buck and his cousin. Yet wouldn't it be better to know?

'Yes. I expect I should. But that's the past –'

'And you want to concentrate on the present! Very well, so you shall. May I stay while you dress?' Her voice defied me to be conventional.

'Of course.' I turned my back to put on my camisole.

'Why, Maggie! However did you get those bruises?' Shiona crossed the room and stood just behind me. She touched the backs of my arms gently. 'That hurts, doesn't it?'

'A bit. I – I slipped. On the boat yesterday. The deck was wet.'

'You fell as hard as that? And never said anything?' She couldn't conceal the disbelief in her tones. 'They – they look like thumbprints! However, you should know. You – you aren't shielding someone?'

'Oh, for heaven's sake!' My laughter sounded unconvincing. 'I thought I was the imaginative one. Whom should I be shielding?'

'If you say it was an accident, then I must believe you. But it's very unusual to fall in that position, so that you bruise both arms and not your back.'

'What shall I wear for my first riding lesson?' I asked a little desperately. I simply must divert her before anyone else appeared. Fran, for instance, who was sharp and unpredictable. 'Would this do?' I held up the black skirt and the white blouse I liked best.

'Very suitable.' Shiona put her head to one side consideringly. 'How do you like this room?'

'It's fine.' I wriggled into the skirt and fastened the waist-band.

'You don't sound too sure about it.'

'I never sleep well in a strange bed. But tonight it won't be strange anymore.'

Shiona went to the window and stared down. 'A lot of Stewarts are buried down there. Drummonds too, of course –'

'And Grahams?'

'Yes,' she murmured. 'Grahams as well. You haven't met Kate yet, have you?'

'No. Does – does she come often?'

'Not really. She's rather a recluse nowadays since her husband died. They didn't seem to get on, yet when he died she was quite affected. Guilty conscience, I expect. I think she spent all her married life thinking about someone else.'

'Father, you mean.' I began to button the blouse. My arms still felt stiff and rather sore. How sad for poor Johnnie Graham always to have been a second best. Buck must have been caught in the crossfire of those tangled emotions. He couldn't have remained unaffected. Was that the reason for that – violence?

'So everyone said.' Her tone was noncommittal, as though she hadn't thought much about it.

'Do people go into the graveyard at night? Tap stones – or anything?' I asked.

Shiona turned her eyes toward mine. 'Good heavens, no! Why? Have you seen anything?'

'Nothing. It was a noise I heard.'

'Oh, you mustn't worry about night noises. The house is old, though it's well preserved. Maidenstane's full of creaks and whispers. Woodwork contracts and expands –'

'It was more like banging.'

'Darling! A little bogle sitting behind the wainscot with a hammer?' She made it sound ridiculous, which it probably was. 'By the way, don't expect to see much of Mother today. It's her day for visiting Aunt Bell. She's a cousin of hers. Not quite right in the head, poor thing. She's in a private home. Mother thinks it's her duty to see her regularly. There's no one else to make the effort. Aunt Bell's parents are dead and she'd no brothers or sisters. She's a distant relative of Kate's too. I'm not sure just how they're connected.'

'How awful for her. For both of them.'

'Yes, isn't it?' Shiona didn't seem unduly concerned. 'And

Father will be busy with his book. We always hold the old festivals here. Lots of places have given them up. The church doesn't approve of them unless they're concealed under the guise of religion! But in this part of the country, the old customs are very much alive. There's a place called Dragon Hole where people still go. You'd find it creepy. Hawks and kites flying overhead and a difficult path leading to the hole. Doesn't hold many. Ten are a squash and the candlelight flickers over the rocky walls – ' She gave a little reminiscent shudder.

'You sound as if you've been there.' I brushed my hair to a semblance of smoothness.

'Do I?' Her voice was evasive.

> 'Butter, new cheise and beir in May
> Connan, cokkelis, curds and quhey.'

'What's that?'

'Oh, just a Beltane couplet. That's the May festival, Beltane.'

'What does "connan" mean? I think I know what the other things are.'

'Rabbits, darling. That's all. Just innocent little rabbits.'

'Oh.'

'Don't sound so disappointed! There's a man in the village called Connan. I think he felt he had to live up to his name.' She giggled softly.

'Oh, why? Does he eat nothing but lettuce?' I turned away from my now neat reflection.

Shiona laughed. She had the most attractive laugh I'd ever heard. 'You're a lovely little innocent. No, you goose, he's got dozens of children.'

'Aren't you exaggerating?'

She smiled. 'A little. Not much.'

We went out of the room laughing. Fran was close by the door. I had the feeling she'd been listening. She looked pale, like someone who had been left out in the cold. I was suddenly sorry for her. Would it be indiscreet to ask if her were coming with us? I had no idea if her disability prevented her from riding. The one thing I was sure of was that I couldn't just walk away without finding out, without making her feel that she was welcome.

'Are you coming, Fran? It's a lovely morning.' I made my tone cheerful.

'Coming where?' A stiff, prickly voice that matched her hunched shoulders.

'To the stables. I'm about to head for a fall. Wouldn't you like to see the great event?'

'I don't ride.' Her face seemed to close up.

'Haven't you ever tried?'

'Maggie,' Shiona said quietly. 'It's not a question of trying. Mother and Father don't want Fran to take such risks. You see – '

'You don't have to explain for me! I am here! There's nothing wrong with my head or my tongue!' Fran's eyes looked huge and unhappy.

'Sorry, Fran.' Her sister was contrite.

'Someone pushed me when I was small. We were all playing, Charley, She-She, Buck, Roddy and me. I was all right then. We were playing at sieges down at the Stone Maiden. I was the defender. And someone came up behind me and gave me a push. I didn't see who it was. We were all dressed up, you see, in robes and helmets and things. Everyone looked like everyone else. Except me. I was the littlest. They all knew who I was. But I didn't know them – '

'It must have been an accident,' I said through stiff lips. But my mind remembered the steamer and the pressure at the rail. Buck had been there just as he'd been at the Stone Maiden when Fran was hurt. 'It must have been. Mustn't it?'

'That's what everyone says. But it didn't feel like an accident.' Her voice was hard.

'It wouldn't. You'd be shocked. All you'd remember would be – ' I stopped abruptly, my hands unconsciously touching my midriff. All I could recall was a futile horror, the sense of being at the mercy of someone so strong that I was pinned, unable to struggle, unable to turn for the briefest look at my attacker. 'Why don't you come? You'll be out in the fresh air. Better for you than – '

'My window seat? Maybe. But I prefer the seat. You go and enjoy yourselves. Don't worry about me!' Fran's voice was high-pitched, mercilessly clear. She went back into her room and shut the door with a bang.

'Poor Fran,' Shiona said softly. 'It was a bad break. Her leg never quite caught up with the other, hence the limp. She can never be convinced it was an accident. Roddy and I were together and Charley and Buck were somewhere else. They'd separated. I suppose they were so afraid of getting into trouble when they realized Fran was so bad that whichever it was hadn't the courage to own up. Roddy explained that I was with him, but the others were under a cloud for long enough, poor things. I could never believe Charley capable of duplicity, but then I suppose I'm biased, being his sister.'

'So you think it was Buck, do you?' My voice was harsher than I'd intended.

'Oh, so you are interested in him!' Shiona said lightly. 'I thought you were right from the first moment at Holyrood. I think he reciprocates that interest. I'm rarely wrong about such things. Only you won't forget what I told you, will you? Fran would never hear an ill word about Buck either –'

'Either?' I frowned.

'Do you think I haven't noticed how you change the subject when he's mentioned? You see? Even now you're scowling because I've spoiled his image for you. But I think when you find out more about Charley you'll come to agree with me.'

'Grandfather seems to like him.'

'He felt he had to make up to Kate and Buck for your father. He always has.'

'I see.' Somehow the sunlight was dimmed for me. 'What was the consensus of opinion about Roddy? About the way he died?'

Shiona whitened. 'It was an open verdict. There were marks on him that weren't explained, that happened before he drowned. Buck said he wasn't at the loch that afternoon, but no one came forward to say they'd seen him anywhere else. There was no proof.'

I thought of Buck's strong body and broad shoulders. I felt a little sick. 'The horses,' I said lamely. 'We've forgotten the horses.'

'So we have,' she answered. 'We mustn't waste any more of this good weather. It's not always like this.' She began to hum absently a tune I recognized but couldn't name.

I followed her out the back door and through the sunken garden where the roses sprawled, heavy in the heat. I was very aware of the old gravestones beyond the wall, leaning and lichened, listening to our voices. Looking back, I could see the steeple and distinguish the window of my room. As I watched, I saw a shadow pass the window and the pale round of a face. A coldness tightened about my spine. The whiteness remained for a second, then disappeared. It would be Ness or 'You', I told myself. But something about the hunched, featureless

5

figure stuck in my mind, refusing to be shut away. The tapping had come from near the window and there seemed no explanation for it. There was no room overhead where someone could play tricks. Only the blue-slated steeple. I had the cold conviction that my bedchamber was haunted. Shiona was still humming and now I remembered the melody. It was 'Early One Morning'. The tune was as haunted as my spirits.

I was tired when I went up to my bedroom. It had been a difficult day. Horse riding is attractive in theory but very different in practice. It's extraordinary how hard it is even to get astride a mount, never mind stay on it. I'd had two nasty tumbles that made my head ache, and our practice field was close by the loch side and in full view of the Maiden. Each time I saw those smooth black limbs I was reminded of Fran and of the game that had ended in disaster. Poor child. My own body ached in sympathy.

Shiona was like a goddess astride the chestnut mare that was her own property. I saw her, in my mind's eye, riding with Buck in the days before they became enemies. She called him a Satan, but Grandfather had been kinder. Whichever was right, he was there for me as he had been that day I'd fallen from the merry-go-round. The fat pony I sat so awkwardly became the white polished horse. There were white and gold swans circling to the music of the hurdy-gurdies, brass poles rising and falling.

But the day's efforts hadn't been wasted. I was almost rid of that vulnerable, sitting-on-a-mountaintop feeling by the time my pony was returned to the stable and I was getting the hang of what to do with my knees and elbows. Shiona seemed very pleased with me. The only thing that had upset me was the fact that Buck – in the flesh and not in my imaginings – had ridden by just as I had my second and more painful fall. I'd become aware of him as I sat up in a tumble of petticoats and laced boots, just in time to see the slight twitch of the lips that passed for a smile and the black gypsy eyes alight with mockery. Shiona had her back to him at the time, but I knew she was conscious of his proximity. Only he had the power to cast a shadow over her eyes and her features, to make coldness out of her essential warmth. Had she been in love with Roddy Graham? That could be one explanation of her revulsion for Buck. But she'd said he hurt people. Took them up and abandoned them when it suited him. Had she meant someone else? The only other girl was Fran, unless it was someone in the village – someone I hadn't yet met. Odd how the impression remained that she'd meant herself. But in that case she couldn't have loved Roddy. It was all very puzzling.

I had a bath before supper in a huge, old-fashioned tub. I reveled in this luxury, feeling some of the stiffness and soreness melting out of me, but secretly horrified when I saw the bruises around my ribs.

Shiona had disappeared after the meal and Fran was still uncommunicative. Grandfather was tired – it wasn't one of his good days – and Aunt Margaret wasn't yet back from the private home where Aunt Bell lived out her life. Uncle Rob retired to his study, and Charley went out to have a last look at his precious livestock.

Now that I was in the steeple room I was reluctant to go to bed. I hadn't forgotten that glimpse of a figure by the window this morning. I was suddenly wide awake and unwilling to undress, to have to blow out the candle. I thought I heard Fran walk by in the passage. The dragging step was like hers. But when I opened the door, there was nothing to be seen and the crack under her door showed no light.

I went to my window. The moon was very bright. The shadows under the gravestones seemed to shift ever so slightly. The leaves on the branches threw moving splatters of blackness over the blanched grass that grew thick and wild where it could. Even the moss on the wall appeared not to be still. It was only my active imagination...

Someone was walking through the graveyard. They moved slowly and silently. From here I couldn't tell if it were a man or a woman. Was it Shiona? She hadn't said where she was going. It must be my cousin. Something in the posture of that quiet figure suggested sorrow. Buck had returned. He had hurt Shiona. I wanted very much to comfort her. I thought I knew why she had chosen the cemetery. It was as close to Buck's home as she could get. Did she still love him in spite of the hurt he'd inflicted?

I picked up my mantle and fastened it over my shoulders, then began to walk downstairs. The turkey carpet dulled what sound I made. I fancied Grandfather called out in his sleep as I passed his door, but I couldn't make out what he said. 'Early One Morning.' Shiona had been humming the sad little song today. 'Oh, don't deceive me, oh, never leave me. How could you use a poor maiden so?' As I let myself out at the back door, I almost hated Buck Graham for making my cousin unhappy. Had he made her love him and then turned her away? Something stronger than that near-hate wanted to believe otherwise. I couldn't identify that new emotion.

There was a gap in the wall beyond the sunken garden. As I stepped carefully over the broken stones I could smell the scent of the roses, half-drowned now in the strong, sad odor of pine and rotting leaves. A stick cracked under my foot. The blood rushed to my face. I was conscious of guilt, though I had only come out here to talk to Shiona. It was the first time I had given my action any real thought. I had stolen out of the house like a criminal. The night scents, the mingled moonlight and darkness pressed around me, curiously alive. No sign, nor sound of the figure that walked alone.

I took a few experimental steps. The grass was long, making soft, swishing noises against my skirt. Again I had that impression of inanimate things that moved on the very edge of vision. The moon was immensely large, bland as a Chinaman's face. I stared downward. Between the leaning stones I could see the Maiden, edged with silver, watching her reflection in the black glass of the loch. On the opposite hill, the dead stone face of the Warrior gazed at nothing in particular.

'Shiona?' I whispered, nervous now that I'd come so far. The grass thinned, revealing cracked slabs of stone under my feet. Carved letters, half-obliterated with moss, weird patterns of lichen, a horrible conviction that I stood on human remains. My breath caught sharply in my throat. It was stupid of me to have come, stupid and dangerous. I had strong feelings of sympathy with Shiona, but I shouldn't have let them carry me so far.

I turned to go back and froze where I stood. Something stood in the shadow of a yew, something tall and dark, that didn't move. Panic spilled over me in little icy spurts. Too tall for Shiona. Anyway, there was something masculine about the outline. Graveyards were haunted places. Only madwomen went into them at night. I gave a small shocked scream and began to run.

Half-buried stones laid traps for my feet. My outstretched hands thrust away dragging branches and propelled me around spongy tombs. I could hear stumbling footsteps not far away. And then I fell forward, my head striking the edge of something large and very hard. Far away, a voice called my name.

I opened my eyes to candlelight. A golden haze obscured my vision.

'I think she's coming 'round,' someone said. I'd never heard the voice before. There's a peculiar horror in awakening to utter strangeness. Not only the voice was unfamiliar. The room that emerged slowly from the yellow mist was equally strange and so was the face that stared down at me. She was very beautiful in an odd, ravaged way. It was the face of someone who had suffered a great deal. High, sharply angled cheekbones, deeply set eyes that could be any color. They were mere dusky blobs at this moment. Her mouth was lovely, well-shaped but determined. The hair that was swathed around her head was dull gold – like the light that became suddenly too powerful for me. I closed my eyes again, my senses swimming like carp in a pool. Or the swans around the Stone Maiden . . .

'Well? What do you think?' A man's voice this time, soft and muffled.

'She's like him. Extraordinarily so.' There was an edge of pain there that told me who this might be, then snatched the knowledge away before the idea had formulated.

This had happened to me before. White and gold horses and swans circling in darkness blurred into a haze, my head thumping and pounding.

'Should I tell them?'

'Not yet.' Through the gap in my lashes the lovely, sad face took shape again. I tried to move my head. A small sound escaped me.

'Does it hurt?' The pain that had surrounded the voice had melted into solicitude. I wondered, weakly, why I was so afraid.

'Yes. It does a bit. Did I fall from the horse? I remember horses – '

'You'll be all right,' the woman said softly. She turned to speak to someone else. 'You'd better go to Rob after all. She ought to stay here as a precaution, but we don't want anyone getting the wrong ideas. Kidnapping, for instance. Better to clear ourselves straightaway.'

Kidnapping? Clearing themselves? What did they mean? Where was I? I began to struggle to raise myself and the mist came blanketing down again.

'We should get the doctor. It's happened before,' the soft male voice said just before night fell for the second time. 'It could be dangerous.'

I woke up remembering everything. A tall bony man took

my pulse and felt my head. He had hollow cheeks and ginger hair. His voice rasped, unlike the one I had heard last night. 'D'ye ken your name?' he asked me suddenly.

'Margaret Stewart.'

'Aye. Aye.' He watched me narrowly. The room shimmered about me in a sheen of silk wallpaper and Chinese cabinets. The bed canopy was of some blue-green material in which the colors shifted and swam like the waves of the sea.

'Where am I?' I asked. 'I should be at Maidenstane. How could I be here?' Confusion settled over me like a blanket.

'You're at Carn Tierlath.'

I stared blankly. The man turned and addressed someone who stood on the other side of an elegant screen that sheltered one side of the four-poster bed. 'She should stay here a bit longer. Let her rest a bit. Keep her quiet.' How familiar this situation was!

'What about them?' someone whispered.

'I'll call there myself. So that they know it's all perfectly legitimate.'

Who were they and what was legitimate? And where, oh, where, was Carn Tierlath? There was the sound of receding footsteps. A shiver of breeze rustled the seawater canopy. The carpet on the floor looked Chinese too, pale, exquisite colors that blended with everything else. I raised my head a little to look out the window, but there was nothing to see but a blur of green.

'Good morning.'

I fell back against the pillow. My eyes met those of Buck Graham. I knew the wild color swept into my face but I was powerless to prevent it. I knew, too, that this was the house on the other side of the graveyard, that the ravaged, beautiful face belonged to Kate Graham, who was once my father's love.

'How on earth did I get here?'

'You seem to be abnormally accident-prone. Last night was the third time I've seen you throw yourself at Mother Earth. Is it some sort of compulsion?' The dark brows were raised satirically.

'Then it was you in the graveyard?'

'If you mean was it I who saw you fall, yes.'

'You didn't follow me?'

'Follow you?' His eyes said that was the last thing he would do.

'Someone did.' I shivered at the recollection.

'Why were you there?' Curiosity took the place of disapproval but only briefly.

'I saw someone from my bedroom window. I thought it was – ' I stopped, remembering Shiona's attitude toward Buck. I became terribly conscious of being in bed, of the nightgown I wore in place of my outdoor clothes, of his impassive stare.

'Oh?' He waited for me to go on with a studious politeness.

'I was wrong. Of course.' I lowered my gaze.

'Oh, of course,' he agreed silkily, his gypsy face all stretched and taut as though he knew quite well who I'd thought was walking in the cemetery.

'Do I have to stay here?' I asked abruptly.

'Doctor Forbes seems to think so. You need remain no longer than is absolutely necessary.' He put a hand on the polished rail of the four-poster. I looked at it warily. It was a strong hand, burned with much sun, a capable, unfrivolous hand. And very strong – I began to wish we were not alone together, and yet there was a secret part of me that rejoiced in his presence, that wanted to go on watching all the tall, dark foreignness of him for as long as he'd let me.

'I owe you some money,' I said, making my voice brittle.

His black eyes flickered. 'You must be mistaken – '

'The fairground. Remember? I forgot my purse.'

He looked down at the polished toes of his boots. 'Oh. The fairground – '

'I still haven't my purse with me. But I wouldn't care to be in your debt.'

'Naturally not. Shall I make you out an IOU?' I was wrong, of course, but I imagined I saw a trace of amusement around his mouth for a moment.

'Don't make fun of me!' I said sharply.

'As if I should dare! I haven't forgotten how you glared at me yesterday – '

'Yesterday?' I frowned.

'Your riding lesson. You were having difficulties – ' He turned toward the window.

'Oh. Then.' If he smiled again, I thought I should strike him!

'Are you feeling better?'

'Much. I'm sure I could go home.' Home. That had come out very spontaneously.

The dark eyes came to rest on my face. 'I'm sure Doctor Forbes knows best. Your head must be made of cast iron. But it's just as well, isn't it?'

'I suppose so. Do you mind? Doctor Forbes said I should be quiet.'

'Hoist with my own petard,' Buck said softly. 'All right, Miss Maggie. I expect Mother will be in to see you soon –'

'Was it necessary,' I asked, 'to come to Berwick to spy on me on her behalf?'

His eyes blazed, then dulled again. 'So that's what you think.'

'That's what I know.'

The hand that grasped the bedpost tightened. I wondered if I'd gone too far. But he said nothing else, only turned on his heel. I couldn't understand why he should mind so much that I'd merely stated the obvious. Perhaps he was only annoyed that I'd found out the reason for his presence in Berwick.

It was quiet after he'd gone. I began to wish that I hadn't sent him away. Not that he would have wanted to stay. I looked, half-dreaming, at the trees and flowers that decorated the lacquer cabinets, the gold-painted dragons and birds. I didn't hear Kate Graham approach, only became aware of someone standing just out of sight and a strong impression of sadness. Had it been Kate who'd been in the graveyard? I remembered the footsteps, the crack of old twigs and the moment when I realized I stood over dead bones and moldering flesh. Or Charley? He'd gone out and I'd received that impression of masculinity about the waiting figure. Or had it been Buck all the time? Charley. He had been under suspicion of causing Fran's accident as well as Buck. My mind scurried from one thought to another to put off the necessity of addressing Kate.

She spoke first. Her voice was very different from last night. 'Buck says you seem better. Margaret Drummond was here, but I told her you were to be kept quiet on Doctor Forbes's orders. She said she didn't realize you were not in the house until Buck called on them.' She had a flowing gown that went very well with the Oriental room.

'She went to see someone called Aunt Bell –'

Kate shivered and moved her position. She put a cigarette into a long jade holder and puffed at it nervously. I had never seen a woman smoke before. It was almost indecent, I thought. 'Yes. Poor Bell. I'll have to visit her myself. She's my cousin, too – second cousin rather. Unfortunately, it upsets me to see people incarcerated. Anything for that matter. I won't have pets in the house or caged birds. Everyone – everything should be free –'

'But what about people who would harm others if they weren't restrained?'

Kate drew on her cigarette. Some of the strain left her fine face. 'You do sound better, don't you!' Her laughter was low-pitched and a little forced.

'I'm all right now.'

'Are you? Sit up then and I'll bring you a cup of tea.'

I pulled myself halfway up the pillows when the dizziness came again.

'You see? You aren't as indestructible as you think. Stay where you are and I'll fetch the tea. Could you eat something?'

'Not really. Later perhaps.'

She moved away, leaving the air faintly hazed with blue smoke. There was something about her that reminded me of Shiona. My cousin was much more like Kate than either Aunt Margaret or Uncle Rob. Perhaps I saw a resemblance because they were both beautiful and had similar coloring.

The Chinese room was more relaxing than the steeple room at Maidenstane with its stark, narrow bed and the tapping that came from a place where no sound should proceed. Not to mention the view from the window! They had meant me to have that room. Shiona and Fran had both made it clear that I had been discussed before my arrival and found wanting. But Shiona had grown to like me since. The thought of my cousin made me feel better. The tapping might be mice or birds . . .

Kate came back with the tea, which was subtly flavored and had a thin slice of lemon in it. 'It's lovely,' I said, enjoying the freshness of it on my tongue. 'By the way, I must tell you. I know who you are.'

'I'm Kate Graham,' she murmured.

'I know about you – and Father.' I couldn't lie here, drinking her tea and pretending. She was being kind and I must be honest.

'Oh?' She crossed one leg over the other. 'Already?'

'I know how you must have felt.'

'Do you? Do you really?' Her eyes were wide open now, the lines in her face more pronounced. There was a restrained anger in her voice and her expression that made me see I'd been wrong in being so free with my sympathy. It wasn't always the answer. Fran repulsed it over her physical hurt as Kate did over her mental pain.

'Could I have some more tea?' Anything to relieve the

73

charged atmosphere. I'd been clumsy. It would have been better to say nothing.

The second cup of tea was not so enjoyable as the first. I wondered awkwardly how to restore Kate's good humor, while a little voice inside me reminded me that she probably disliked me very much but had succeeded in concealing the fact until I'd been stupid enough to bring the past out into the open. 'What did the doctor call this house?' I asked in an effort to break the uneasy silence.

'Carn Tierlath. It means Charlie's Hill. After the Bonnie Prince. He used to come over here from Maidenstane. He was fond of this little rise. He planted some blue convolvulus where the end of the garden is now. This house, of course, didn't exist then. I believe the convolvulus only grows in one other place. Skye, or close to it. He brought the seeds with him when he came to conquer his birthright, only it didn't work out that way. There was Culloden – it was all finished.' She shrugged her shoulders.

'Do the flowers still grow?'

'Oh, yes. The Stewart children took some of the seeds back to Maidenstane. You'll see them there, but ours are the original ones.' She was looking at me intently as she spoke and I had the certainty she wasn't really thinking about the prince and the blue convolvulus. Had my father really loved her as a girl, held her in his arms, kissed her and promised to marry her? The idea seemed to have no reality. And where had Buck obtained his dark gypsy looks? There was no resemblance between him and his mother. What had Johnnie Graham been like? If Buck had taken after his father, I couldn't believe that Kate hadn't loved him. He'd never have let the shadow of another man stand between him and happiness. He'd have been far too forceful and dynamic.

'This room,' I ventured. 'It's most unusual. But beautiful – '

'My husband was very knowledgeable about antiques. He was a specialist in his way. He taught Buck, my son, what he knew. Buck buys and sells now for clients wanting specialized articles and not wanting to make expensive mistakes. Johnnie was responsible for furnishing this room, for instance. We have a Tudor room too, and a Stuart, Regency, even one after the French eighteenth century. That's why Buck was in Edinburgh. He's usually here, looking after the estate. But we've a good factor too. He copes well in Buck's absence.'

This was living on a grander scale than at Maidenstane and immeasurably far above our modest way of life at Berwick. The little old house, my sheltered convent education, the shadows that gathered in the stairwell, the whitened step, the waves of scarlet tiles that surmounted gray stone, I saw them with a terrible clarity. Father must have loved my mother very much to give up all this.

'He must lead a very interesting life, your son. I – I suppose Maidenstane *is* called after the Stone Maiden?'

'Yes.' Kate snapped off the word as though she didn't care to think about the woman in the loch.

'It must be a place of enormous interest.'

'Oddly enough, very few people go there. I haven't been for years. And Buck hasn't for some time. Not since someone drowned . . . ' Her voice trailed away uncertainly. Someone drowned. The ghost of Roddy Graham seemed to hang over the room, vaguely threatening. There had been unexplained marks on his body – just like the ones that marred my own flesh. Buck was usually with his cousin. He had been there when I was attacked on the steamer. He'd been on the Maiden when Fran was disabled for life. How could I be attracted to someone like Buck? I should do as Grandfather Stewart suggested and take a good look at Charley.

I fell asleep when Kate went, to dream of the devil on a white horse.

6

Fran came to see me later in the day. 'Well,' she said sharply. 'If you wanted to bring yourself to Buck's notice, couldn't you have chosen a less painful way?'

'If I were going to be personal, you made the most of *your* opportunity, coming so swiftly on the heels of my disaster! Didn't you, cousin Frances?'

For a moment, I thought she was going to fly into a rage. Then she laughed. 'I'm so glad you aren't going to be peevish and martyred.'

'No. I'm just going to be peevish.'

She giggled. 'You look pale and uninteresting.'

'Isn't that supposed to be pale and interesting?'

'Egotist!'

We were both laughing now. Fran's face changed, became cautious. 'Why on earth did you go out like that? Last night, I mean. I thought you were only going to the bathroom.'

'And I thought you were asleep! I was going to talk to you but your light was out.'

'I – I was tired of reading. I often lie in the dark and think.'

'Is it a good idea?'

Fran shrugged. 'I don't always go to sleep quickly.'

'You need more fresh air.'

'You sound just like Mother. I used to have all the fresh air I needed –'

'Fran. How much do you remember about that day at the Maiden? It's – it's not just idle curiosity. It's something I'm trying to work out in my mind. Are you sure you didn't recognize anything about whoever it was?'

'I didn't see them. One minute I was alone, then – push from behind!' Her freckles stood out in a sudden pallor.

'How did you get back home?'

'Father was there. He'd come to fetch us. None of us knew. He'd been watching us play.'

Uncle Rob. He'd been on the steamer. I'd seen him on the staircase with Buck. He was tall and very strong. He must have resented the fact that Charley wasn't to have Maidenstane even if he'd appeared to be open-minded about it. But why Fran?

'What's it like where you were defending your fort or castle or whatever it was?'

'It was the top of the Maiden's head. I know it looks bare and exposed from here, but there are lots of bushes growing 'round her head and shoulders. That's what gives her hair that realistic look. You could crawl in between the bushes and no one could see you properly. There's quite a drop on the other side onto rock –'

'I must go and explore,' I told her quickly. 'There are so many things I still have to see. I'm just beginning to realize that.'

There was a small sound on the other side of the screen and I had the uncomfortable certainty that someone had stood there listening. Or were they still there, only a few feet away?

'I like this room. Mrs. Graham says her husband knew about antiques.'

'He was a nice man. Clever too.'

'Was he like Buck?'

'Oh, not at all. He was quiet, rather elegant. A narrow, rather Spanish sort of face.'

'You seem to remember him well.'

'He hasn't been dead for long. Just after Roddy – '

'Oh, I'd imagined it was much longer. What happened to him?'

'Congestion of the lungs. He'd got wet and hadn't looked after himself properly afterward. Maybe he just wanted to die.' Like my mother, I thought. Only he had a different reason. Her love for my father had been returned, Johnnie Graham's had not. Did Kate have an uneasy conscience as Shiona had suggested?

'Where's Shiona?'

'Riding the hooves off that poor horse.' Fran's voice was cold. She seemed not to care for her sister.

'I don't suppose it minds. I'm sure she wouldn't ill-treat it,' I protested.

Fran yawned. 'I think I'll go. When will you be back?'

'I'm not sure. Your departure is awfully sudden, isn't it? Aren't you supposed to humor invalids?'

'You never told me why you were in the graveyard.' Fran sat down again purposefully.

'Oh.'

'Thought you'd diverted my attention, did you?' Her eyes were on mine, bright and curious.

'I wasn't trying to. We just got onto other things.'

'You did, you mean.'

'Didn't Buck explain? I saw someone from my window walking about between the stones. Then that banging started again, near the window. The sounds you seem not to hear.' I stared at her and watched her bite her lip. 'You know something about those taps and bangs, don't you? Anyway, I thought I'd see if it was Shiona down there. I'd lost the inclination to go to bed. The room's haunted, isn't it? That's why you all thought you'd put me in there. For a joke – '

Fran laughed again, a little uncertainly. 'What an over-stimulated imagination! Why should we do any such thing?'

'Because of Charley?' I suggested carefully.

Fran chose to ignore this. She stood up and tidied her long

hair, smoothing the skirt and blouse to neatness. Was it because she might meet Buck on her way out? It could have been Buck who attacked her on the Maiden. Presumably she knew this. And yet I'd gathered she bore him no resentment. No visible resentment – odd how alike our reactions were where he was concerned.

'Going, Fran?'

How quietly he moved! Buck was there beside the screen, dressed in dark trousers and an open-necked white shirt that showed much of his chest. He was very dark-skinned. Fran had said Johnnie Graham was Spanish-looking. Perhaps the dark coloring was all he'd passed on to his son.

'I was.' Her face was quite pink and her mouth showed a tendency to smile. She looked unexpectedly pretty.

'I'll walk back with you.' His eyes met mine and I knew that the gentleness there wasn't for me. 'Doctor Forbes will be back. He may let you go home tomorrow. I'll tell Rob. Oh, and I'll be looking in to see old Mr. Stewart. Have you any message for him?'

'Yes. Ask him if his manhood's been placed in jeopardy lately,' I requested flippantly.

His brows drew together in a frown. 'Will he understand?'

'Naturally. Don't forget, will you? And give him my love.'

'What a very untypical girl you are! It seems to run in the family. Fran, too, and – '

'She-She?' Fran suggested when he hesitated. His features set into a mask. There was a curious, taut silence. He looked more like Heathcliff than ever. It occurred to me that the Brontë women had been even more untypical than we were. Imagine a minister's daughters inventing people like Heathcliff and Mr. Rochester. Ouida, yes, but for such sheltered women to have such strong, creative natures! Jenny would have been fascinated by Buck and the aura that surrounded him, of suppressed violence and darkness. I watched his strong, booted legs walk away, heard the soft shuffle of Fran's feet on the polished boards beyond the Chinese carpet. There was a hostile silence after they were gone.

I was depressed. The rest of the day would be an anticlimax, I knew.

Kate Graham brought the doctor in not long afterward. He made me sit up and I was less dizzy than I had been in the morning. The headache too was diminishing. 'She'll do,' he pronounced. 'Back home tomorrow, Miss Stewart.'

'Tomorrow?' My reluctance to leave here surprised me. The doctor misunderstood.

'It wouldn't be a good idea to go tonight. Anyway, you couldn't be in better hands.'

'Mrs Graham's been very kind.'

'Kate,' she said. 'No one calls me Mrs. Graham. It makes me feel old.'

I already thought of her as Kate, I reflected.

'Wait till afternoon before you go. And you'll let me know if there's any setback?' Dr. Forbes took himself off well satisfied.

Kate brought me a tray. So far I'd seen no sign of servants, but they must be here just the same.

Outside someone was whistling 'Early One Morning'. My appetite suddenly vanished. It would be Buck. They must still think about each other in spite of the estrangement. I was ashamed to discover that I'd rather Buck and Shiona were enemies than friends. That tune meant something that neither wanted to forget.

I was much better the next morning. Kate made me stay in bed until after lunch, then I was allowed to go to a rather Roman-looking bathroom, not at all the sort of room one expected in the remoter areas of Scotland. There was a good deal of marble and opulent-looking bottles and flasks of colored glass, expensive soap. A huge mirror with a gilt frame showed me a healthy enough reflection. Fortunately the blow on my head had left no bruising on the face. A tentative exploration discovered a still-tender swelling. Rejuvenated by my luxurious soak, I dressed carefully. My hair, for all my brushing, refused to lie down. I wished, uselessly, that it were smooth and elegant as Shiona's – or Kate's.

Buck was in the drawing room when I went downstairs. 'Mother wondered if you'd like to see the garden before you go?' He was more formally dressed than yesterday and I guessed he was to be my escort back to Maidenstane. I hesitated only briefly. If anything happened to me, it could be laid directly at his door. I fancied I was safe enough on this occasion.

'I'd like that.'

'Good.' He opened a french window and let in a rush of buoyant air and the smell of growing things.

'Did you give Grandfather my message?'

'Of course.' He stood aside to allow me to precede him onto a flagged, colonnaded walk.

'I thought you wouldn't,' I told him, breathing in the spicy scents with pleasure. Ivy climbed up white pillars. Turning to look at the house, I was conscious of a sense of familiarity. It was squarish and built of pink sandstone. There were white ironwork balconies. It was a feminine house, contrasting with the masculinity of Maidenstane. The two buildings reminded me of the Maiden and the Warrior.

'Oh? And why shouldn't I deliver your message? I'd be intrigued to know.' The dark gypsy face looked down at me. His mouth was curved in the slightest of smiles.

'I thought you might be afraid he'd only laugh at you.'

'Is it so terrible? To be laughed at?' He shrugged.

'It depends on who's doing the laughing, I suppose. Why does this place look so familiar? Oh!' My voice choked briefly. 'I've remembered. I was looking at a very similar house that morning on the steamer. Just before – ' I stopped abruptly.

'Just before what?' His voice had changed subtly. I was conscious of his intent stare.

I couldn't answer straightaway. There was no real proof it had been Buck. Yet who else could it have been? I know I'd found out that Uncle Rob had been in the vicinity when Fran had had a similar experience, but I couldn't believe that a father had tried to destroy his own child. A fragment of a conversation came back to me. Something Grandfather Stewart had said. 'He couldn't take on another man's child' – that was about Josh Davidson – 'It's fortunate we don't all suffer from such unwillingness.' Had he meant Uncle Rob? It seemed too ridiculous, only I had firsthand knowledge that such situations existed.

'Just before it began to rain,' I replied a little lamely.

'Mother said you had some bad bruising. Apart from the bump on the head.'

My face flamed. How would he feel if I shouted, 'You put them there! You know how I came to have them!' I couldn't, of course. Instead, I said, 'They must have happened when I fell. In the graveyard.' My voice, to my relief, remained level.

'She says they weren't new. And it must have been an odd accident that marked you back *and* front.'

Good gracious! Was it necessary to examine me so thoroughly? Now that I come to remember, I fell against the ship's rail. I – I slipped on the wet deck.'

He gave a little grunt and took my elbow to change my course of direction. We were in the shrubbery, not unlike the one at the back of Maidenstane. There was a grass plot at the end of it, and, sheltered by the wall, a sprawling mass of glorious blue that made my breath catch in my throat. 'Oh, how lovely! What are they?'

'The morning glory. A blue convolvulus supposedly brought over from Normandy by –'

'Let me guess! Prince Charlie?'

'Why, yes. Are you psychic?' His brows rose.

'And they only grow in one other place. Skye.'

'Now that's where you're wrong. It's Eriskay. They grow in Prince's Bay. You've been talking to Mother, haven't you? She never gets details right. She's absentminded –'

'I should have said she was anything but that. Her prolonged interest in my family, for instance? I'd have described her as very single-minded.' We stood glaring at each other, the banter and the blue flowers forgotten.

'You still see her as planting spies all over Berwick, don't you! It really wasn't like that. Perhaps she did find it hard to forget your father. I could almost hate him for causing such unhappiness. Mother's a constant sort of person –'

'She'd have been unhappier still if they had married. Can't you see that?' I fixed my eyes on the stretch of wild moorland on the other side of the wall. A kite hovered over it. It made me think of Shiona's Dragon Hole, above which birds of prey flew. Clouds cast moving patches of blue shadow over all that bareness.

'You may be right. But wouldn't it be fairer to forget what you've already heard and take Mother as she is? I think she likes you.'

'Does she? That's very magnanimous of her –'

'I wish you meant that. But I suspect you'll hang onto all those preconceived notions. You're too young as yet to be generous –'

We began to walk back toward the pink bulk of the house, both breathing rather heavily, Buck with repressed anger, I with trying to keep up with his long strides. Hydrangeas bordered the colonnade in splotches of blue, pink and lavender. White butterflies tinged with green settled on a low wall separating the flagstones from shallow, moss-covered steps.

'Mr. Graham – ' I stopped and rested one hand on the nearest pillar.

6

'Buck,' he growled. 'Must you be so formal?'

'Buck,' I repeated. 'I'm sorry if I sounded ungenerous. It's not a habit of mine. Your mother's been kind. I will admit, however, that I've been confused about certain happenings since I left Berwick. I can see I have to keep an open mind and not let others make it up for me.'

'You would be wise. By the way, you must have made a hit with Fran. I can't think of anyone else she'd visit.'

'Oh? I hadn't realized it was such an unusual event. Poor Fran.' The dark look came back to his face as I spoke. I would have given anything to know what he was thinking about. When he answered, the subject was different. 'I – I couldn't help but see your riding lesson. You could be good if you relaxed a little. Don't hold yourself so stiffly. Give a bit more with the movement of the horse, and never pull too hard on its mouth. That can hurt. But your posture was promising.'

I flushed. 'I hadn't realized you'd been there so long.'

'You were much too occupied to see me. But that's how it should be.'

'Shiona rides magnificently,' I couldn't help saying, just to watch his reaction. His mouth hardened. There was a grating quality about his voice when he answered. 'She's a splendid horsewoman. You – you get on well with She-She, do you?'

'Very well indeed.'

He wanted to say more. I could see it in his face. He crushed down the impulse. 'Mother will want to see you before I take you back. It hasn't tired you, marching you 'round the grounds?'

'Not at all. I'm glad you let me see the prince's flowers. I'm very interested in history.'

'You should get on well with Rob.'

'Oh, yes. His book. Shiona says –' I stopped.

'And what *does* she say?' Buck asked softly. 'I can't believe you've forgotten.'

'She says the old festivals still have their place in spite of the church's disapproval.'

'Yes. The country's slow to give up what it enjoys. Farming communities are superstitious in the main. If you look in the kitchen at Maidenstane, you'll still see the corn dollies hanging on the wall. On Saturday it's Midsummer Eve. The minister will say it's John the Baptist's Day, but we know it was Balder's long, long before John the Baptist was born. Folks around here take boats on the loch and throw flowers around the Maiden.

And some climb to the Warrior looking for yarrow and vervain and fern. And you'll see fires burning –'

I wished he had not stopped talking. Now that all the hostility and passion was burned out of his voice, it was pleasant, oddly seductive.

'But Rob will tell you all about that,' he went on brusquely, as though aware of my thoughts. 'A clever man. There's far more to him than most people see. A fair man too –'

I thought that was true. Uncle Rob seemed to hold no grudge against Buck for all that he might have injured Fran. Or was there some other reason for that? Was it because Uncle knew Buck wasn't responsible? Was he well aware that he or perhaps his beloved Charley had done the damage? The thought was chilling. Although Fran was an odd, withdrawn, bookish girl. Had her imagination run away with her? She'd been much younger then. She could have been living the past. A toe caught in heather roots, a stumble, a headlong fall. If she'd struck her shoulder at the beginning, she could have deceived herself –

Kate appeared just as the silence lasted too long for comfort. 'You'll come back, won't you? I know this wasn't the sort of visit one normally looks forward to, but it hasn't been too awful, has it?'

'It wasn't awful at all.'

'Good. I thought it might have put you off.'

I shook my head. 'It hasn't. I only hope I wasn't a nuisance.'

'You weren't. Buck, don't forget to say that Doctor Forbes wants to be informed if Maggie has any kind of relapse. And in any case, he'll be calling in a day or two. I think that's everything.'

'I'm sure it isn't necessary,' I objected.

'But heads aren't brass cooking pots. They'll only stand so much. And there was that other time, wasn't there?' Kate lit another cigarette in the long green holder and threw the taper into the fireplace.

'Other time?'

There was a long, tingling silence. She knew all about what had happened at Berwick and Buck still expected me not to suspect that they'd been prying. I didn't like to contemplate these intelligent, attractive people watching me and mine. Everyone was entitled to his privacy. No one liked to think one was like a goldfish in a bowl.

'Well,' I said flatly. 'I do thank you. '

They looked at me for a moment. Kate puffed at her cigarette, the smoke hazing the long, elegant lines of her body in the flowing gown. Even her clothes were different from everyone else's. I knew when I was back at Maidenstane that this would seem like some impossible dream. And yet this place was mine for the taking. I knew too that Kate found me just as fascinating as I found her and Buck. We seemed caught in some odd, warped relationship that mattered to us all.

'She'll be back,' Buck said as he took my arm, his dark face shuttered.

All the way home to Maidenstane I wondered how it would end.

I wrote to Aunt Sarah and Jenny. They were, of necessity, superficial letters about everyday things. I said nothing of Buck Graham or Kate, but I dwelt on the kindness of Grandfather Stewart and of the Drummonds. The account of the journey took up quite a lot of space and I included descriptions of the Maiden and the moors that began where the garden walls ended. The letter writing took up the two days of rest enforced by Aunt Margaret, who had been disturbed by the graveyard episode.

'You could have lain out there for hours!' she told me. Her genuine concern warmed me.

Shiona had been delighted by my return and had given up her beloved horse riding to sit with me, surrounded by silks and ribbons and all the paraphernalia of the workbasket. She was trimming a dress for Saturday. Fran hadn't joined us. It made me feel uncomfortable, the way one kept away if the other was with me. If I devoted all my time to Shiona, I should never see Fran. It seemed a pity the sisters shouldn't get on better together.

'What did you think of Kate?'

I had to admit she was beautiful.

'Just imagine! She might have been your mother.'

'No, she wouldn't! It wouldn't have been me. It would have been a girl who was a mixture of Father and Kate. I'm somebody quite different. One's mother determines all kinds of things in one's nature.'

'I suppose so. But you look like your father. Everyone says so. That could have stayed the same.'

'Charley looks terribly like Uncle Rob. They're more like brothers, aren't they?'

84

'Yes. Except for Father's penchant for the past. Charley has his feet planted very solidly in the present.' Shiona gave her warm, affectionate laugh.

'Isn't there some girl? He's very good-looking.'

'There could be. He's grown rather secretive of late. When a man has something to hide, there's usually a petticoat at the end of it.' No trace of amusement now.

'Grandfather doesn't think so.'

'Grandfather's confined to his room. He doesn't see what I see.'

'Who is it?' I picked up a length of blue velvet ribbon and stroked the plushy surface absently.

'Of course, it could be all on her side –'

'On whose side?' I cried.

'Cathy Forbes.' Shiona's needle flashed in and out of the tawny material.

'Forbes? That's the doctor's name. Is she some relation?'

'His daughter. She's eligible, of course. There aren't many girls around her who are, but Cathy's one of them. There's the solicitor's daughter too, but I think she has other plans. She usually accompanies her father to Carn Tierlath when there's any estate business. Sometimes asked to dinner too.' Shiona stabbed a pin into a velvet cushion with unnecessary force. So she did still think of Buck.

'What are they like?'

'Cathy's little and dark – more your type.'

'And the solicitor's daughter?' I prepared myself to dislike this unknown girl.

'Elizabeth Stewart? She's fair, blue eyes, pretty if you care for insipid women.'

'Stewart?'

'I suppose she's a distant relation. All the Stewarts in the district are connected in some way, though you'd have to go back a long way to prove such liaisons. Anyway, you'll be seeing them soon enough. They'll be on the loch for the Midsummer Festival and at the bonfire. Their brothers too.'

'Don't you mean the Festival of Saint John the Baptist?' I inquired mischievously.

Shiona laughed. 'I suppose I do. But Midsummer is so much more evocative! I can't bring to mind any picture of poor old Saint John. Yet Midsummer reminds me' – she turned her face away abruptly – 'of so many things. I think I've sewed enough for one day, Maggie. You can't ride yet but I'd like to. Would you mind?' She had obviously remembered something painful to her. It seemed a pity that all the things I wanted to know brought back memories that hurt.

I went up to Grandfather's room after Shiona had gone. Fran was there, sitting on the side of the old man's bed. I fancied his eyes lit up at the sight of me. 'Shiona's gone riding,' I said. 'I can't just yet.'

'Think you'll take to it?' Grandfather asked.

'Oh, yes. Buck said – ' I stopped, very aware of two watchful pairs of eyes.

'Well? What did he say?'

'He thought I'd do well. He suggested a few things that might improve matters.'

Grandfather grunted. 'And how d'you like being here?'

'Very much.'

'You aren't going to go running back to your Aunt Sarah?'

'I can't. Not if I want her to marry Josh.'

'Is that the only reason?'

'Of course not. You know that. There's something different about you. What is it?'

'Different?' His frosty eyes glinted.

'You've got a different feather in your bonnet.'

'He broke the other. Rolled over on it in his sleep,' Fran told me, grinning.

'Another reason why you shouldn't wear it as a nightcap,' I suggested.

'When should I wear it if not here? I can't get out, can I, child?' There was a look of real deprivation on his face. I realized that it must be very frustrating for someone with a keen mind to be confined within a few square feet of space. I came near to understanding Kate with that realization. She, too, regretted that people and animals must be incarcerated. It was so wonderful to be free, to be able to see the world, to have the Midsummer Festival to look forward to as I did.

'There are corn dollies in the kitchen,' I said. 'Will you take me to see them, Fran?'

The kitchen was a huge, stone-flagged room with a cat by the hearth where a large fire burned. There was an enormous, black-leaded stove and a vast array of pans and skillets, copper jelly molds, wooden spoons, and a scoured preserving pan. A store cupboard stood open, revealing bottles of gooseberries and plums and cherries and jars of jam and pickles. A smell of baking bread and spice hung on the warm air. On the dresser with its rows of plates and saucers stood a jar containing sprays of a small plant I didn't recognize.

'Saint-John's-wort,' Ness said, looking up from her busy stirring. 'We'll have peace and plenty now. That's protection against witches and like badness –'

'Where did you get it?' I was interested.

'Won't do you no good to tell. It's got to be found by accident. You go for a walk and keep your eyes open while you're about it! There's fern seed too, but make sure the fairies don't see you pick it. Put a sprig of rowan in your pocket. Bad little creatures, the fairies are. Steal you as soon as look at you, they would.'

'What would you do with the wort if you find it?'

'Hide it in your bodice. Keeps off the second sight, the evil eye and – death. There's enchanters still where you'd least expect them,' Ness informed me quite seriously.

Buck, I thought to myself, there's an enchanter if ever there was one. And Shiona too. There was more than a trace of witchcraft and magic about my cousin.

'Here are the corn dollies,' Fran called out, growing impatient. I went over to the corner beyond the dresser where she was waiting for me. There was something curiously human about the little figures that hung there. 'That's the mother,' Fran said, pointing to the larger of the two. I stared, fascinated, at the dried clay face and the bead eyes, the baby dress gathered at the waist, the piece of rag that covered the top of the head like a scarf, showing only wisps of corn. I thought her unexpectedly sinister. The maiden was more attractive in her silk trimmed with lace and the soft white bow that clasped her waist. The shower of corn that made up her head was pretty. The mother showed stems tied with string for her feet; the maiden's were concealed under her becoming skirt.

'Gruesome little thing,' I remarked, still disturbed by the corn mother. The set of the beads in the dirty clay gave the face a knowing look that made my flesh creep. 'I don't like her at all.' I touched the shawl briefly.

'We get used to them,' Fran told me. 'You'll see how they're made after the harvest. Usually these are taken down on the Eve of Saint Bride. The horses eat them. I wonder why these were forgotten? Oh, yes. It was – poor Roddy –'

'You mean the drowning?' I breathed, unwilling to disturb her train of thought.

'That's right.'

I became aware that Ness had stopped stirring and was listening intently. Fran intercepted her gaze and plucked at my arm. 'We'll never find Saint-John's-wort if we stay here all day.'

'Well, don't be missing for your dinner!' Ness called crossly. I suspected her annoyance was due to the sudden halt in the conversation. Local folk were still interested in the topic of Roddy Graham's untimely death. I had a horrible feeling I knew how he had died. His attention distracted and strong purposeful hands at his back, thrusting without mercy. It didn't bear thinking about. And Buck was always with him . . .

We went out the back way so that no one would see us. I was more than a little tired of bedrooms and being made to rest. The air was filled with a pine-laden freshness, and the cornfields were patches of yellow catching all the sunlight.

'Let's walk in the graveyard,' Fran suggested. 'Unless you're afraid to.'

'Of course I'm not afraid.' I suspected she had some undisclosed motive. Her next words proved me right. 'You want to know about Roddy, don't you?'

There seemed no point in dissembling. 'His name does keep cropping up. Yes, I do.'

We clambered through the gap in the mossy wall. The leaning stones didn't look frightening as they had in the moonlight, only sad and neglected. A vague air of grievance permeated the place. Fran limped the way I had gone on the night of my accident. I followed, the events of that ill-fated excursion filling my mind until Fran said, 'Roddy was a good person. People tended to play on that. His parents died – like yours – only he was younger. He'd already spent a number of holidays with the Grahams and got on well with Buck. He didn't look like him. He was much more like Johnnie Graham, Buck's father. They were more like father and son than uncle and nephew. Anyway, they more or less adopted Roddy. He and Buck had the same tutors and you never saw one without the other. That sort of thing.' Fran's voice sharpened. There would be no such liaison for a crippled girl, especially one so aware of her deficiencies. Even if anyone held out the hand of friendship, it would, like as not, be slapped away.

The shadows of the stones sloped blackly over the pink grasses. The trees seemed to press closer. 'The Grahams spent a lot of time with us. Everyone thought She-She and Buck would get married eventually – and then, all of a sudden, it was She-She and Roddy, and Buck was left out of things a bit. But there was something wrong about the whole thing. Roddy wasn't happy. He didn't say anything but he turned quiet and moody. It was unlike him. He and Buck still went riding and swimming together. Not long before – before he died, Roddy tried to tell me something. He'd called for She-She and I was in the drawing room while he waited. I can't remember what he said now. A few halting words, something about Buck – I wasn't to blame him – but She-She came down before he got any further. He worshiped her, I could see it in his eyes. Perhaps it's just as well they didn't get married. I think he'd have been a doormat, poor Rod. I think he was trying to say that Buck didn't mean to hurt me. So I suppose it was Buck all the time. Only the funny thing is, I just can't believe it or stop liking him. Isn't it stupid?' Her poor voice was sharper than ever. I discovered we had stopped on the half-buried gravestone that lay sunken on the path, the same one that had so upset me previously with its suggestion of covering bones and the remnants of flesh and hair.

'Whose grave is that?' I asked Fran huskily, and moved aside in an attempt to decipher the overgrown lettering.

'The first Charles Stewart to live here after Maidenstane was built. The one Prince Charlie visited. No one knows much about that visit – '

'Apart from the convolvulus being planted.'

'So you know about that! Kate and Buck, I suppose.'

'Yes.'

'He was supposed to leave something else. A silver punch bowl and six matching goblets – '

'Silver?'

'All of them. With a white rose design. They aren't in the house. But Father and Buck Graham still believe they exist, that they're somewhere here, waiting to be found. They'd be worth a fortune to a collector. The prince gave them to this Charles, only he had to hide them because of the defeat at Culloden. If anyone had seen them he'd probably have been accused of treason. Somehow, they got lost – '

I stared down at the cracked slab with its patterns of lichen. Fran had moved away. 'Here's Roddy's grave!' she called out. I skirted the rounded remains of smaller upright stones and looked at Roddy's. It was very simple. Roderick Graham – aged twenty-three. Johnnie was buried beside him. There were flowers on the graves and I knew where they'd come from. They were blue – blue convolvulus, probably the rarest flower in the British Isles. A yew overshadowed the burial place. I had seen that waiting figure by the yew. Kate was tall and inclined to dress oddly in clothes that hid her femininity. Had it been Buck's mother walking in the moonlight, who had followed me so purposefully? For some reason I thought of the corn mother, an inanimate object but with a kind of unpleasant intelligence about the manufactured face as though something evil looked out of the china blue eyes. Blue flowers, blue beads, both communicating something unchristian.

I wished futilely that I hadn't asked Fran about Buck. Her replies had only made matters worse. Much worse. She'd made it seem as if Roddy had some proof that would convict Buck of assault.

'I know where we might find the Saint-John's-wort,' Fran said. 'Coming?'

I nodded, avoiding the flagstone that covered Charles Stewart's resting place. I'd had enough of graves and reminiscences. Perhaps I should have sought out Charley. Charley would have talked of the present or the future – anything but the past.

7

Midsummer Eve began with the smell of baking. The fragrance of cakes and bannocks and pies rose to all the bedrooms, spreading an air of expectancy. Ness and 'You' must have been up extremely early. From my bedroom window the graveyard was still misted with blue. That haze probably meant heat. I hoped passionately that this was so. Rain would spoil the entire occasion. I wanted very much to sail on the loch with all the young people who would be our visitors this evening. There was to be a special supper. We were to climb to the Warrior where special Sun Stones still stood. Sun worship had existed there since this place had been inhabited. Fran said that lovers first drank at the well, then went to the Troth Stone, which stood apart from the Sun Stones, and clasped hands through the hole near the top of it. This was as good as a declaration of marriage. Some divided a six-penny piece between them, each wearing the half on a chain.

I took off my nightgown and wondered if Buck had ever held anyone's hand through the hole in the Troth Stone. He certainly wore no half sixpence on a chain, for I'd seen his bare chest more than once. I wriggled into my clothes and tried to push down the feelings of excitement and anticipation that were so like the pleasure that preceded the May Fair at Berwick. From the vase on the chest of drawers I took my sprig of Saint-John's-wort and placed it in my bodice. 'Protection against witches and like badness,' old Ness had said. Did one need such protection in the nineteenth century? It seemed incredible. Then I thought of Fran and Roddy and, touching the still-tender places around my midriff, decided it wasn't so impossible.

Surveying my neat blouse and black skirt, my well-brushed hair, I regretted that I was not so beautiful as Shiona or Kate. But did looks matter so much? Father had abandoned Kate for Mother, who was certainly far less striking. And Shiona had implied that she had been put aside by Buck Graham. It was a habit of his, she'd said, to pick people up and make them love him, then end it when his interest had evaporated. It was all immensely puzzling.

I pinned my cameo brooch onto a black velvet band that Shiona had given me from the selection in her workbasket, then fastened it around my throat. I fancied it made me look older, more interesting. The blouse was plain but the little pearl buttons gave it more distinction. Shiona would have liked me to have the turquoise dress, but she hadn't yet offered it to Fran. If Fran didn't accept it, I would fall heir to it.

I opened the bedroom door and stopped, sickened. Something was dangling from the lintel, a little swaying figure with a dusty clay face and malicious eyes of blue glass. The small straw feet brushed my cheek. The skirt gave off a smell of damp and spiders.

I looked along the passage. Fran's door was open about an inch. She'd probably expect me to scream but I didn't intend to give her that satisfaction. It must have been Fran. I'd let her know the figure repelled me. Poor Fran. She'd been hurt, her life spoiled. Something in her made her want to hurt others in retaliation. One had to feel pity. I reached up and pulled at the string that kept the corn mother hanging there. The little creature tumbled into my hands and I hated the feel of it. Taking it inside the room, I pushed it into the chest of drawers. The drawer was no sooner closed than the muffled tapping started. It was almost as though the mother were knocking at the inside of the drawer, clamoring for release. I backed away, all my pleasurable anticipation drowned in revulsion. If I were a more timorous character, I wouldn't stay here another day! Perhaps that was what someone wanted . . .

I went out into the passage and called, 'Ready, Fran?'

She emerged immediately, almost as though she'd been waiting for that summons.

I smiled. 'It's going to be a lovely day. There's a heat haze over the moor.'

'Is there?' Fran's voice was flat. 'I – I don't think I'll go out. I never like it if it's hot. It makes me tired.'

'You needn't do anything energetic. But you'd get tanned. Sunlight's good for you.'

'There's not much point. I can't get up to the Warrior. It's quite a climb.'

'But you could sail on the loch. Just imagine the boats in the moonlight and all those flowers. Everyone'll be there. And so will you. You've just got up on the wrong side of the bed, haven't you? Wear that turquoise dress and you'll look as pretty as anyone. Shiona's got it ready downstairs.' I refrained from saying that I wanted it myself.

'Oh, that.' Fran's eyes sharpened but I could tell by her mouth that she desired the gown a great deal.

'Buck seems to like that color,' I went on cheerfully. 'He admired it in Edinburgh.' I thought a white lie was justified under the circumstances. He hadn't actually said he liked the dress. But he had stared at it as if he approved. Even Shiona had noticed.

'Well, I might.' Fran's face had softened. I hoped I hadn't raised her hopes too much. Anyway, there were going to be other men in the party. Cathy Forbes and Elizabeth Stewart had brothers who had been invited. Perhaps Fran already had her eye on one of them.

'There's no might about it,' I told her. 'You'll wear that gown if I have to stuff you inside it!' That made her laugh. Some of the excitement that had evaporated when I found the straw figure returned. If it was Fran who put it there, she meant no harm. It was only one of her disconcerting jokes like saying she couldn't hear the tapping from near my window. Or had that been the truth? Was I the only one who did?

Breakfast was an interesting meal. Uncle Rob talked of the Midsummer Festival, pointing out that this was the counterpart of the Yule celebration. His travels had uncovered half-forgotten facts, that the Scandinavian influence – they supported the Balder legends – was still strong in Orkney and Shetland. Balder was the god of light, and the days that would now begin to shorten threatened Balder with the darkness that was his death. He should have worn Saint-John's-wort, I thought, conscious of the sprig I had tucked inside my bodice. It would ward off second sight, enchantment, witchcraft, evil eye and death. And what of the condition that Shiona called *temps perdu*? Would the plant ward that off too? It hadn't happened to me since I arrived here.

Uncle Rob showed me a jar containing branches of elderberry and rowan and roses. 'It's the time of roses and love, Maggie. It's for lovers and fire – ' And I thought of love and flowers, seeing young couples jump over flames, hand in hand, then climbing in dusk to the Troth Stone. There was a curious sadness in the thought. No one knew me well enough to ask me to join in the time of roses. Everyone else had known one another since childhood. Bonds were already forged. Who could want to partner me? And then I remembered that this wasn't the last time. The festival took place every year! I would get to know people, have time to develop relationships. Only a romantic would expect to go out in moonlight and be pursued by some personable man who appeared out of nowhere. 'The elderberry's for protection,' Uncle Rob was saying. 'And there's a job for you girls this morning. Pruning the roses.'

'Why today?'

'Because the rosebush that's pruned today will be blooming far into autumn. We'll get scissors from Ness,' Shiona said. 'It always seems to work.'

I wondered privately if it wasn't more likely that the sheltered seclusion of the sunken garden was really responsible for the long-lasting blooms, but the Drummonds seemed to believe that the Midsummer pruning was what influenced that longevity.

'I like the black ribbon,' Shiona said when we were out in the garden snipping industriously at the rose stems. 'I'm glad I gave it to you. How grown-up you look.'

'Do I?'

'You've grown up tremendously since that first moment I saw you standing so nervously in the station,' she told me. 'You were petrified, weren't you?'

'Not really. There was something you and Uncle didn't know.' I told her about the heavy swell in the plaid suit and how he had pestered me because of their lateness.

'What a popular little soul!' she commented, cutting deep into the heart of the bush she was concentrating on. 'And then to engage Buck's interest so thoroughly. I thought he'd never take his eyes off you when we were at Holyrood. He'd better watch out if he tries his tricks on my cousin. Don't' – she stared at me seriously – 'don't let him hurt you, Maggie, will you? I was quite worried when I knew you were under the same roof. He can be quite violent.' She shuddered then and I wondered what she was remembering. Had Buck assaulted her, and did Shiona turn to Roddy as a result? Buck might have resented the transference of her affections to the man he regarded as a brother and constant companion. That might explain the drowning, the marks on Roddy Graham's body. I found myself looking at the pruning shears with distaste, the sharp sounds of Shiona's slashing into my mind in the most unpleasant way.

We went riding later. Aunt Margaret was too busy with her preparations for tonight to worry about the effects of a tumble on my accident-prone head. I think she was only too glad that we were to be satisfactorily occupied. We had, after all, spent the entire morning on the roses and in gathering flowers and she had sufficient help with her culinary efforts already. I followed Buck's instructions and found that I did, indeed, sit the pony's back all the more comfortably. We went up a sheep track onto the moor instead of staying in the meadow by the loch. It was delightful to amble along with the glen all laid out below in a shimmer of blue and gold, the cloud shadows swooping over the fields and woods like the shadows of kites and hawks. The loch was black, as it always was, and the huge stone figure of the Maiden sprawled close to the shore, the dull green of her hair spreading down to the water. I noticed we would have to row to the other side of the loch to climb up to the Warrior. I saw the laden boats in my mind's eye, plowing wet furrows in the moonlight and people laughing and throwing flowers onto the shining surface of the water. There would be fires and the Sun Stones. It all seemed old and wicked . . .

Shiona put her mare into a gallop, but I was content just to watch her flying form ahead of me. She went farther and farther away until she and the chestnut mare were only a moving dot, barely distinguishable from the waste of heather.

The sound of water trickling attracted me. It was very hot. I had been right about the heat haze. I tied the pony's bridle to a stunted bush and climbed down a stony declivity to the mountain stream that gurgled over a bed of pebbles. The cupped water was delicious, like nothing else I had ever tasted. I wiped some over my temples and wrists and sat down to contemplate the shifting lights and brown darknesses between the stones. Shiona was coming back now. I could hear the horse's hooves drumming on the ground, a hard determined sound that roused me from delightful lethargy. I turned to wave to her.

It wasn't Shiona's chestnut mare I saw. A big dapple-gray with a silver mane and a dark man on his back. A centaur, Uncle Rob had said. A devil, my cousin had suggested. They were both right. There was something distinctly satanic about Buck Graham today. Poetry too in the fusion of his body and the mount's. It was as if he'd grown there like a tree in a very old wood, its roots embedded for eternity.

The gray was slowing down. Buck dismounted. 'Are you all right?' he called.

'Why shouldn't I be?' In spite of myself, Shiona's warning rang in my ears. I thought of poor Roddy trying to tell Fran that she mustn't blame Buck. The lethargy fled.

'All alone in the wilderness?' he mocked.

I should have said I wasn't alone, but something stronger than truth had taken possession of me. I watched him come toward me, and subconsciously, my fingers reached up to touch the place where the Saint-John's-wort was hidden. A charm against enchantment and that was what exuded from every pore of Buck Graham's body.

'What are you doing up here?' I asked with deceptive calmness. 'I thought you'd be far too busy selling antiques – or looking after your stock.'

'Well informed, aren't you?'

'The antiques, you mean?' I shaded my eyes from the sun and stared up the broad length of him. Light shone on his boots in spite of the thin film of dust. 'Your mother told me.'

'I am looking after my stock. Some sheep have managed to get through the fence. There was a hole I haven't seen before.'

He frowned. 'Anyway, there's no sign of them. I'll have to bring Caesar with me.'

'Caesar?'

'My dog.'

'Oh. It's marvelous here, isn't it?' I didn't care for the way he loomed over me, or for the continuing frown. But I could have kept him away. All I'd needed to say was that Shiona would be back at any moment and I knew he would have gone immediately.

'Isn't it rather foolish of you? To ride into all this solitude just after that accident?'

'We just ambled along – '

'But it's all new to you. The pony might have stumbled.'

'I'm not made of china.'

'What an argumentative creature you are!' he said, exasperated.

'I've no intentions of going through life as a yes-woman,' I told him and was secretly pleased when he smiled, not a grudging relaxation of the features, but a smile that reached his eyes.

'You're impossible! Are you looking forward to tonight? You will be there?'

'Very much. Wild horses wouldn't keep me away.' I was watching him and his eyes were different now. I had the sudden, wild conviction he was going to say something important. Then his gaze shifted, the black eyes flickered and narrowed.

'I thought you were alone?' he said softly. He hummed a few notes of 'Early One Morning'.

'I was at the time.'

'I was going to offer to take you back, but I see it isn't necessary,' he remarked, his voice drained of expression. 'Good afternoon.'

His eyesight must have been very good because he was at the bush where the pony and gray were tethered and halfway back the way he'd come before Shiona reached me.

The guests began to arrive early in the evening. The big room with the velvet-covered furniture gradually filled. Estate workers in their Sunday best came diffidently to be received by Charley and Uncle Rob. They seemed too shy to look properly at Fran, Shiona and me. We all were waiting expectantly, Fran in the turquoise dress in which she looked unusually attractive.

I had brushed her hair for her, taking a long time over the task. It had never looked so well. Shiona, as always, appeared beautiful without apparent effort.

Cathy Forbes was shown in, accompanied by her brothers Shaun and Angus. Cathy was just what I'd expected, tiny and sloe-black. Even her eyes gleamed like jet. Shaun and Angus were taller, broader versions of their sister and so alike it was difficult to tell them apart. I found their soft, accentless voices charming. I thought it odd that none of his children in the least way resembled Dr. Forbes, who was rawboned and red-haired.

Elizabeth and Graham Stewart arrived soon afterward. Shiona had done Elizabeth an injustice, I decided. True, the girl had pale coloring, the lightest of blue eyes and almost white hair, but there was character in the well-modeled face and her bone structure was exquisite. The straight hair hung in a waterfall down the narrow back. She turned to look at me and I saw that the lashes that framed her large eyes were just dark enough to make them arresting. She and Buck would look magnificent together. Graham didn't seem to resemble her in the least, being brown-haired, brown-eyed and unexceptional in appearance. But there was a kindness about his mouth and his gaze, especially when it rested on Fran, who was sitting quietly close to the green-shadowed window. He nodded and bowed to the assembled company, then made his way between the chairs and sofas to stand beside her. Elizabeth joined Cathy and the Forbes brothers. Not once had Cathy even glanced in Charley's direction. I thought he looked particularly handsome tonight in kilt and stockings, frilled shirt and velvet jacket.

Just as I decided this, Charley came up to me. 'Has anyone introduced you to our guests?'

'No. Not yet.'

'Where's She-She?' I fancied he frowned.

To my surprise, my cousin was no longer in the room. I hadn't heard her leave. Of course I'd been watching everyone else with great interest.

'Come on, then. Angus, Shaun, this is my cousin, Maggie.'

I could see by their eyes that they knew all about me, my father and Kate. It wasn't difficult either to tell that they wondered if I'd prove a kind of femme fatale that my mother must have been to steal the prospective husband of the loveliest woman in the district. I began to feel uncomfortable. Cathy

97

and Elizabeth chatted in a friendly fashion, but I sensed a wariness that could have stemmed from the same source. Naturally, I couldn't have expected to arrive in such a close community without the inevitable conjecture and gossip that always resulted from the appearance of a stranger. From their conversation it was easy to see that local events did, indeed, have a considerable interest for them all.

'Is Buck going to be here?' Elizabeth asked eventually, her eyes searching the corners of the room.

'So he said,' Charley told her.

'It'll be funny without Roddy,' Cathy murmured. 'I wonder – ' But she said no more. There was no need. All those attractive faces registered the same doubt, calculation and a certain amount of rejection. Roderick Graham – aged twenty-three. That's what his tombstone had said. There had been blue convolvulus spread on the grave. I had assumed that Kate had put them there. Had it been Shiona? Maidenstane also had its morning glory. And my cousin had left this gathering as though she too found it lacking without Roddy's presence. Or was it Buck's?

Elizabeth was asking me, a little curiously, about my accident. I received the implication one only had to blow one's nose in this neighborhood to be remarked upon. And then, Shiona was there again, with her mother, Ness and 'You', handing around the refreshments and glasses of cordial, something stronger for the men. Fran, I noticed, was smiling and bright-eyed, and Graham Stewart showed no sign of leaving her side. He was, Charley informed me, newly qualified in his father's firm of solicitors. I liked his air of quiet studiousness, his consideration for my crippled cousin, who could so easily have been overlooked. I didn't think he was the type Shiona had pronounced Buck to be, the kind who takes people up and gains their affection, then pushes them aside.

There was much more noise now that the food and drink was circulating, then, suddenly, there was a curious hush. I looked up from my plate. Buck was standing in the doorway, staring across to the little group of which I was a part. Elizabeth reacted by becoming a little paler. His eyes moved over the assembled company and came to rest on Shiona. Their gazes held for an eternity. The hush was covered up by a host of little meaningless noises, a rush of artificial conversation that deceived no one.

I was aware of an unwelcome pain that reduced me to leaden

silence. That look that had passed between Buck and Shiona consolidated my conviction that they still loved each other. There had been some misunderstanding that had put hate and suspicion in the place of love, but there remained sufficient to burst out of cover one day, to burn as brightly as ever it had in the past.

Shiona moved toward the tenants and farm workers as if in a dream. Buck's eyes focused and singled me out of the throng. I watched, hypnotized, as he came toward me, elegant in the fitted coat and dark cravat, his face abstracted.

'So you got home safely?'

'Of course. Why shouldn't I?' I knew that Elizabeth Stewart was listening.

'I told you this afternoon. You should have stayed longer in the paddocks. The moor is rough.'

'I tried doing what you told me. Improving my posture and so on.'

His eyes gleamed. 'Did you? I'd like to see for myself if there's any difference.'

'I didn't fall off at all. Not like last time.'

He laughed softly. 'I need more proof than that. Will you ride with me? Tomorrow?'

Elizabeth made a small impatient gesture and began to talk rapidly to Charley. I was conscious of pity for her. She had defied public opinion in visiting Carn Tierlath with her father in order to seek out Buck, who had presumably encouraged her, and now he gave her neither a look nor a word. I knew I should refuse his invitation, but a part of me that I despised longed to accept.

'I'm not really good enough,' I said more harshly than I intended.

'I don't expect miracles.'

'You certainly won't get them either!'

'How fierce you look. It always surprises me that small people can occasionally be so determined.'

'And what are you used to? Subjection? How dull that must be.' I was aware that Shiona stood there with a tray of glasses. I seized one defiantly.

'That's whiskey,' Buck pointed out maddeningly.

'I know,' I told him. 'I intended to take it.'

'Are you sure –'

'Of course I'm sure.'

He took a glass himself and Shiona hesitated, then passed on toward the Forbes boys. She had on the tea-rose gown. The color glowed against all the dark coats and subdued men's clothing. I noticed there were roses pinned in the honey-colored swathe of her hair. The time of roses, Uncle Rob had said. Roses and fire, protection against enchantment. Shiona was the most beautiful of witches and Buck had hurt her. I wanted, ignobly, to hurt him in return. Always, when they were both with me, I was conscious of conflict, of being divided.

I took a great sip of the whiskey and only stopped myself by a great effort of willpower from coughing. I could feel the tears rise to my eyes, blurring my sight. The colorful gathering swam in front of me like the first sight of the rose garden from these same windows.

'Do you still intend to finish that?' Buck asked suavely. He plucked the glass out of my hand. 'I'll fetch you something more innocent. Stay there.'

I wiped my eyes surreptitiously. Elizabeth had turned a cold shoulder and the Forbes menfolk whispered together. Cathy was talking to Charley, her black eyes sliding toward me as she did so. Tomorrow everyone would know that I was unused to whiskey. They would also know that Buck Graham had singled me out for approval and wanted me to ride with him. Would I too be set aside when my face no longer fitted? Buck was back before I carried out my intention to leave the room. 'There you are. That's more suitable for you.'

I accepted the glass of cordial silently. Even Ness had her eye on me. I was reminded of the corn mother episode and the horror of that little dangling figure swaying so near my face. I turned to look at Fran. She and Graham were still close in conversation. I found it hard now to believe that she could have done something so distasteful. And yet it wasn't harmful in itself. Why, if she liked me, as I felt she did, had she tried to frighten me?

'Have you cut flowers for the boats?' Buck asked, watching me over the rim of his glass.

'Yes. This morning after we pruned the roses. And Fran gathered some more this afternoon. There are several baskets-ful outside.'

'Good. It's very beautiful, the flower festival.'

'Are you going to climb to the Sun Stones?'

'Everyone does. I hope you slept well. You're unlikely to see your bed until morning.'

'So long?'

'The sun. We must wait for the sun. You'll need your cloak. It can be cold.' Buck showed no sign of interest in anyone else. Elizabeth looked coldly angry now, though he seemed not to notice.' You must come in my boat,' he went on, finishing the whiskey without it having any noticeable effect on him.

'Why?' I was nothing, if not direct.

'Because you are different. Because everyone else – ' His voice dropped to a whisper.

My gulp of whiskey had made me bold. 'Believes you killed Roddy?' I suggested, whispering too.

'Brave,' he commented, 'as well as fierce. You shouldn't have mixed those drinks. You're becoming incautious. But you will come with me, won't you?'

'Because I'm new and untried? Because you haven't had time to get tired of my face yet?' I murmured unevenly.

'Is that what you believe?' His eyes seemed to say that what I had suggested was too preposterous to be taken seriously. I wanted desperately to be convinced that it wasn't true.

'No. No, I don't.' My voice was husky.

'Good.' He smiled and my heart leaped. Liaisons, Fran had said. Boys and girls paired off. So did men and women. There was nothing in the least juvenile about what I saw in Buck Graham's face, or in what I felt at this moment. It wouldn't last, of course. It could never last – this enchantment. And wasn't I protected against it? He would never be able to hurt me as he had hurt Shiona and Elizabeth, for I had the antidote tucked in my bosom as other women had done these hundreds of years. I had my sprig of Saint-John's-wort and it had been found by accident. I had not been told where to find it.

His fingers came out and pressed mine briefly.

We went upstairs for our cloaks. Shiona hadn't waited for Fran and me. I watched the peach-colored skirts disappearing around the bend of the stairs and I felt like a traitress. Fran and I went into Grandfather's room to tell him where we were going. We had developed the habit of spending part of each evening there, talking or reading to him. His eyesight had deteriorated, taking away some of his pleasure in books. Some of our excitement communicated itself to Grandfather. 'Oh, we had some fine times,' he said without self pity. 'Your grandmother and I visited the Troth Stone. It was a beautiful night, just like this one.' His blue eyes stared at the dark patch of window as though he could see beyond it. 'Alex, too, and

Kate – ' He had forgotten that I was Alex's daughter. I thought of Father climbing up to the Warrior and the Sun Stones, Kate beside him. Tonight I would do the same with Kate's son . . .

Up on our own floor, Fran and I reached the door of my room. By the light of the candle I could see the little hole where a nail had been, 'Fran,' I said, 'why did you hang the corn mother over my door?'

She turned a blank face toward mine. 'Why did I do what?'

'That's where the nail held the string. It was there first thing this morning – '

'You're imagining things, Maggie.' Quietness was giving way to anger.

'I'll show you. Come in. I put it in a drawer. You were the only person who knew I disliked it.'

I put the candle down on the top of the chest and pulled the drawer out. Fran and I looked down at the folded undergarments. 'I told you it was imagination, didn't I?' she told me scornfully.

'It must be one of the others,' I said without much conviction. It had been the top drawer. I was sure of that. We peered into the other drawers without success. I began to wish I hadn't mentioned it. Fran was regarding me very oddly. 'Perhaps you dreamed it.'

'Oh, no. It happened. I know it did – '

'You don't think it had anything to do with your fall, do you?' Fran suggested carefully. She looked extraordinarily different in the half shadow of the room, all the sharpness and shrewishness gone, the intelligence softened by the consciousness of her own attraction. She wanted to hold onto the magic of tonight and I was spoiling it for her.

'Of course it hadn't. Forget it, Fran. Get your cloak. I'll see you downstairs. Perhaps I did dream it. Anyway, it doesn't matter.' I spoke rapidly as I reached for my own cloak and fastened it. Although I pretended composure, my fingers trembled and a chill lay over my precious happiness. Fran hadn't sounded like someone who had played a silly trick and was trying to get out of the consequences. But she was clever – clever enough to work out a proper reaction to cover up guilt. What did it matter? I asked myself as I ran downstairs again. No harm had been done.

I went to the kitchen, seeing that Ness and 'You' were still occupied in the sitting room. The tap was dripping, giving the place a curious atmosphere of occupancy. The corn maiden and the mother both hung on the wall, just as they had been yesterday. I stared at the malicious eyes in the clay face, and it was as if those unmoving features reflected a hatred that some human person felt toward me. The glow of the oil lamp made the blue beads glitter with small points of light. A draft from the door caused the light doll to sway ever so little, the face turning and changing with the movement. Tricks, I thought bleakly, foolish, meaningless tricks. But I knew they covered up some nastiness, something unpleasant and frightening, something not yet finished.

Everyone was ready when I returned to the hall. There was a bucket of pitch close by the porch and the men dipped brands into it and set them alight. Flickering gold lay on the paths and on tree trunks, spiraling to the dark islands of pine boughs and shivering back again, nebulous waterfalls. Fran, her arm through Graham Stewart's, did not look my way. I was attacked by useless regret. I should have said nothing. My relationship with Fran had been progressing satisfactorily. Now she would avoid me, spending more and more time in her room, her legs tucked up on the window seat. How could a few mysterious bumps from the wainscot hurt me, or a sheaf of corn dressed in baby clothes and scraps of material from someone's workbasket?

People were forming into little groups. Men and girls waited, arm in arm. Shiona was with the Forbes brothers. She had one arm in Shaun's and she was smiling as she talked to Angus. Her fairness complemented their black eyes and hair. Buck had the same kind of darkness but his skin was browner. Elizabeth emerged from a room that had been put aside for coats and repairs to disordered hair. She looked glacially cool, her features seeming to have sharpened and hardened in some subtle way. She joined the group that comprised Cathy's brothers and Shiona. It was obvious they intended to join forces for the evening. Their chatter excluded everyone else.

Aunt Margaret bustled out, looking for Fran. 'You stay with Maggie. Do you hear?'

Fran replied sulkily, 'I hear. But she'll be doing the climb –'

'Graham, you'll fetch her back then, will you? You don't mind?'

'I don't mind.' What a pleasant voice he had. 'I can always join the others later.'

'I don't want to spoil things for you.' Fran's voice had risen imperceptibly. Graham bent his head and said something in a low voice. She hesitated, then began to walk toward me. Was it my imagination, or did she hold herself straighter? Her limp seemed less noticeable. 'Mother wants me to stay with you. Until you leave the boat, anyway. You needn't worry about afterward – '

'I know,' I said in a low voice. 'I'm not deaf.' She had spoken as though I hadn't been there. It was more hurtful than if she'd sounded angry. There was method in Aunt Margaret's madness, of course: If I were keeping an eye on Fran, Fran was also in a position to keep an eye on me. Doubtless, my aunt had also asked Shiona to remain with me on the climb to the Sun Stones for the same reason. We all were unattached girls who could be swept away on a tide of unaccustomed feelings, and although this new world was much more lax than the stuffy Victorianism which brought up its young women with only the marriage market in view, there must still exist some form of chaperonage. I might be going with Buck this evening, but I was unlikely to be alone with him at any stage of the proceedings. I was surprised to discover relief superimposed over disappointment.

'Ready?' Buck asked, making me jump with nervousness. I had neither seen nor heard him come. Like the day on the steamer when someone unknown had come up behind me. What would have happened if Uncle Rob hadn't started to come up the stairs to the top deck? Or had it been Rob?

The enchantment was running out of the evening like flour out of a split sack.

'Aunt Margaret wants Fran and me to stay together,' I told him, avoiding his eyes.

'And Graham's coming. He's rowing me back later. That is all right, Buck, isn't it?'

'Perfectly. There's plenty of room for four.' There was an edge to his voice. 'And if anything goes wrong, it makes it easier to lay the blame at the right door, doesn't it?'

'It isn't like that,' Fran retorted, sounding much more like herself. 'But you know mothers! Men are all rapacious beasts with slavering jaws, waiting to devour their spotless virgins. She didn't mean anything else. Honestly.'

'If you say so. Did anyone tell you how charming you look, Frances Drummond?' Good humor seemed restored in Buck's even tones.

'I did,' Graham Stewart said quietly.

There was a silence in which Elizabeth's high-pitched laugh rang out like a warning. Buck raised his head. His eyes flicked over the little group which was now joined by Charley, looking immense in the torch glow, and the tiny doll-like form of Cathy. Shiona was laughing, seeming not to notice us at all. Pain stirred in me. But it was Buck she was ignoring, pretending not to see. It had nothing to do with me. Nothing at all ...

The girls all began to pick up baskets of flowers while their escorts held the torches to light the way to the loch. Uncle Rob, Aunt Margaret and Ness were calling goodbye from the open door. Our footsteps crunched over the pebbles that lay scattered over the main path. The scent of the flowers I carried rose in little eddies of sweetness. There was a smell of pine and cut grass, a suggestion of mountains crouched in distance, the moving points of stars overhead.

Fran could not hurry, so we were left behind the other groups. Graham showed no sign of impatience. Aunt Margaret must have had great faith in him to entrust Fran to his sole care after the flower festival. They talked comfortably as they went like people who knew one another well, but all the time I had the certainty it was Buck my cousin Fran reacted to. More than once I had caught her profile turned toward him, sensed a flow of feeling that moved from her to him. Could it be Charley she thought responsible for her lameness? It had to be Charley or Buck. Roddy and Shiona had been together. Roddy had said so and everyone said Roddy was a good person. Everyone had liked him. People still put flowers on his grave –

'A penny for those deep thoughts,' Buck said softly, the others being occupied.

I cast around for inspiration. 'It – it's always seemed a long way down to the loch when I'm riding but we must be nearly there.'

'Was that all?'

'Yes.'

'I could have sworn there was more.' He lifted the brand and the light struck my eyes, revealing indecision, an air of guilt I hadn't had time to hide. The brightness revealed the shapes and colors of the flowers I carried. Roses, sprawling masses of velvety spirals and folds and curled petals, and an incredible blue I recognized to be Prince Charlie's morning glory.

'There she is,' Fran said, breaking a curious, suffocating pause that had lasted much too long. She pointed ahead. Blotting out the stars and the sky were the great still shoulders and head of the Stone Maiden.

8

Enchantment was returning slowly. Drawing close to that huge, reclining figure had something of the sensation of belonging to Lilliput. The stars seemed as big as silver lamps suspended against velvet. The last of sunset lay in peach-tinted splendor behind the slate-colored mountains. The undersides of clouds were ribbed with apricot. There were patches of gray and violet and lavender. The dark glass of the loch reflected small boats rocking close to the shore and the roseate shadows that were swans. The boats looked strange and beautiful with their garnishings of flowers. One, in the glow of the burning brands, was trimmed to resemble a Viking longboat with dragon prow, another was like Noah's Ark, one like a swan. The largest had a model of a castle on a mound set near the prow; the smallest was a bird's nest out of which rose a bird whose glorious blue I recognized. Even in torchlight, the brilliant color could only be that of the prince's convolvulus.

There were screams and shouts as the young people began to step into the boats. Men picked up girls so that they wouldn't get their feet and skirts wet and deposited them on the flower-covered seats, handing in the baskets of blooms they had carried from Maidenstane. Some had musical instruments, pipes and fiddles, and sounds floated over the water. The screams changed to songs.

By the time we reached the edge of the loch all the boats had drawn away except the one that contained the blue bird. Fran and I were given the torches to hold.

'It's beautiful,' I said. 'Beautiful –'

Graham picked up Fran and set her down in the nest. Her turquoise-colored skirts showed under the cloak. She looked very happy, though I thought I detected a trace of wildness in her pleasure. Her smile faded as Buck swung me over the gap between shore and boat to put me down beside her.

'Aren't you glad you came?' I asked, settling myself on the seat.

Fran watched Graham wade through the shallows to climb carefully over the decorated side of the boat. 'I'm glad.' Her voice was brusque. Had I been wrong about Fran and the corn mother? She was certainly acting as though she had a grievance. I stared at her uncertainly. 'I'm sorry if I was wrong,' I told her. 'Truly, I am. Don't let's spoil the evening. I want to be your friend, not your enemy.' I kept my voice low so that Graham Stewart wouldn't hear. Fran was looking uncertain now and I pressed home my advantage. 'It wasn't you. I can see that now. One should always be sure before one speaks.' I pressed her hand and felt an answering response.

'What are you two hatching up?' Graham asked smiling.

'Wait and see!' Fran retorted and now she was cheerful, her look including me again. Part of me responded to her changed attitude, but the other wondered who could have overheard my remark in the kitchen. Ness, who had obviously been listening. But who else? I gazed over the spreading ripples. Charley, Shiona and their group had the large boat with the castle on the crag. I could see their silhouettes, gold-rimmed, Elizabeth's pale blonde head against the vast slaty-blue bulk of the Maiden. The sounds of the pipes drifted in the still air, small and incredibly sad. I seemed to see the pallor of Roddy Graham's drowned face, floating, submerging, reappearing . . .

Buck sprang into the boat, tilting it dangerously, then he was sitting facing me, his face in shadow, his thigh close to mine, his physical presence banishing ghosts and conjectures most decisively. Fran dipped her hand into the basket of roses and threw petals over him. He put his head back and laughed, and the moonlight showed up the strong, dark column of his throat, the darkness where his eyes were. He and Graham began to row. There was something acutely pleasurable in the sensation of gliding over the loch's surface, the tips of the oars dropping beads of colored light. A smell came from the torches composed of resin and tar and flame.

The Maiden was quite close to the shore. I pictured a boatload of children in daylight, a trip that had begun in pleasure as this one did but had ended in tragedy. Was Fran thinking of that occasion now? And what lay behind Buck's expression?

People were disembarking on the Maiden. I could see the flicker of their torches climbing higher and higher until that huge, uncaring head was ringed with lights like a birthday cake.

'Do you want to get off?' Buck asked.

'No,' Fran said too quickly. 'Unless – unless Maggie wants to.'

'I'd rather stay on the water,' I answered. It was true. Here on the loch was peace and beauty. Something about the reclining woman repelled me with its suggestion of violent passions unleashed, of wickedness. There could be none, I tried to tell myself. It was all mountains out of molehills, this awareness of something monstrous, a cold, calculating mind that waited to mar and spoil. Yet the remnants of pain in my body, my cousin's lameness seemed to point to a campaign of destructiveness. And there was the episode of the corn dolly . . .

The sky was dark at last and the mountains etched in the color of bluebells. The Warrior loomed vast and glacially hard under a shawl of pale cloud. Everything was clear. We were enclosed in a ring of enchanted hills that would hold us prisoner till morning, and when that morning came, we would be high on one of those hills with the first rays of the dawn striking the Sun Stones. The night melted about us in shades and planes of purple and grape and hyacinth, out of which flame flickered, sank and expanded like jungle flowers vying with the real ones we carried.

A boat was approaching perilously close. The black silhouette of the castle showed me that this was the large one manned by Charley and the Forbes brothers. One of their oars scraped against Graham's. Shiona's face showed out of a golden gloom like a mask from an Egyptian tomb. I was conscious of a queer, uncomfortable leap of the heart.

'Be careful!' Graham shouted. 'You'll swamp us.'

'We're the kings of the castle,' Shaun called out mockingly, 'and we're hunting birds. You're all birds!'

'Don't be a fool,' Graham admonished. 'You're too close! It's dangerous.'

Fran's face was terribly pale. Kings of the castle. That's what they had been playing that day she was hurt. But Shaun hadn't been there. He couldn't know what memories he was reviving. Buck knew. His brows had drawn together in a frown I recognized too well. His mouth had hardened into a straight, uncompromising line. His oar dipped deep into the loch water, the little boat drew away, followed by a chorus of catcalls and laughter. A shower of blossoms rained around us. I stood up and threw some of ours. The catcalls changed to something more good-natured. Graham was rowing strongly now, and the distance between the two vessels grew greater by the minute. I was suddenly aware of the skirl of the pipes shivering over the water from the direction of the Maiden. It was the essence of all loneliness, a sound to cut one to the heart.

'I don't suppose they meant any harm,' Graham was saying. 'But I'll have a few words to say to Elizabeth when I see her again. It wouldn't have been a joke if they'd overturned us. You can't swim, Fran, can you?'

'No. I . . . can't swim.' Her knuckles were stretched tight.

'The Forbes boys are usually so considerate,' he went on. 'Do you think the girls might have been egging them on? They probably didn't realize the danger. Anyway, they'll never overtake us now. Too much weight to pull. We had the advantage.' Graham's voice was very soothing and some of the strain was leaving Fran's face. She smiled tentatively. I took my cue from Elizabeth's brother. 'I can't see anyone for miles. Are those lights over there some of the farm people on the bank?'

'Yes. That's where the climb begins. We go one way and some go through the farmyard and up the back. The Stewarts of Dunholm have been taking up the requisites for the fire. It's all ready by now, I expect.'

Buck had said nothing for some time, but his rigid back and compressed lips spoke of tightly reined feelings. Shiona said he could be violent. As I watched him covertly, I believed this to be true.

'Let's just float for a while,' Fran suggested and now she sounded quite normal. 'I don't want to go back just yet. That's lovely, that drifting sensation. Like being one of those swans.'

Some of the tenseness went out of Buck's attitude. He pushed the oar into the rowlock and leaned back. The swans bobbed on the edge of vision, white now in the strong moonlight. The beauty of the night, the faint music, the lap of the water, the proximity of pearly feathers, the perfumed strangeness of the boat, all conspired to bring back enchantment. I found myself wondering if Fran had Saint-John's-wort hidden in her underclothes, or was it vervain or yarrow or the seed of fern?

'Rob knows all about Midsummer Eve,' Buck said, breaking the silence. No one mentioned John the Baptist. There was a queer sense of time past, of ancient custom that had nothing to do with things Christian. For the first time I believed in a devil like the one described by a witch called Agnes Sampson of North Berwick, a devil with 'a nose like the beak of an eagle, with great burning eyes in a terrible face, with hairy legs and claws for hands and griffon's feet. Yet even her devil had turned out to be mortal. He was Francis, the nephew of Mary, Queen of Scots' husband, Bothwell. Perhaps the devil I sensed emanated from some human frame, the body of an attractive man. The loch abounded with them tonight . . .

'Father knows everything,' Fran stated with pride. She was relaxed now, as we all were, though her fingers plucked at the petals of flowers in her lap. 'He had a Hebridean grandmother, you know. She came from Clach Mhiceil. Something dreadful once happened there – ' She stopped tantalizingly.

'Is that all you're going to say?' Graham asked lazily, his gaze fixed on her.

'It's not very nice – ' Her eyes gleamed provocatively.

'Since when did that stop you?' Buck teased. 'Anyway, there's nobody particularly nice on board. Except maybe Maggie.'

'You can leave me out of the eulogies,' I said. 'I'm as nasty as anybody. Aren't I, Fran?'

'All right.' Fran laughed and I saw, briefly, how she might have been but for the accident, all her features soft and compliant, nothing of malice or spite to be detected now. 'It was about the local churchyard – great-grandmother's – not ours at Maidenstane. The dead were all given an unpleasant sort of half-life. They climbed out of their graves – I presume they dug themselves out – then they walked about Clach Mhiceil, terrifying everyone.'

I shivered. It wasn't the kind of story one would want to dwell on late at night, when one's bedroom window overlooked a graveyard, the stones of which one could see all too clearly most evenings.

'Maggie's scared,' Fran remarked gleefully. 'Perhaps I shouldn't finish it.'

'Of course I'm not. Do, pray, go on.' The blind face of the moon seemed to assume a shining cruelty. Buck and Graham began to row again.

'The people who hadn't been dead for long didn't look too bad,' Fran continued in a small musing voice, 'but the others!' She allowed us time to conjure up a picture of bones and corruption. 'Father said there was no priest on the island so the half-dead couldn't be exorcised. His grandmother's folk and their neighbors decided they must leave their village and go to the mainland, only the boats wouldn't hold them all. Some were left on the rocks while all the time the half-dead got nearer and nearer. Then, suddenly, a cockerel appeared on a rooftop and crowed –'

'Three times, I presume?' Buck inquired unexpectedly, the oar tip dripping diamonds.

'You've heard it before!'

'No, I haven't. A lucky guess.'

'And they all vanished back to their graves,' she ended quickly in case he forestalled her.

'Did it – did it ever happen again?' I asked, my skin still goose-pimply.

Fran smiled and some of the moon's coldness was mirrored in her face. 'Not yet.'

'A charming tale to tell one's children by the winter hearth,' Buck observed. 'You'd terrify the poor little mites out of what wits they had.'

'You make it sound as if they weren't likely to have many!' Fran retorted. 'Pig!'

'Unintentional, I assure you.' Buck's tone was ironic.

'I'm like Father. I don't think folk legends and festivals should be gradually lost. Nor all the old crafts that one handed down from father to son. I'll write books about them too when I'm older.'

'Wouldn't you rather marry and have children?' Graham asked. 'Or is that too ordinary?'

There was a long silence. Fran tore up some more rose petals and flung them into the water. The swans drifted up inquisitively, imagining them to be crumbs. 'Dear me,' she murmured at last. 'Could that have been a proposal? And in front of witnesses?' Her voice was husky. 'I might conceivably hold you to that, Mr Stewart.'

'I might just conceivably want to be held to that.'

This time the silence was different. I was beginning to feel like an eavesdropper.

'Pigs could fly!' Fran cried harshly. 'They most certainly would if I ever took any notice of you.'

'They're just as likely to do that as for the dead and buried to pay social visits in South Uist,' Buck drawled in a bored way. 'Look. They're starting to light the fires. I think this is where we leave you, Fran, to continue your discussion alone with Graham. There's the landing place. Ready, Maggie? We're going to talk about moon paste and fairy arrows – '

'Yes. I think so – ' I could see, by the water's edge, the shapes of some of the other boats, the Viking ship, the swan, the Noah's Ark. The castle on the mound wasn't yet there. There was no Shiona or Charley to keep an eye on me for Aunt Margaret. Once I stepped off the boat, I was on my own.

Buck jumped ashore, his heels crushing the shingle just under the water. The keel scraped harshly. I stood up and waited. His arms reached for me, grasping me by the waist. I was handed onto the rim of damp sand in a flurry of skirts and petticoats and quickened heartbeats. Fran stood up, dangerously unsteady, and threw flowers at us. Petals clung to my cloak and hair and fluttered onto the tide line. Buck's shoulders were patched with white. It was curiously like being . . . married.

'I'll be back. Later . . . ' Graham's voice was dying away as he pulled vigorously at the oars. The sound of laughter was carried faintly down the mountain. Moon paste and fairy arrows, Buck had said. Witchcraft and enchantment. But nothing could happen. I was protected. The awful thing was that I didn't want to be, not standing under the Warrior with the track just visible in torchlight and moonlight and the stone face of the Maiden raised toward the mountaintop. Something in her immobility and intentness made me think of the story of her efforts to rejoin the Warrior in his armor. She could never go to him, but sometime he might come down from the mountain, his slaty armor pounding the hillside. Nothing seemed impossible on Midsummer Eve.

'Come,' Buck said and now his voice was impersonal. 'This is the way.'

I followed, the light of the torch shining on the scattered stones on the path, the dark rosettes of bilberry, and on the broad back that was turned against me.

The Midsummer fires burned so brightly that there was no need for the torches. They were doused in the stream and left ready for the journey homeward. Ale and whiskey had been transported to the Sun Stones, and the faces of the men, at least, were flushed and excited. Girls giggled and squealed, and I wondered uneasily what Aunt Margaret would think of it all. But Uncle Rob believed in the old customs. He would have brought his bride up here. My aunt, as a girl would have looked like me, I reflected.

I turned and looked back over the loch. It seemed a long way below. I could just make out the tiny dots that were the swans floating close to the landing place and the long, moving object that must be the last boat just arriving. Shiona would know I was here as soon as she saw Fran and Graham on their way back. I'd be glad when she got here if the truth were told. Buck was helping to twist straw around a wooden wheel which had been dragged up by some of the farm lads. It was to be rolled down the slope later, once everyone had arrived, and with it would go all ill luck. The revolving wheel was a representation of the turning sun. Everything went back to the sun, or the lack of it, in country communities, and so far the church had made little difference to deeply ingrained beliefs. Soon would come Saint Peter's Eve, the fishermen's celebration, and still later, Lammas, the autumn festival.

I closed my eyes against the night sounds and sights to breathe in what seemed like the smell of clover. 'Tired?' Buck asked, close to my ear. I shook my head. A broad-shouldered man pulled at a girl's hand and dragged her, shrieking, to jump over the edges of the bonfire. She snatched her skirts away just in time. He held her to him when they reached safety, and, bending his head, kissed her mouth as though he would never stop. I wondered how I could ever have connected marriage and that which was associated with it with James. He and Jenny seemed part of another life, a life with no spark in it, no warmth and feeling. The fire, the flames, the kissing, that did seem part of life with a lover, a husband . . .

Above us, the Sun Stones brooded, the pink light of the fires washing over them, giving the impression that they moved just a fraction. The smooth, curved surface that was the Warrior's armor glistened over soil that seemed inadequate to keep it there. I was suddenly uneasy, imagining it beginning to slide, gently at first, then faster and faster, flattening everything in its way.

'It doesn't look safe,' I told Buck. 'Has no one said so before?'

'Many times. It'll give way one of these days. There's little one can do about it.'

'It could kill,' I pointed out.

'It'll not shift in summer when the mountain's comparatively dry. It's torrential rain that'll move it one day. No one

8 113

comes up in winter. Think of all the centuries that have passed since this place existed. Hundreds of years ago people undoubtedly talked of its dangers and it still remains.'

'I suppose that's how the legend came into being.'

'Legend?'

'The Stone Maiden and the Warrior. How they were separated by witchcraft and have tried, ever since, to come together. If he fell, he'd just about reach her, wouldn't he?'

'Just about. I'm not much given toward legends.'

'Fran and Shiona crawl with them! I suppose it's Uncle Rob who indoctrinated them.'

'Probably. They don't worry you, do they?'

'Not always.'

'Then they do! I guessed as much when Fran was on with her "half-dead" tale. She's a very imaginative child.'

'Not really a child,' I couldn't help saying. We were, after all, the same age.

'She finds it difficult, I think, to separate fantasy and actuality,' he went on.

'I don't agree. I think Fran is always very well aware of what's happening. She can be very shrewd.'

Buck said nothing but I knew he was watching me. My hand moved, of its own accord, to the place where the Saint-John's-wort rested. 'How is your mother?' I asked.

'Quite well. She wants you to visit her again.'

'Because I resemble my father?'

'Because she took a liking to you.' There was reproof in his voice. I flushed. 'Doesn't she hate me, because of him? That's what – '

'Is that what you were told? Well, I did warn you that the Drummonds have strong imaginations!' He laughed in an unpleasant way and kicked out at a pebble.

'I don't always believe everything I'm told.'

'But it does remain at the back of the mind, doesn't it? I know. I do know.'

'It would be better if we were to drop the subject of our relatives, wouldn't it? Don't things ever get out of hand? Up here, I mean?' The scene around the fire was assuming a kind of bacchanalian boisterousness. Leaping figures washed in firelight, unbridled laughter, a strong hint of sulfur and brimstone. My senses responded alarmingly.

'They work hard for few pleasures,' Buck told me. 'Have you seen the Troth Stone – '

'No.'

'It's not far. Would you like to see it?'

'I – I don't see why not.' If my voice wasn't quite steady, he seemed not to notice. I felt his hand cupping my elbow. We moved away from the bonfire and went to the left where the cool sound of dropping water made an antidote against the crackle of flame. A little well, shining under the stars, was surrounded by straggling bushes where fragments of material fluttered in the breeze. Little prayer rags, I realized, tied there by women on holy days. The stream went on above the deep round of the well. The Stone grew out of the darkness, broad as a man and higher than my companion. Through the hole that was level with my eyes, I could see a star. The whisper of the stream was like the murmur of couples who had once stood here. Grandfather and Grandmother Stewart, Uncle Rob and Aunt Margaret, Father and Kate Graham, who was once Kate Buchanan. There was an immense sadness in standing in a place where so much of young love and passion clung. Something inside me shuddered and was still. The atmosphere had changed subtly. The man who had been Buck Graham was someone else, someone taller and slimmer, whose face I knew well. And there was a girl, a girl like Shiona, who laughed and tossed her heavy gold hair. She put her hand through the hole in the stone and the man took it in his, bent down and kissed it gently, released it again.

'You shouldn't have done it!' I cried out. 'You really shouldn't – ' There were tears on my cheek, blurring sight. I blinked them away.

'What shouldn't I have done?' Buck asked softly. The night was as it had been, the images of Father and Kate dispelled.

'Did I say that?' I asked. 'I can't think why.' How did one explain *temps perdu* to anyone but Shiona? It was quite impossible. But I knew now that what Shiona had told me was true. Kate had been very much in love with my father. There had been no mistaking the look in her eyes. Perhaps she had taught Buck that it was safer never to give one's love completely, to draw away before one was committed utterly.

I had been right. This was a sad, unhappy place and I didn't want to stay in it. Turning, I began to run down the slope toward the well.

There was someone at the well. I came to a standstill, breathing fast, my ribs still vaguely uncomfortable from the bruising. I put out a hand to steady myself, and it brushed one of the fluttering rags that dangled from the holy tree. The touch of it was unpleasant with its suggestion of an enormous moth struggling to become free.

'I was worried about you,' Shiona said and her face, in the moonlight, did indeed show concern. 'Especially when I saw that – ' She hesitated and stared up the mountain.

'That Buck wasn't at the bonfire either? You needn't have bothered. He's behaved perfectly.'

'Then why are you running away from him?' Curiosity edged her voice.

'It wasn't from him. You see, it happened again. *Temps perdu.* At the Stone.'

'Oh. Poor Maggie.' Her tone was warm and full of affection. 'What actually did take place?'

'One minute I was standing there with Buck, then everything felt different. I saw my father and Kate. They were holding hands through the Troth Stone. It was true, what you said. She was terribly in love with him – '

'Of course it was true. She'd be the first to admit it. Poor Kate.'

'He must have thought he loved her. At the time.'

Her hand came out and touched my cheek. 'One can never be sure of anyone. That sounds hard, perhaps, and quite cynical. But it is true. I know. And so does Kate.'

I listened and the sadness that had been at the Stone was in me. It seemed the most terrible thing in the world that one couldn't trust any longer. Without trust the world was an empty, meaningless place. The remainder of my life seemed to stretch away, littered with the tombstones of destroyed relationships. The water of the well, quite suddenly, smelled sour and disagreeable.

'You're cold,' Shiona said softly. 'You shivered. Come back to the fire. I'll take you.'

I looked back the way I had come. 'But what about Buck? I should explain – '

'How,' she asked practically, 'without sounding a bit "Aunt Bell"?'

'Aunt Bell' I repeated with distaste.

'Crazy,' she told me. 'She is, you know. They don't dare let her out. She'll always have to stay where she is.'

'What form does her madness take?' I followed Shiona, half-

116

regretting my undoubted curiosity about Aunt Margaret's mysterious and unhappy cousin.

'She can't bear to be thwarted in anything. She attacks the person she imagines has deprived her of what it is she wants and doesn't get.'

'But one can never have everything one wants,' I said slowly. 'I don't know that it would be very good for the character to have everything tossed in your lap.'

'Still. It's lovely to occasionally get your own way.' Shiona smiled and stared ahead to where the fires burned even higher, a shower of sparks exploding to rush into the dark sky and be lost as though they had never existed. Were feelings really like that? Was no emotion based on security? I was filled with an acute anxiety for Shiona. Perhaps she believed this at the moment, but later, when she'd found someone more constant, she would change, wouldn't she? I made myself think of my parents, of Aunt Sarah and Josh Davidson, of people like Graham Stewart. And most of all I was relieved that I hadn't ever encouraged James into thinking I could be more than just Jenny's friend. It must be dreadful to hurt someone as Kate and Shiona had been hurt. I put my arm through Shiona's and felt an answering pressure. 'You've made such a difference to my life,' she whispered as we drew close to the largest fire. 'I don't know what I'd have done without you, Maggie. You won't change, will you?' I knew what she meant. She was thinking that I might let her down, allow my feelings toward her to turn cold. What Shiona needed at present was to feel loved and wanted. How could anyone not love her? Whatever it cost, I must remain constant. Not that it would be a hardship . . .

'I won't change,' I said. 'I never would.'

She laughed her soft, warm laugh. 'I might have known you'd say that. You're a sweet, affectionate girl and I must introduce you to those who'll appreciate you. And how beautiful you look with your hair all windswept like that and your eyes all big and fey-looking. You look like a witch, Maggie Stewart, a high-class, quite enchanting witch.'

The Forbes brothers – I still found it difficult to tell them apart – were dancing around the fire's perimeter – sunwise, of course. Everything was performed with the sun in mind on this night of the year. Charley and Cathy were jumping over one of the little fires, and I saw him snatch her up just before her skirts were in danger of being set alight, to hold her up in

117

the air as a father would hold up a small, noisy daughter. I wondered if it wouldn't be better to tell Grandfather about Charley than to let him think that his grandson and I might ever marry. But perhaps Charley was only fascinated by Cathy's smallness and childishness. He might have no intention of becoming too involved with Miss Forbes. If Buck hadn't asked me first to accompany him tonight, Charley might have come looking for me. There was Maidenstane, after all, to be considered. Charley Drummond felt passionately about the place – everyone said so. It was his life. He could even come to feel that way about me.

'She-She!' one of the Forbeses shouted. 'She-She! Where the devil have you been! Come and dance!'

Shiona pulled at my hand and we ran. I rather awkwardly, toward them.

'Ah, the retiring Miss Stewart!' Angus said gravely, or was it Shaun? It could be disconcerting to be married to a man who looked so much like his brother. Not that either was likely to fall in love with me the way they both looked at Shiona. Anyway, I preferred a man to be entirely individual, like Buck Graham. Buck – always Buck.

The brothers separated to allow my cousin and me into the riotous circle. They were witty and high-spirited – even their natures seemed identical – and there was no more opportunity to brood about the disposition of Maidenstane or of my dark gypsy of a neighbor who was reputed to be violent and even murderous if the business of Roddy was true. I'd be better pushing him out of my mind completely.

The heat of the fire forced us to jettison capes and jackets and the men to roll up their shirt sleeves, showing strong arms and portions of sunburned skin. They sang queer Gaelic songs I couldn't understand, but it was quite easy to dance to the lilt of the fiddles and pipes. My feet and body seemed to move of their own volition as though I had performed these steps all my life. It was exhilarating to be pulled, to be swung off my feet with the flames and the stars whirling and the breath cut off in my throat. I found myself laughing and singing with the rest of the wild company.

'Not so retiring, after all,' Shaun whispered close to my ear. Or was it Angus? I laughed again because it was so ridiculous to be flirted with by someone with two identical images. Shiona's hair was glorious in the reflected flames, although the roses were tumbling out of the disorder of that once perfect swathe, and there were little curls and fronds around her temples and brow that hadn't been there when we started out. I remembered Fran with a pang of pity. If only she had been able to be here. How she would have enjoyed all the fun and color, the noisy excitement.

I became sharply aware of Buck Graham. He was with some of the farmhands, helping to prop the decorated wheel against a boulder in readiness for its launching. He looked up from the task to encounter my gaze. Shaun was leaning close to me and whispering that this was the best Midsummer Eve he could ever remember and did I know anything about anatomy. Anatomy? Belatedly, I remembered Dr. Forbes who, incredibly, had fathered these dark, dashing children. My lips formed the word 'no' as in a dream.

Everything seemed to stop under the impact of Buck's scrutiny, the gaiety, the crackle of the furze and sticks and dried fungus, the whisper of the water, the spinning of the stars. There was a vast, dusky quiet in which only his face existed, had shape or form. There was no friendliness in the look, only something repressed, something that had once been – what? Nothing I could identify. 'What do you want of me?' I longed to cry out. But no words came. The music and singing and movement came rushing back like dam waters released, filling up that brief vacuum.

The fires were dying down for lack of fuel. Everything that could burn had been thrown onto the flames. The embers sighed and crumpled, putting out little but transitory fingers of heat. I moved away toward the place, lower down the slope, where I had put my cloak for safety. No sparks could touch it there. It was oddly cold and quiet away from the crowd. I knelt on the ground and put the garment around my shoulders. I seemed curiously shut off from everyone in this small hollow.

A pebble shifted and rolled toward me. A shadow fell over the spot where I knelt. 'Why did you run away?' It was Buck's voice, and I thought I recognized a kind of defeat in it. I raised my eyes and could see little but his outline rimmed in the dying glow of the fires, giving it a satanic appearance. I thought, with a jolt of the senses, that Agnes Sampson of North Berwick must have seen Bothwell's nephew, Francis, under just such circumstances. The air was charged with devilry and suggestions of orgies and witchcraft. I was protected. I must keep that at the forefront of my mind. Protected . . .

'I wanted to join the others,' I told him. 'I promised Shiona – '

'I see.' The defeat seemed accentuated, and I was conscious of a sharp uprising of pity. But why should I be sorry for him? I couldn't matter. He hurt others because his mother had been hurt. She had influenced him to destroy in women what my father had spoiled in her. It wasn't his fault, but what he did was wrong – wrong!

The ground shook unexpectedly. Buck sprang around with a sharp exclamation. 'Get up! For heaven's sake, girl, don't be so slow!' I heard a series of bangs and bumps, a slither and jolting that grew steadily nearer. I couldn't move. He bent down and jerked me to my feet, then flung us both sideways to fall on the stony ground. Something crashed close to my head, then went bounding and tearing down the steep hillside. I shuddered, then became aware of the hard pressure of his body against me, the banging of his heart against my breast. His head moved slowly. I could sense his eyes searching my face. Then his mouth covered mine and the whole meaning of the Midsummer Festival became known to me. The world was all flame and heat and color, whirling and spinning, carrying me to – destruction? Everything in me responded. And then I remembered what had happened. I knew what that leaping juggernaut had been. It was the wheel, the great circle, the representation of the sun that carried away bad luck. It had almost carried me with it. I began to tremble with reaction, to struggle away from Buck.

He didn't try to keep me there. The reason was obvious. All the little roseate figures by the fires were running toward us. The singing and playing was over. And from below there was a great splash as the wheel found its last resting place in the waters of the loch.

9

I was out in the rose garden when I heard Uncle Rob and Aunt Margaret talking. My first instinct was to call out, but because they were discussing Aunt Bell, I stayed where I was and did nothing. The Drummonds were not a satisfactory family to question, I had discovered, and I had my share of curiosity about the unfortunate woman.

'I'm seeing Bell tomorrow,' my aunt said. I could hear her pulling out drawers and pushing them back again. 'Kate says she'll come this time. I think her conscience has been pricking her. Anyway, she ought to go. She's as much a relation as I am and last time I was there Bell was worse. She won't know us soon.'

'Don't take it too much to heart,' Uncle Rob advised in his deep voice. 'It's none of your doing, or anyone else's for that matter.'

'It's easy to say that,' Aunt Margaret said quietly. 'There! Look at this photograph. You'd never think she'd turn out as she has, would you? As bonny a girl as you'd ever find. She should never have had a child. Never! It worries me, Rob. It's all so close to yours and mine. I've had terrible doubts – '

'Doubts are not certainty,' my uncle said firmly. 'Only Roddy could have answered those – '

'And now he's dead.' Her voice was nearly a whisper. I stirred uncomfortably.

'As you say, Roddy can never tell us about that last afternoon. He could have taken cramp. The loch's aye been cold and it was early for swimming.'

'Buck – '

'You'll not speak of him. Even to me. I won't listen.' I had never heard such a note in my uncle's voice before.

'But Maggie. Is she – safe? She seems attracted. They've been in each other's company a fair amount. Kate said she was bruised.'

'She fell, didn't she?'

121

'She'd have needed to fall in every direction to sustain the marks she had.'

My ears had begun to burn. It was all very well to listen to snippets about some unknown woman, but the conversation had taken a horrible and disconcerting turn.

'Should I warn her?' Aunt Margaret asked miserably. I was touched. She obviously had no wish to hurt anyone needlessly.

'We don't know. You could be spoiling something. Suspicion ruins relationships. We've never been able to lay anything with certainty at that particular door.'

'But it fits! Oh God, it does fit.' It was a cry from the heart. I moved away silently, my spirits crushed. It did fit. Even to me the jigsaw was nearly complete. But only nearly. There was still the element of doubt. And why should Buck have saved me from the wheel if he intended to kill me on the steamer and had only been prevented from this by the advent of Uncle Rob? Close to yours and mine. Only the distance of the graveyard apart. Those drawers pulled out and slammed shut. There was a little desk in the room that overlooked the garden. I remembered seeing it. I wanted passionately to see the photograph for myself. Bell's child might resemble her.

I found myself almost running for all my tiredness. All my senses were flooded with pain. It had been late when we got back from the mountain. It had been the most wonderful night of my life. I still felt his arms around me, the whole vibrant weight of his body on mine, our mouths clamped together as if they would never come apart. He had wanted me. I knew this with some curious certainty I could not properly explain. Only for him it couldn't last, while for me it was everything I had ever dreamed of. Buck could have no lasting feeling for any woman. I had known it all along. I had relied on the powers of a plant that was the antidote against enchantment, but Buck had been stronger.

And now my curiosity had ruined the memory of Midsummer as it had been spoiled for Shiona and Elizabeth Stewart. I would be one of them when his fancy for me was burned out like the fire on the hills last evening. Even with my eyes shut I could still see the first red ray of the light as it struck the central stone of the circle like a daub of blood. We had watched the magical reawakening of the sky, the floods of brilliance, the curved upheaval of the sun spilling its cascades of color to ripple and spread and shift in every direction. There had been no need to kindle the torches from the embers of the bonfires. We all had stood silent, wrapped in our cloaks, stupefied into stillness by that sheer magnificence of visual splendor.

No one had been able to explain how the wheel had moved of its own accord. Buck had admitted placing it in position. He'd pushed a smaller stone under it to act as a brake until the time came for its launching. Had he done it in such a way that it must, in a short time, work loose? The soil had crumbled in the place where the stop stone had been. Had he realized, just too late, that he would be suspected and snatched me to safety in order to appear innocent? But that warm, enveloping embrace, the kiss that had aroused me, how had he made that semblance of wanting so convincing? Because I had wanted to be convinced, I told myself, and hated that readiness to see only what I desired to believe.

I had reached the graveyard, and some strong compulsion made me step over the crumbled stone of the gap to stand under the mourning trees. The ground sloped away toward the loch and the uncaring bulk of the Maiden. The swans were in her shadow, their plumage mysteriously blue. The little boats still rocked, their garlands already fading. Everything fading . . .

Seen from this distance, the Warrior did not appear unstable. Last night, for one heart-stopping moment, I had imagined that the soil under the stone that comprised his armor had given way at last and that the thing that was crashing its way toward me was an enormous slab of rock. But it had been the wheel that Buck had helped decorate, had placed in a spot from which it had broken loose just as I became vulnerable.

'Maggie?'

I swung around sharply. Kate was standing by the Graham memorial stones, a bunch of lilies and honeysuckle in her hands. She looked much too young to be the mother of a young man.

'You were far away, weren't you?' Her voice reminded me of things I had forgotten. Of a rose-red house with lace balconies, white pillars where ivy climbed, a confining wall against which blue convolvulus climbed, a Chinese room and a screen where someone stood unseen. There were rooms filled with antiques chosen by Buck and his father – if Johnnie Graham *was* his father. There was Bell who had given birth to a child, Bell who couldn't bear to be thwarted, who resorted to violence when she couldn't obtain her own way. Kate and Johnnie

Graham had adopted Roddy. Why shouldn't they have adopted a previous child? It had been a loveless marriage. Perhaps it could only have been made tolerable by the introduction of children. I became conscious that Kate waited for me to answer her. 'I was thinking. About last night.'

'Oh, yes. Last night. It's some time since I participated in the festival.' Her face was now bent over Roddy's grave and I was unable to study her expression. But her voice was level, giving away nothing of her emotions. I watched her shift away the blue flowers that decorated the mound and begin to arrange the fresh flowers into the shape of a cross. There were none left for Johnnie's grave, I noticed. Oh, poor, poor Johnnie. How could he have borne to spend his life in her presence and to know he meant less than someone else's child?

'You look well in the crimson dress,' Kate told me.

'It's new. I had it specially for coming here,' I explained.

'But you look much too pale,' she said reprovingly.

'I am rather tired. And it's hot – '

'Come and have a cup of tea. And you haven't yet seen the house properly.'

I hesitated.

'I'm all alone.' Was she trying to tell me that Buck was out? That it was therefore safe to visit Carn Tierlath? Had someone told her about the wheel?

'That would be pleasant.' She hadn't asked me why I wandered here alone. I was grateful for that.

'Come then. Would you carry these dead flowers? We can put them on my compost heap. It's just over the wall there.'

I obeyed, though I couldn't help wishing she had cleared the convolvulus from her husband's resting place as well. Neglected Johnnie – Was there nothing of tenderness left for him? Perhaps she had tried to love him. I hoped so.

I deposited the flowers in the place she indicated. The sky was clouding over and a purple heaviness weighed down the sky. The gravestones were tinged with pale violet. 'There's going to be a storm,' Kate observed, leading the way to the colonnade and pushing open the french window. 'Hurry!' Already large drops were splashing onto the flagstones.

'Just in time,' she went on. 'What were you doing when I saw you?'

'Thinking.'

'And I mustn't pry too closely! It's all right, my dear, I can

124

take a hint. But why were you alone? You are happy with the Drummonds, aren't you?'

'Why, yes. It's just that Shiona wanted to have a gallop and I'm not good enough yet and Fran is rather wedded to her library. Habits die hard. She's always been an insatiable reader and even my presence can't break the habit. Not that I'd want her to, on my account.'

'Of course you wouldn't. Poor Fran – '

I saw my advantage and took it. 'It was that accident that spoiled things for her. I heard about it.'

'I wonder just what you did hear,' Kate said quietly, tugging at a brocade bellpull. 'There are several versions of that occasion and none of them match. I sometimes wonder if the child didn't just fall and wanted attention afterward. Or she could have been thwarted by one of the older children and decided they should share her tragedy. I seem to recall she was a rather self-willed child. Oh, Mary' – this to a neat maid who appeared in the doorway – 'tea please. And bring some cakes.'

Thwarted. Self-willed. Wanting someone to share the blame. This was a new angle on those other versions. But wasn't it natural that Kate should look at the accident in this way? Two of her family had been involved, although only one of them could have been responsible if there ever had been a fatal push. If – There had, of course. My own experience on board the steamer bore this out. Or had that been the work of some unbalanced stranger and nothing to do with either Graham or Drummond?

'Thinking again?' My inattention had not gone by unnoticed. Kate was tidying her dull-gold hair at a gilt-framed mirror, but I knew she watched me at the same time. I nodded. 'It's all still so new here and yet I feel as if I've never been anywhere else – '

'It does have that effect, this part of the country. It's lovely, isn't it? Especially in autumn.' In autumn the last sheaf of corn would be cut and new corn dollies made. The clay face of the corn mother swung in and out of my mind with a horrid persistence.

'Child,' Kate went on. 'Is there something you're trying to tell me?' She sounded concerned.

What was there to tell? The queer, hollow tapping from the wainscot, always in the same place? The dangling doll? The figure in the graveyard? The wheel? There was nothing tangible. Nothing at all. The sound of the rain became suddenly loud, and there was a brilliant flash of lightning, an ominous roll of thunder that banged and echoed and died away sullenly. Kate forgot her question. She ran to the windows and drew the curtains of gold silk. 'Mirrors attract lightning,' she explained, lighting candles with quick, nervous gestures. The ensuing glow showed me a face no longer so young or beautiful as I remembered it. For the first time it seemed possible she could be Buck's mother. There was even a faint resemblance of bone structure and expression. But Kate, like Aunt Margaret, was Bell's cousin. There were bound to be nuances of likeness and habit, even disposition.

'I hear you're going to visit Aunt Bell. Tomorrow.' I couldn't prevent myself from saying the words. Fortunately Kate didn't ask where I'd obtained that information. She frowned. 'Yes. It is necessary.'

I wanted to ask why it was necessary, but there could be no possible excuse for me to do so. The young and pretty maid came back with the tea tray, which she placed on a low pie-crust table close to comfortable-looking armchairs upholstered in yellow brocade. There was a horse-shoe-shaped chair covered in moss-green velvet and one or two padded footstools. All the furniture in the pleasant room escaped the rigid, uncomfortable lines of present-day sofas and so-called easy chairs. In fact, the entire room lacked Victorianism completely. It was entirely pleasing, as gracious and uncluttered as Kate in her loose, attractive garment that was neither gown nor peignoir, but somewhere just between the two. How Kate would have detested our parlor at Church Street with its mustiness, the glass dome covering the branches, grasses and stuffed birds, the shell casket, the poker-work letter rack, the framed sampler, the articles of cork and beadwork, the ship in a bottle! She made me feel unsophisticated and rather crude, though I was sure this was unintentional. I couldn't ever imagine her sending anyone a valentine on die-stamped paper, with a sentimental motif of violets and roses and gilded curlicues. Or press ferns and flowers or do ordinary things like modeling with damp bread. Any ornaments that were in this room had elegance and style. Were these qualities enough without the saving grace of affection? Wouldn't Johnnie Graham have been happier with less perfection and more warmth?

'Here you are, Maggie.' The smile she gave me was warm

126

enough, though there were vague reticences at the back of her eyes that put me on my guard. I had the feeling she knew something concerning me that she was unable to put into words. The thunder was still rumbling across the heavens like giants trundling cannonballs.

The lemon tea was delicate and quite delicious, the little cakes light and golden. I asked Kate about the ornaments and she lost her abstraction. The glass was Amberina, a gorgeous pale amber shading to ruby. The Chinese bowl was Wan Li and quite old, early fifteenth century. There was some Vincennes porcelain and a Medici jug containing branches and flowers, everything blending with the gold color scheme. When I admired the silver teapot on a stand, she told me it was made by Peter and Anne Bateman in the last century. The sugar was in a seventeenth-century caster and the jug was Irish silver. Everything had a history. Part of me was fascinated, but another was not quite comfortable surrounded by such treasures. I felt that here things were more important than people. I hoped I was wrong.

The last growl of thunder died away right on cue as we finished our tea. 'Come and see the other rooms,' Kate invited, drawing back the curtains to reveal a drenched garden and the flags of the colonnade glittering with water. The sky was not so dark but there was no blue in it. There was a threat of further disturbance later. The upstairs rooms were fascinating. The Tudor bedchamber was dark and heavy with oak. An enormous four-poster, draped with red, took up a great deal of space. A nonsuch chest stood against a wall, and Kate opened it for me to show coarse, well-laundered sheets overlaid with dried lavender. A closestool and a copper bed warmer completed the furnishings. The French room was quite different, all blue satin and brocade and delicacy. I could imagine all this dainty, gilded furniture rising of its own accord and floating against the painted ceiling. I should be afraid to move about in this place for fear of breaking something.

The Stuart room was the one I liked most. It seemed the only real, habitable chamber in the house. The four-poster had a slept-in look as if it had been newly vacated. A pair of boots stood in the fireplace, large, masculine boots, I noticed with a quickening of the pulses. There was a Queen Anne bachelor chest with one drawer not quite closed and a gilt-framed miniature on top of it, a bureau with the lid down, revealing an assortment of papers and pens and a silver inkstand. There was an ink stain on the carpet underneath it and I almost rejoiced in the blemish. This room was lived in, used, without the sterility of those showplaces I had just been taken into.

'Oh, dear,' Kate said seeing the inkblot. 'And the window's been left open. The rain's come over the sill. I'd better close it, although it does seem a bit like locking the stable after the horse has gone.'

I went over to the bachelor chest and looked at the miniature. A boy's face stared back at me, a long, Spanish-seeming face, dark-eyed, dark-haired, extremely handsome in a gentle kind of way. A house robe hung to one side of the chest, a slightly shabby garment, red and warm.

'It's Buck's room, of course. He never puts his boots away. On his gown.' Kate opened a press and tidied away the offending articles, then smoothed the pillows and bedspread. Some of the impression of life evaporated. Was that why Father had stopped loving Kate? It made his defection easier to understand. Perhaps she had tidied away his attempts at showing his need for more than a stylized neatness. Or was Kate only old-maidish because of her early rejection? She certainly wasn't inhuman. She'd proved that by her dislike of caged creatures. What an odd mixture she was! I felt I should never understand her.

'Oh, I see you're looking at Roddy's portrait,' Kate had come up close behind me and I was very aware of her at my shoulder, the strong warmth of her body.

'Roddy? I thought it must be – ' I stopped, not wanting to be indiscreet.

'Johnnie? No. It's not my husband, though it could have been, I suppose. There was quite a strong resemblance.' Something cold had crept into her voice – something I didn't care for.

I went on looking at Roddy Graham's pictured face. There was something wrong about its presence here. Why should Buck keep a reminder of a boy he had fallen out with, a boy he was suspected of killing? And right here in his room? It didn't make sense. But, then, it could denote cunning. How better to divert suspicion? Like engineering that accident yesterday and then 'rescuing' me. What was true and what false?

'I think I'd better go home,' I said flatly. 'They don't know where I am.'

'Come back again. Promise?'

'I promise.'

It was a promise I wasn't at all sure of keeping.

I saw Buck on the way back to Maidenstane. I was still in the shelter of the graveyard trees when I saw him up on the moor. He looked more wild and Heathcliff-like than ever, with his hair and his shirt plastered to his skin, and a drenched collie running alongside his horse. An untidy huddle of sheep preceded him. He was as much of a bewilderment as Kate. An antique collector on one hand and a farmer on the other. I watched him from behind my barrier of wet leaves and branches, remembering the Stuart bedroom, the polished boots that had offended Kate's tidy eye, the well-used house robe, the open bureau and the inkblot. They all were bound together in a picture of reality, the man, the moving creatures, the room I had just left. They were an entity.

He must have been fond of Roddy to keep the picture in his room. The memory of that miniature reminded me of Bell's photograph. I waited till Buck was out of sight, then made my way quickly and quietly to my uncle's sunken garden. My feet were very wet from walking through long grass. I hardly noticed them. Would the morning room be empty? It was a long time now since I had heard Aunt Margaret and Uncle Rob talking there. If I once saw the picture of Aunt Bell, I would know for sure. Doubt hammered at my mind. But I would never have another peaceful moment if I didn't see it. I wasn't doing any harm. It wasn't as if I intended to steal something. Not all my excuses removed the feeling of guilt.

I opened the garden door very quietly. The little hall was dark now that the sunlight was gone. It was quiet as the grave. The door to the morning room was slightly ajar. I pushed it open, feeling like a criminal. It was stupid really. I did have the freedom of the house. I was one of the family after all. Listening until I was certain that no one else was in this part of the house, I went toward the desk. My short time in Kate's 'museum' had given me an eye for Queen Anne bureaus. This was of the same period. It was walnut-veneered on bracket feet. There were keyholes. Were the drawers locked?

I found myself tiptoeing as I approached my object. There was a long drawer under the sloping lid, then two smaller ones underneath it. I pulled out the top drawer carefully. It was filled with the usual stationery, blotters, inkwell, pens and nibs. No photographs. I replaced it gently. There was nothing of note in the left-hand small drawer. The other slid out smoothly. The photograph lay on top of a bundle of letters and neatly folded papers. A dark, gypsy-looking woman with wild hair stared back at me. Not even the tightly buttoned, conventional gown could make her look ordinary. Her eyes weren't dark; they were several shades lighter than Buck's. They needn't be brown either, for the entire picture was in shades of buff and sepia. But the features were like his, the cheekbones high and strong, the outline firm and square, the expression rebellious.

I pushed in the drawer with a sudden sharp movement. I felt vaguely sick. I had often wondered how Pandora felt when she opened the forbidden box and now I knew. She had seen darkness and disease. I had done likewise.

'Looking for something, Maggie?'

I turned around slowly. Shiona stood there smiling, her eyes full of dancing lights in spite of the room's dullness.

'I – I thought I'd write to Aunt Sarah again. I need paper and an envelope.'

'They're all there,' Shiona said cheerfully, tossing back her hair. 'The top drawer.' She went to the desk and fumbled for a moment. 'There you are. I expect you didn't want to pry without permission. You don't have to be like that here. You belong.'

'Still, I'd rather – '

'No one would have refused you. It's only a sheet of paper, after all. I had a wonderful ride!' Her cheeks were glowing with recent exertion.

'Oh. Weren't you caught in the rain?' I remembered Buck with his wet hair and clothes.

'I got back just as it began. I was lucky. You've been out, haven't you? Look at those wet footprints! No wonder I couldn't find you. But the rest of you's dry. How did you manage it?' She sat on the edge of the table and swung a booted leg.

'I was in the graveyard – '

'Again?' Her eyes were curious. 'You don't seem able to keep away from it. What's the attraction?'

'It's peaceful. And it has the advantage of proximity. It was too hot to walk far.'

'Is that all? You aren't being morbid, are you?'

'No. I've never minded graveyards. After all, there's nothing there. The important part is already taken care of. What's left behind is only – '

130

'Nonessential? Refuse?' Her voice was mocking.

'Yes.'

'You do believe in an afterlife, then?' She smiled slightly.

'Why, yes! Don't you?' I watched her with a vague disquiet.

'Not really. I think all that stuff about getting one's rewards in heaven is nonsense. If one really wants something badly enough, one has to fight for it here on earth.'

'Is there anything you want as much as that?' I asked slowly.

She stared down at her boots. Her lashes made little shining crescents against her cheeks. She looked like her own room, full of secrets no one would ever find out. 'If there was,' she replied, 'I'd keep it to myself. Never show your trump card! It makes one vulnerable.'

'If you'd been a man,' I told her, 'you'd have been a general. All plots – and tactics.'

'Of course!' She laughed. 'But you still haven't told me about your wet feet and dry clothes. Did you take refuge in a tomb?'

'I was invited to Carn Tierlath.'

She was silent for a moment. 'Oh, Maggie. After all I've said. After that wheel business. On the mountain – '

'It wasn't Buck who asked me. In fact, Kate made it quite clear that he was out before she pressed me to go. And it did save me from a drenching.'

'That's different.' Some of the tenseness went out of her attitude. 'I'm fond of you. So you mustn't mind if I fuss. You seem to be the only person I can really talk to these days. I wouldn't want you to be hurt. In any way – '

'Why can't you talk to Fran?'

Again that silence. Then Shiona said, 'It's she who puts up the barriers. Really it is.'

I believed her. Poor Fran. She really was jealous of her sister. It must be galling to be a cripple in the same house that contained Shiona. I could sympathize with her viewpoint.

'She was like that with Graham Stewart last night. As if she couldn't bring herself to let him come too close.'

'You think he wants to?' Shiona raised her eyes and I read the interest there.

'I'm pretty sure of it. I think that eventually he'll succeed. Oh, I'd really love that to happen. Why shouldn't Fran have some happiness?'

'Why not?' All the warmth had returned to her voice and her features. 'Did you know you made quite a hit with Shaun Forbes, by the way?'

'No.' I blushed stupidly. 'Who says so?'

'He did, of course. Do you like him?'

'He was quite fun up at the Sun Stones. I can't say I liked his behavior much, earlier in the evening.'

Shiona frowned. 'Why? What did he do? I'll certainly talk to him if he misbehaved himself with my favorite cousin!' She sounded indignant.

'It was that business on the loch. Fooling about so near our boat. Fran was quite upset. You must know she can't swim.'

'Yes. I do know. We told them off in no uncertain terms, don't worry! They had a bottle with them – more than one in fact – and although Charley tried to stop them, they had some drink in them apart from the little they got at the house. The Forbes boys are inclined to be repressed at home – the doctor's a bit of a Tartar – so they break out with a vengeance when they get the chance. They didn't realize they were annoying anyone – '

'It wasn't annoying. It was frightening. Buck was quite angry – '

'Buck has no room to talk!' Her eyes flashed ominously. 'No right at all!'

'Perhaps not,' I replied evenly. 'But if he was on bad terms with Roddy and, as some people obviously think, had a hand in his death, why does he keep a portrait of him close by his bed?'

Shiona turned white. 'You've – you've been in his room?'

'Oh, it isn't what you think! Kate showed me 'round Carn Tierlath. And that included Buck's bedroom. You didn't really imagine – ' For the first time I was furious with her.

'No. I didn't,' she said quickly. 'I was just surprised. But Buck can be very persuasive when he wants to be. And he has a certain crude magnetism – ' Her mouth shaped itself into a beautiful scorn. 'He sets out all his attributes on a stall and one just takes one's pick. I'm only sorry I fell for all that emptiness. You see, there's nothing underneath. Nothing at all.'

'Not even violence?'

The sky was clouding over again and the room was filled with a brooding dimness.

'Oh, there's that, all right. I've had firsthand experience of that,' she said bitterly. 'But there's nothing warm, nothing lasting. No tenderness.'

I thought she was right about the last remark. That embrace, that kiss. They hadn't been gentle. Not in the least. But they hadn't seemed false. I remembered the photograph of Bell, and I didn't want to pursue the subject of Buck any further.

'Have I destroyed any illusions?' Shiona asked, so gently that I could have cried.

'Illusions? About a man I've only seen half a dozen times? Of course not. Truly.'

'Methinks – in the words of Shakespeare – thou dost protest too strongly. Am I right?'

'No, you aren't,' I said shortly. 'I think I'll go and write to my aunt.'

'Have I hurt you?' Her voice was filled with compunction. 'It's the last thing I'd want.'

Yesterday at this time I could have denied it. But in between then and now had come the Midsummer Festival, the time of roses and fire and love. I wanted to say 'No', but the word stuck in my throat.

'I'll write my letter,' I said at last and went away, leaving Shiona in the room of shadows.

There was a further storm that evening. The lightning blazed down onto the gravestones as I stood by the window, just before getting into bed. There seemed a curious, horrifying life about them and I was reminded of Fran's story of Clach Mhiceil and the half-dead. It was even worse after I got into the narrow bed and blew out the candle. The house was quiet apart from the occasional low taps I had grown accustomed to but which I had failed to trace to any source. Mice behind the wainscot or birds up in the eaves. That must be the explanation. It must . . .

Something brushed up against my door, something soft like a robe trailing. There was no sound of footsteps as there would have been if it were Fran. I waited, breath held, but there was nothing else. Only that stealthy rustle – then silence.

Disappointment weighed down my senses. I may be haunted, but what did it matter? The flavor was gone from my life and could never be put back. I had eaten the apple of knowledge and it was bitter. The picture of Bell hung over my closed eyes and nothing could keep her face from burning a hole in the darkness. Over and over again I saw her gypsy features

that melted and gathered together again to show me Buck
Graham. And each time his mouth was pressed down on mine.
I could feel the weight of his body as I had on the mountain,
urgent and demanding. It was no vision of poetry and distance.
It was warm and immediate, tantalizingly real.

I fell asleep to dream of the Maiden, her head ringed with
lights, and Fran hurtling downward to fall in a still heap on
the rocks below. Someone rose up in the center of the ring of
torches, and it was the devil Agnes Sampson had seen, all dark
and grotesque, with hair and hooves and eyes burning. He
played on a set of pipes, and all the gravestones moved, dis-
gorging what lay beneath. The half-dead moved, rattling and
scraping and crawling, answering the music of evil. And, as I
watched, the face of the devil became clear. Buck's face, looking down at Fran's crumpled body and laughing . . .

Fran was there in the room. I pushed myself up in bed. Pink
light came in through the window, bathing the wall beside my
head.

'You screamed,' Fran said quietly.

'I hope I didn't disturb anyone else.' My whole body
trembled.

'I'm sure no one could hear but me. We're the only ones at
the top of the house. And Charley and Father sleep like the
dead – '

I shuddered involuntarily.

'Nightmare?'

'Yes.'

'It isn't this room, is it?' Fran asked carefully. 'Does the
atmosphere disturb you?'

'No. If you want to know, it was your beastly story! Clach
Mhiceil? Remember?'

'I'm sorry. It seemed such fun on the loch with everybody
hanging on my words. And it was true. It is in Father's notes.'

'I'm sure it is! Are you cold, Fran? Put my house robe on if
you like. It's on the back of the door. But you needn't stay if
you don't want to. I'm awake now and I won't go back to sleep.
I won't be doing any more screaming.'

'I'd like to stay. Just for a little.'

'All right. Come and sit on the bed. Warm enough?'

Fran wrapped my robe around her and nodded. She looked
toward the window. 'A red sky at morning, the shepherds'
warning.' Shepherds' warning. Buck was a shepherd as well as
all those other things. Was he also a murderer? Had he killed

Roddy, tried to kill Fran and me? Were Kate and Johnnie his parents? Or was it Bell who was being visited by Kate who thought it 'necessary'?

'You've changed,' Fran told me. 'You seemed quite a child that first day. But now –'

'And now?' I challenged. I had stopped shaking.

'You make me feel years younger.' She sounded rueful.

'My birthday's May. I'm Gemini. That probably explains it, Two-faced.'

'So am I. What date are you?'

I told her.

'You'll never believe it! So am I! That means we're twins. Why didn't anyone know?' She was quite excited.

'Because Father was outlawed. Remember? He wasn't likely to say just when I'd been born. And I don't suppose anyone asked.'

'It is a coincidence –'

'Actually, it often happens in families. And our parents were brother and sister. Alike in looks too, just as we are.'

'Do you really think we look alike?' Fran was touchingly pleased.

'Extremely. Can you bear it?'

'I suppose I'll have to, won't I?' She giggled endearingly. Her pleasure seemed genuine.

'I didn't see Graham again. Didn't he come back to the Sun Stones after all?'

Fran's voice changed subtly. 'He changed his mind. He came in and spent the rest of the evening with Father and me. Mother never stays up late now.'

'That must have been nice. I like Graham.'

'Yes,' she said carefully. 'Everyone does.'

'Then why did you do your temperamental act in the boat? He couldn't have made it plainer that he was staking a claim.'

Fran hunched her shoulders. 'Does a forester lay claim to a damaged tree? If he's got any sense, he picks a perfect one. Anyway, there isn't all that much choice, is there, around here? Cathy's got her eye on Charley, the Forbes frères have a penchant for She-She. Elizabeth –'

'And Elizabeth?' I prompted shamelessly.

'She'd let Buck walk all over her if he wanted! It's all on her side, though.'

'Oh? I thought I was told he was interested too? Once –'

135

'Who said that? I think Buck finds her attentions embarrassing. No encouragement there.'

'How do you know?' I clasped my hands around my knees.

'Oh, Buck still talks to me. He thinks I'm still in pigtails and teeth braces.'

'Graham's interested in you in spite of all that damaged tree rubbish.' My heart was lightened, inexplicably, by the revelation that Buck hadn't encouraged Elizabeth.

'Oh, Maggie. What's the use?' Fran's voice was low. 'He's only seen me in long dresses and that turquoise one *is* an improvement. Even I could see that. But – well, marriage isn't a particularly private state, is it? Whoever marries me is going to see all of me. I couldn't stand it if he drew away from what's usually disguised.'

'Your leg, you mean. Did you ever stop to think that Graham's known you for a very long time? He's heard all about what's happened to you. He'd have to be blind, deaf and dumb not to be perfectly aware of any of the facts. He's a solicitor. Solicitors have to have good heads on their shoulders. They're trained to go into every possible eventuality, to be able to recognize truth from falsehood, never to rush into anything. They're notoriously cautious people. Oddly enough, I knew one in Berwick, and odder still, he was attracted to me, but that's beside the point. So a small thing like your limp, for instance, isn't much weighed against your intelligence and your sense of humor. And the sympathy that made you come in because I was having a nightmare – '

'Brought on by me.' Fran's laugh was half pain.

'Yes. I was dreaming of your festering half-dead all marching down to the loch – '

'How horrid for you! So long as it isn't this room that puts you off.'

'It isn't.' I was sure Fran was about to tell me of the ghost that haunted this place and I waited for her next words. Before she could speak, there was a light tap at the door and I heard Shiona say, 'Maggie? Are you alone? I thought I heard something.'

'I've got a man in my room!' I called out. I could see Fran withdraw into herself. Her eyes lost all expression. There was something more than jealousy there, only I couldn't identify the emotion.

'Maggie?' Shiona's voice was sharp and I couldn't help laughing.

The door opened. She stood, framed in candlelight, looking like an angel in a fall of white cambric and little satin bows. She looked at us, frowning. We sat like two children caught eating bread and jam.

'I was just going,' Fran said, getting up.

'You needn't –' I began.

'See you later.'

Shiona stood aside and let her sister pass. The she turned to me. 'I'm sorry. I didn't mean to interfere. I thought I heard a cry. Like that time in Edinburgh. Remember the bed with the rusty-red curtains? Well, I listened for a little while and I suppose I heard Fran walking about. So here I am.'

'Come right in,' I invited. 'You did hear something. I had another nightmare. Fran heard me as well. Then we got on talking. And that's all.'

She came over to the bed and put a hand on my forehead. 'No fever. That's good.'

'I'm not ill,' I protested uncomfortably.

'Too many things have been happening to you. Falling all over the place. Seeing through cracks in time. Nightmares. The steamer –'

'The steamer?' A warning echoed in my mind.

'You said you slipped on the deck. You did, didn't you?' Her voice sharpened with suspicion.

'Yes. I'd forgotten I mentioned it.'

'And then there was last night –'

'Shiona. Buck pulled me out of the way of the wheel,' I reminded her.

'Whitewashing himself! It was a splendid way of making himself a hero in your eyes. Don't you see that?'

I was silent. I had worked that out for myself. Odd how reluctant I was to believe it, though.

'Mother's away today. I'm in charge. Why don't you have a rest in bed? The weather's still unsettled and we won't be able to ride. Horses don't like storms.'

'I'll think about it.'

'We've lots of books. Read. I'll bring you meals on trays. Spoil yourself,' she urged.

'I don't know. It's still early. Let's go back to sleep, eh? We'll decide later.'

Shiona went reluctantly. I didn't go back to sleep, of course. She seemed to know what had happened to me on the steamer. Had she put two and two together to make four? She was so fiercely protective toward me, so determined that no harm would come to me. I had the feeling she knew about those strong, cruel hands at the ship's rail, that I had placed another stone on the wall of Buck's guilt.

10

I hadn't seen Buck or Kate all week. It seemed like a lifetime. It had poured with rain all day after the nightmare incident and I'd been happy enough to stay in bed with a book. It kept me out of the way of Fran and of Shiona, who must be allowed no more fuel against Buck Graham. She might voice those suspicions to her mother and father, and they already had sufficient of their own, judging by what I'd heard.

Aunt Margaret brought me back a present from her trip to see Bell. She called me into her little sitting room the following morning. There was a large box on the table and I wondered what was in it.

'Uncle Rob and I would like you to have this, Maggie. It's by way of being a sort of thank you.'

'Thank you?' I raised surprised eyes. 'It's I should be giving you presents!'

'Not only,' she went on, 'have you cheered up your grandfather out of all recognition but we've noticed a tremendous difference in Fran since you came. We don't say much but we do have eyes and ears. She's a different girl. I even have hopes – ' She stopped, but I thought I knew what she was going to say. That she and my uncle were aware of Graham's interest in Fran and would be pleased if the relationship between them were to develop. I hoped so too, with all my heart.

'There's a special celebration for Lammas. Supper and singing and a spaewife to tell fortunes – '

'No dancing?'

'Not on Lammas Eve. We want no witches and trows coming to the house!'

'Trows?'

'Trolls, I suppose you'd call them.' She smiled and indicated the box. 'That's to wear for the supper. It would be fine for Michaelmas too. There's a ball at night, dancing then of course, and the old millers' play. That's after the horse races. We noticed, you see, that you'd nothing light and pretty, and our girls are both supplied at present.'

'I have the red gown – ' I began, fumbling with the soft nest of paper inside the strong cardboard container.

'And very nice it is too, though not what I'd call a party dress.'

The tissue was opened at last and I took out a gown of soft magnolia-tinted voile, very light and filmy, not at all like the heavy materials I usually wore. It had lace at the neck and sleeves, a widely gathered skirt that would float beautifully when worn. There was a stiff, rustling underdress and a waistband of narrow black velvet with long ends hanging down almost to the hem. I was so touched I couldn't speak.

'You do like it, don't you?' Her voice was anxious.

I went to her wordlessly and put my arms around her. The answering pressure of her embrace was like being held by a mother. 'Did you know,' I said, my words muffled in the folds of her dress and the little capote she wore over her shoulders, 'that Fran and I are twins?'

She held me away from her, the large blue-gray eyes questioning.

'We are! We compared birthdays. Isn't it remarkable?'

'Remarkable,' she agreed. 'That makes even more of a bond, doesn't it?' It was in that moment that I loved Aunt Margaret as I'd wanted to love my own mother.

'It's the most beautiful present I've ever had. And the velvet band Shiona gave me will match it perfectly. I'm so very lucky.'

'You get on well with Shiona, don't you?' She turned away to fiddle with one of the ornaments on the mantelpiece.

'Very well. I'm extremely fond of both Fran and Shiona. Charley too, only I don't see him much. He's always so busy.'

'Yes. He loves Maidenstane. He'd work twenty-four hours a day if he could.'

'It should be his, shouldn't it?' I said slowly, folding up the dress. 'I'm going to tell Grandfather so. He told me about it being Father's right, only he turned his back on it and left someone else with all the work. He couldn't have expected to find it still here all these years later, waiting for me – '

'Entails are difficult to break.'

'Graham Stewart and his father could think of some way – '

'You must realize it isn't only you who's involved. You'd be taking away your own child's inheritance. Your son.'

I was conscious of an almost physical shock. 'My son?' The words conjured up a picture of a sturdy child with an olive skin and gypsy-wild hair, black eyes that could look right through people. There could never be such a child. I must turn my back on Buck Graham. It was the sensible thing to do – the only thing.

'The time to cross bridges is when one comes to them,' I said surprisingly calmly. 'Thank you for your gift. I'll look forward to wearing it.' I began to fold the pretty garment. 'Did Kate go with you yesterday? She said she might when I saw her last.'

'Yes. She went. It was she helped me choose the gown. She and Buck are going to London in the next few days. One of Buck's contacts has some antique or other he's been angling for, for some time. And Kate has a cousin in Hampstead she hasn't seen for a while.'

'Oh. I – I don't suppose they'll be here for Lammas then.'

'They may. It's doubtful.'

The future seemed suddenly bleak.

'Are you very disappointed?' Aunt Margaret asked and there was a queer note in her voice I couldn't recognize. I fancied she disapproved of my interest.

I laughed very creditably. 'Of course not! I might be if Shaun couldn't come.'

She looked up at that and I saw relief in her face. 'Shaun always comes.'

'Good,' I replied with a false pleasure. I picked up the dress box and took it up to my room. I hoped I hadn't given my aunt the wrong impression, but it would never do to let her think Buck mattered to me. Even if he did.

It was six days before I saw Buck again. I was down in the paddock waiting for Shiona. My horse cropped at the grass, and I was looking across the water to the slaty-blue bulk of the Maiden. She seemed not so graceful from this angle. Today I thought her broad and powerful as some Ethiopian ogress. The sun lay on the granite smoothness of the Warrior's armor and cast black indentations into his nostrils and eyesockets, the groove that separated his lips. And I thought, with a futile regret, of the night that I had lain in close embrace with Buck, remembering his strength and the pressure of his mouth on mine. I should never feel like this about any other man. Never . . .

Someone was riding down the road toward the village. I turned away from the Maiden and the armored knight. It was as if I had conjured Buck out of the empty air and my own memories. He pulled at the rein when he saw me, dismounted and came across the scented meadow. He was close to me and part of me wanted to keep him there, while the other half cautioned me to retreat while there was still time.

'So, you found your sheep,' I said, being afraid to remain silent any longer.

'How did you know that?' His eyes slanted down and there were little sparks of sunlight dancing in their blackness.

'I saw you.'

'And why didn't I see you?'

'I was in the graveyard –'

'Hiding? From me?' His mouth was harder than on that night in the mountain. Midsummer, roses and fire. The time of roses – and love. But it couldn't last. It hadn't.

'From the rain,' I said mechanically. I had the sensation of being manipulated.

'My mother said you'd been at Carn Tierlath. I'm sorry I wasn't there.' Conventional words that meant nothing. His mother. Was she his mother?

Our eyes met and didn't look away. I was in danger of being swept away on a tide of darkness, of brilliance, into the deepest, blackest pothole that had ever existed. I would never be able to climb out of it. Not ever – He was Agnes Sampson's devil. If he took his boots off, I should see cloven hooves . . .

I knew that he was going to kiss me. The conviction spread to every part of me. And if he did, I'd never be able to escape. I'd cease to be my own woman. Then one day I'd be outside the charmed circle of his affection, like my cousin whom I loved, and there would be nothing. Nothing . . .

'Aunt Margaret says you're going to London.' Somehow, I'd taken my eyes from his and was walking toward my mount. I could hear him following me, each thud of his boots like a heartbeat, destroying my composure.

'Tomorrow.'

'Oh.' Emptiness yawned beyond today. 'She said there was some antique –'

'Silver. Queen Anne teapots shaped like melons – or gourds – ' He made it sound like poetry.

'I see.'

'They were beautiful then. Not the ugly overornamented things they produced later. And there's rather a fine silver punch bowl my agent's unearthed – '

'Wouldn't it be marvelous if Prince Charlie's punch bowl and goblets ever came to light? Has no one searched?' I knew my voice wasn't steady.

'Everyone has looked. Maidenstane was turned upside down, not to mention the garden.'

'Perhaps they'll never be found.' Still, I couldn't meet his eyes again.

'Perhaps.' His voice had sunk to a husky softness.

'I must get on with my practice. I want to be proficient before the Michaelmas races.'

'Samhuinn. It was Samhuinn before Saint Michael ever drew breath.'

Some of the tension was leaving the air around us. I relaxed.

'Samhuinn sounds better, certainly. Uncle Rob says Michael was conqueror of the powers of darkness. A knight on a white horse. I suppose he'd be like Saint George – '

'I suppose so.' I thought he sounded amused.

'He says people steal their neighbors' horses for a night and no one can make much fuss so long as they're returned safely, sound in wind and limb. And folk give each other presents – '

'What shall I give you?' The words dropped into a pit of danger.

I flushed. 'Nothing! I don't expect – '

'You can't stop me if that's what I want to do. There's another custom. I wonder if Rob mentioned it.' I wished he'd stop infusing his voice with sheer seduction. Crude magnetism, Shiona had called it. I disagreed for once. There was nothing crude about Buck at this moment. I found it increasingly hard to appear detached.

'Which custom?'

'Men are allowed to take the companion of their choice to ride behind them on horseback. Even their neighbor's wife, should they be inclined – '

'Oh. Doesn't that lead to trouble?'

'It's custom.' He shrugged.

'Like stealing the horses?'

'Yes. You look as if you don't approve.' He was laughing at me but I couldn't object.

'Well, I won't be surprised if I see you gallop off with Aunt Margaret or Ness,' I told him. We were both laughing now, but there was something under the laughter that wasn't in the least trivial. Although he hadn't said it in so many words, I knew he wanted me to ride behind him at the Michaelmas procession. We would go around the loch and up the mountain by a more gradual route than the one that was used at the flower festival. We would ride thrice sunwise – and my arms would be around him.

'I must get on with my practice,' I said for the second time and ran my hand down the warm smoothness of the animal's neck.

'The saddle could be better placed,' Buck commented. 'See? That's safer.' I saw his hands on the girth straps and on the polished leather. He loosened buckles and pushed and pulled and tightened with a smooth expertise I admired.

'I'll remember,' I told him. Why hadn't I let him kiss me? The moment was past and it might never come again. But wasn't that what I wanted? To stay at a safe distance? His shadow fell over me and I knew I had been wise. And there was still Michaelmas . . .

Out of the corner of my eye, I saw something move. 'Shiona's coming. She promised to let me gallop today. Not very fast. More of a trot, I suppose you'd call it.'

He looked at me, at my white blouse and black skirt, at my disordered hair. 'You should have worn a hat. For protection.'

'I didn't think – '

'Well, remember next time, won't you?' he said gruffly. 'I must go now. I have some arrangements to make about to-morrow's journey. Take care. Remember.'

'Will you be back for Lammas?'

'I don't know yet. When Mother gets to Hampstead, she's difficult to shift. There are the theaters and exhibitions and so on – calls on relatives and friends.'

'I see.' I looked at him then, emboldened by the knowledge that Shiona would soon be with me. His eyes promised things I could never accept, a wild rushing into sensuality and something more. Something I wanted but must do without if I were to survive. He moved away. I released my breath on a sigh.

'What did he want?' Shiona asked as she rode up to me. There was a high color in her cheeks, a rim of sunlight around the swathe of her hair. She looked like a goddess.

'Nothing much,' I said carelessly. 'He said my saddle wasn't in the right place. It probably wasn't. It looks much more secure now, I have to admit. Oh, and he and Kate are off to London tomorrow.'

'Oh.' Her eyes were shadowed now and I knew that it was his doing. I'd be a fool if I rode with him at Samhuinn. But knowing one was going to be foolish didn't seem to prevent the act. People persisted in what they wanted to do in spite of the possible consequences. Something stronger than themselves seemed to take over.

'I've dropped my handkerchief,' Shiona said. 'I'll get it before we go.'

I could see the patch of white a little distance away. 'It's all right. I'll fetch it.'

The grass reflected the warmth of the sun. It was losing some of its greenness. The heat bounced up from the ground carrying with it the heavy scent of clover. The handkerchief, when I retrieved it, gave off the unmistakable smell of Roddy Graham's perfume. Roddy was the key to all the mysteries that beset this place. And Roddy was dead. Depression settled over all the other emotions I had just experienced. One could shrug off noises in the night, a face at the window, a sense of haunting. Even the dangling figure of the corn dolly. But a dead man was different . . .

'Thank you, darling.' Shiona's voice, warm and lazy, banished most of the feeling of fatality. Most, but not quite all. She tucked the white linen square into her waistband and smiled down at me. Gratitude rushed over me in waves of comfort. I'd never be able to understand her complete and generous acceptance of me. No blood sister could ever have shown me more love and affection. Remembering that interview with Aunt Margaret and the unfolding of Fran's prickly nature, I was conscious of a contentment in this, my family from now on. It was amazing that they all liked me.

I swung myself into the saddle quite easily. I was no longer a beginner expected to ride ponies. Following Shiona's example, I nudged the horse's flanks and pulled gently at the bridle. The animal responded to my actions like a piece of smoothly oiled machinery.

'A little faster,' Shiona said and I increased my urgings.

Something was wrong. My quiet brown horse no longer obeyed me. Its hooves pounded on the hard, dry earth like war drums. The wind rushed through my hair. I clung to the bridle, digging my feet into the stirrups, feeling my body being flung from side to side. Bushes and trees flew dizzily past. Terror grew and threatened to overwhelm me. I screamed. Then Shiona drew alongside, her face pale and distraught. Her hand shot out to grasp my wrist. 'Take your feet out of the stirrups!' she ordered sharply. 'Don't be afraid. I'm holding you. Nothing will happen. Trust me.' Her hand was very strong and I was glad to do as she told me. There was a sickening moment when I swung loose, dangling over her mare's rounded belly like a flour sack, then she had pulled me up and over its back while she brought it to a standstill. My own mount had stopped its frenzied gallop and was trotting across the field as if some devil had gone out of it.

I slid to the ground, shaking, hysteria welling up inside me. 'Well, I did say I was going to try a gallop today, didn't I!' I was laughing now but it wasn't a pleasant sound. Shiona dismounted and came to me. I felt the sharp slap of her hand across my cheek and shrank back. But it was what I had needed. I was quiet now, quiet and bewildered and my face hurt. I put my hand up to the sore place.

'I'm sorry, darling,' Shiona said gently. 'But that's the only cure.'

'Yes.' My lips were stiff with the effort of not crying. She put an arm around my body, and something cold and frightened in me melted and was banished. She had been forced to do what she had done. It didn't mean that she disliked me. It was the proper treatment for hysteria. My stomach began to stop its uneven plunging and threshing.

'I wonder why Fleur ran away like that?' Her voice was puzzled. 'Come, Maggie. I'd like to examine her.'

We went to the now quiescent beast and Shiona examined the brown hide minutely. She loosened the girths when she found nothing unusual about its limbs or hooves. Turning it upside down she gave a sudden exclamation. 'Look at that! There! You do see it, don't you?'

I saw it with a feeling of sickness and a growing disappointment. A burr was stuck to the lining near the rump end of the saddle. The horse wouldn't notice much until my shifting weight pressed on it.

'I should have examined the saddle more carefully before I put it on,' I said miserably. 'I laid it down on the grass. It must have happened then.'

'Maggie – ' she began.

'It was my own carelessness,' I insisted. 'I should have been concentrating. Poor Fleur. I hope it didn't hurt her too much.'

'You're doing yourself an injustice – ' she protested.

'I didn't say thank you,' I went on, refusing to let Shiona put into words my own terrible conviction. 'I'm glad you were there. I suppose I might have broken something.' I had broken something. My heart. I'd never believed hearts could break. Now I knew it was true. It made it easier to understand my mother. For the first time I felt a dreadful anguish for her suffering.

'You look awfully white,' Shiona ventured sympathetically.

'I'm perfectly all right,' I told her. My eyes felt hot and dry as though they could never shed tears again. 'Let's carry on with the lesson, shall we?'

Shiona didn't argue. I threw the burr away and replaced the saddle. I remounted and, without waiting for my cousin, galloped across the wide paddock. The shape of the Stone Maiden seemed to fill the skyline, hard and uncaring, consciously cruel. I hoped savagely, that she never attained her desire. The Warrior had not yet descended the mountain. I prayed he never would.

The following days were only made bearable by the gentleness of Shiona and Fran's newly awakened sense of participation in things around her. Shiona took me riding, often, I was sure, when she would rather have been alone. Fran found an assortment of paints and brushes and coaxed me into taking her for watercolor outings in which we attempted to capture the essence of the Maidenstane country in rather variable pictures. I'd always loved art, and though each painting wasn't always a masterpiece, the odd one sometimes had a kind of truth that pleased me.

Charley was genuinely impressed and would break off from his outdoor chores if he saw us sitting with our stools and easels. He would stare at his large, capable hands as though comparing them with Fran's slight fingers and careful brush-strokes. There was one of my pictures of the loch and the mountains that he was particularly fond of. I intended to have this framed and give it to him if ever he married Cathy.

Shaun and Angus Forbes called at the house more often since the water festival. I could now tell the brothers apart quite easily. Their likeness was based mainly on coloring and something elusive, something of expression that was difficult to pin down. Shaun's eyes were slightly longer and narrower, his mouth more agreeable, his voice a shade less deep than Angus's. He moved his hands more, prowling about where Angus was content to sit still. I liked Shaun and he made me laugh. I had imagined after the business of the burr under the saddle that I never would again.

I was more resilient than I had imagined. I suppose I've always been reasonably optimistic. After two days of torture, I found myself going over and over again that adjustment of the saddle. I'd been there, watching Buck. Surely I would have seen him do it, if he had placed the burr underneath? Nevertheless, he had loosened and shifted it. It wasn't impossible that he'd tampered with it. The burr had been near the back of the saddle. On the other hand, I had laid the saddle down in the meadow, and it could, reasonably, have been my own carelessness. Once doubt had crept in, I blamed myself. Because I'd rather have done something stupid than believe Buck capable of calculated wickedness, I told myself ruefully. But my heart grew lighter with each passing day. It was fortunate Shiona had been there. I shivered when I thought of what could have happened if I'd been dragged along with one foot in the stirrup. Lucky too that my cousin had such strong wrists. If it had been Fran who was with me, there could have been no such rescue. I owed Shiona a great deal.

They had both seen my new dress and admired it unselfishly. I had put it on for each sister in turn and a queer little quiver of pleasure had run through me as I saw my reflection. She couldn't be me, that slim, dark-haired creature whose image I saw in the glass.

'You really do have a quality of feyness,' Shiona said, smoothing down the long strips of velvet that comprised the sash. 'I told you that you looked like a very superior witch and it's true. Even your hair has a sort of beautiful wildness. You'll never succeed in taming it. Not that you should. It makes you stand out of the rut. I much prefer individualism. Who wants to be a little cog in the marriage wheel? All most people think of is preparing their daughters for wifehood in the wrong sense. Dancing masters and music lessons! Elocution and deportment! How ridiculous to have one's back strapped to a board for hours on end, to walk about with books on one's head. How pointless to understand the mechanics of whom to receive and whom to ignore, and not be encouraged in what really matters – '

'What really matters?' I turned from the mirror and my overskirt floated in the draft from the door. I fastened the black band around my throat. It really matched the waistband very well, the cameo brooch finishing off the effect perfectly.

'The same thing that matters to all couples. How best to please each other in more intimate ways. Men are taught to put women on impossible pedestals. Who wants to be on the same level as some expensive antique one hardly likes to touch for fear of breaking it? I would want to be – '

'Go on,' I said, half-amused and half-embarrassed by these new facets of my cousin's character.

'Used,' she said abruptly. 'As women were meant to be.'

Her words conjured up that kiss on the mountain, that last meeting with Buck in the paddock, the knowledge that Shiona could be right. Convention and coldness were no foundation for keeping a husband once you'd found one. There was contact, physical attraction, a response of the senses that no one human could or should ignore.

I took off the dress and hung it up carefully.

'Got over your near-disaster?' Shiona asked casually as I changed back into my blouse and skirt and began to brush my hair. All of a sudden I felt it ought to be tamed like the dangerous feeling aroused by Shiona's odd conversation. She'd missed one or two things I'd felt should have been included. Consideration and tenderness, for instance.

'You mean the other day? Fleur?' I replaced the brush slowly.

'That's what I mean.' Shiona got onto my bed. She was lying on one elbow in the same attitude as the Stone Maiden.

'It didn't take much gettting over,' I replied untruthfully. 'Taught me a lesson.'

'What sort of lesson?' Her eyes were very direct, her expression severe. She wanted me to say that I would never again take Buck on trust. Some awkwardness in me refused to comply with her wishes.

'Not to lay saddles down in meadows, of course. What did you think?'

'It obviously doesn't matter what I think.'

'Oh, but it does – '

'It can't, when you refuse to listen to sense.'

'Please, Shiona, don't go on about it. Everyone's entitled

148

to – what did you call it a few minutes ago? Individualism, wasn't it? Doesn't that mean having a mind of one's own?'

She laughed unexpectedly. 'Hoist with my own petard! I really ought to keep my mouth shut, shouldn't I! Exhorting you to be a rebel on the one hand and then trying to stifle you on the other. It serves me right.' Her eyes were dancing with mischief and the sunlight brought out all their resemblance to peaty water rushing over the bed of a stream.

'You'll look lovely tomorrow night. I take it you'll be wearing the new dress?' she went on.

'Is it tomorrow? Lammas?'

'Yes. Had you forgotten?'

'Not really. It seems to have come with a gallop after seeming to be far away. I expect it's because I've been so busy. Painting with Fran –'

'You've worked wonders with little Sis. I commend your patience,' Shiona said.

'It's not a matter of patience. I like her.' I was conscious of a brief irritation.

'You like everybody, don't you?' She smiled maddeningly.

'You make me sound abnormal. Is it unusual to want to see the best in people?'

'Perhaps I'm the one who's wrong. I just hate being hypocritical.'

For a long, terrible moment we seemed to be on opposite sides of a chasm. I couldn't bear the thought of us being at loggerheads. Nothing was worth being outside Shiona's friendship. 'You like me, anyway,' I said. 'And that matters.'

'We ought to be able to speak our minds and not become acrimonious.'

'Yes.'

'I must try to have a bath. I feel sticky.' She got up in one lazy movement.

'All right.' I went to the door with her. She stood for a moment, her gaze drawn to the nail hole above the door, where the corn mother had hung that Midsummer morning.

'What have you been up to? Hanging charms against witchcraft? Rowan branches?'

I hesitated. The last thing I wanted was to reopen the business of the corn dolly. I could just imagine what Shiona would make of it, championing me as she always did. She would blame Fran, and I didn't want to spoil our pleasant relationship over something that didn't matter anymore. 'No,'

I answered. 'I've no idea how that got there. Probably been there for ages.'

'It couldn't have been. It was painted just before you came.' Shiona frowned. 'Quite recently in fact.'

Fran's door was open a little and I was certain she could hear our conversation. She wouldn't be able to complain about my handling of her sister's question, though. Perhaps my dislike of having to lie had shown in my voice. But she had rather asked for it!

Shiona went. I hoped she wouldn't mention the matter to Aunt Margaret and Uncle Rob. Not that she would. It was far too trivial. But somehow the peace of the afternoon was spoiled. Whatever I did, the shadow of the corn mother remained, subtly threatening, reminding me that someone had disliked me, had wanted to frighten me.

The morning of Lammas was interesting. Shiona and I got very little riding done. The men were tarring the tails and ears of the livestock which had been brought from the hills and tying red and blue threads near the tops of their tails. Ness was having an orgy in the kitchen. She'd put a ball of cow's hair in the milk pail to keep away witches. I made a silent vow not to have any until the festival was over. Now she was very busy, aided by poor ginger-headed 'You', in setting out a cheese of curds and making a porridge with caraway seeds. There was smoked ham on a marble slab, and the table bore the ingredients for vast numbers of scones, oatcakes and pigeon pie.

I couldn't help looking at the wall beside the dresser. The two corn dollies still hung there. There seemed to be a leer on the face of the corn mother. Her blue bead eyes were peculiarly unpleasant, her clay face dustier than ever. She looked as if she had never been moved. My heart jumped uncomfortably. Had I imagined it all as Fran suggested? But there was the nail hole to prove it. Even Shiona had noticed it. The dress of the corn maiden reminded me of my new party gown with its white gathers and edging of lace. But there was no real excitement in the thought. Buck wouldn't be at the party so it would lack something essential.

'What are you looking at?' Shiona asked curiously. Ness lifted her eyes from her pastry bowl as if she wanted to know what we were talking about. I'd noticed this curiosity before.

'Just these.' I indicated the corn figures. 'I just thought that was a bit like my new dress.'

'Oh, you're there,' Fran said from the doorway and I saw that her eyes, as mine had been, were fixed on the hanging dollies. 'I was looking for you.' She saw Shiona then and went on, 'But it doesn't matter if you're busy. I was going to do some gardening and thought you might be interested.' Fran and I had taken over the gardening. It wasn't too arduous for her and got her out in the fresh air. We had made a difference to the rose beds already.

'Do go,' Shiona said, 'I'm going up to the moor. I'd like to be alone for a bit.'

'Very well. Let's get the shears and things, Fran.' I reflected that Shiona never made a fuss about my now frequent forays with her sister. I found myself wondering what she did when she was by herself. Did she meet someone up there in all that waste of heather? It wasn't impossible. She was beautiful, desirable, and she had confessed that she wanted to be more than something merely to look at from a distance. I only hoped she didn't mean to be more liberal in her actions than was safe. For the rest of the morning, I found her face superimposed over the shapes of roses and bushes, floating between the branches of trees, constantly before my eyes.

Over the midday meal I found myself looking at her frequently. She appeared much as usual, her face becomingly flushed as always when she'd been riding fast, her hair just sufficiently disarranged to look achingly becoming, just escaping untidiness.

'Fran!' Aunt Margaret said suddenly. 'You – you're brown!'

'Have you just noticed?'

'Yes. It must be your gardening! And quite truthfully, the rose borders have never looked better. Charley never has the time and your father's too busy with his book. It's quite a help, you and Maggie doing so much.'

'Do you want any more notes written?' I asked. Uncle Rob had praised my handwriting one day and I had been invited into his sanctum many times since to take down the sentences he delivered in his deep, pleasant voice. Sometimes I found his eyes fixed on me with their so penetrating darkness, and then I wondered again about that day on the boat. I had still not quite excluded him from suspicion. Almost but not quite. He had, after all, been on the Stone Maiden that day of Fran's accident. And he was such a strong man.

'You could help me for a while this afternoon. Unless you've other plans?'

'I haven't'

'Good.' He smiled. 'In an hour's time then?'

'Fine. I'll look in and see Grandfather first. There may not be much chance this evening.' The stirrings of excitement were there now. The house would be full of young people and that was always pleasant. If only Buck were to be present. But how did I know he wasn't back? Sometimes I didn't see him for days on end, even when he was at Carn Tierlath. He could be there, at this moment, in the rose-colored house with the white balconies, thinking about tonight. Or was he wondering what had gone wrong with his plan that afternoon in the paddock? He must know by now that I was all right. He'd have heard if I'd been hurt. The excitement changed to something very different.

Grandfather looked tired and frail, the angle of his bonnet not so arrogant. He had the plaid pulled up to his chin in spite of the fact that it was August and quite hot. I had intended to speak to him about the business of Charley and the estate, but this was clearly not the time. I picked up the book from his bedside table and began to read where I'd left off yesterday. It was *Great Expectations*. Grandfather was very fond of Dickens. I was fascinated by the odd, unhappy Miss Haversham. She, too, had been left at the altar in her wedding finery. All the time I was reading, I thought of Kate. She hadn't gone to the wild extremes that Miss Haversham had, allowing life to fall into dust and decay around her. But her life did seem as much a sham. She had made neither herself nor Johnnie Graham happy. Her adopted son had died mysteriously and her own child – if Buck was her child – had all but been accused of causing that death. Perhaps she too should have shut herself up with the memories she had kept alive. It would have hurt no one except herself. But maybe she had thought she could make Johnnie happy. It could have been a risk he was prepared to take. He must have known all the facts. Everyone else seemed aware of them.

I left Grandfather when he'd fallen asleep in midsentence. I straightened his pillow gently and smoothed his bedclothes. He looked very peaceful, his fierce eyes closed and his features still. With no effort at all, he had replaced that other loved grandfather.

Uncle Rob was in his study when I went down. He was sorting through a frenzied pile of notes that would have horrified any perfectionist. They seemed to have no form or order. His thick hair was rumpled, his cravat carelessly knotted. Every-thing else took second place to his work. Or was Aunt Margaret an exception? They seemed fond of each other in an undemonstrative way. I hoped he did put her first. I had grown extremely attached to my aunt.

When my uncle had found those papers he needed next – we were at present dealing with the practice of handfasting, which apparently still reared its unseemly head in isolated parts of Scotland in spite of the hostility of priests and ministers – we settled down to work. He read out the sentences in his slow precise enunciation and I copied in my best copper-plate. The nuns at the convent had been complimentary about my handwriting and I prided myself on its constancy. 'That's marvelous,' Uncle Rob said, peering down over my shoulder. 'When the time comes for my book to be printed, they'll have no trouble with your portion of it.'

'It's interesting,' I answered. 'I'm learning as I go.'

'My own girls could never settle to it for long. Fran was better, but her writing was erratic to say the least. And Margaret has her own duties. She keeps busy.'

'I don't think I'll get tired of it,' I told him. 'It's even more fascinating when one participates in these events. I'll never forget Midsummer Eve – '

No. I should always remember that. Even if that wild embrace, that almost savage kiss had only been the result of re-action after near-tragedy, it had happened. It could never be taken away from me. And there was tonight. Then there was the horse festival, the conquering of the powers of darkness – and later still, the cutting of the last sheaf of corn in which the Corn Spirit lived. It would be made into a corn dolly – a mother or a maiden. There was much to look forward to. But first there was Lammas.

The house was a hive of activity when I left Uncle's study. My wrist ached a little from so much writing, but I was satis-fied with my work. I'd enjoyed my copying, my reading to Grandfather, the gardening with Fran, yesterday's painting, the horse riding at which I was becoming proficient. It was some time since I'd had a tumble. And, of course, I always inspected the underside of my saddle with scrupulous care before buckling it to Fleur, which seemed to have become my personal property.

I changed into the magnolia-tinted dress, brushed my hair and powdered my nose with a hare's foot, rubbed rose-colored salve onto my mouth. Shiona looked in briefly to give me some of Roddy Graham's scent. I wished I'd had the strength of will to refuse it, but I couldn't bear to disappoint her. The musky odor hung about the room, and each movement of my head sent a fresh spiral of perfume before my face. It haunted me, reminding me of a drowned face in the Maiden's shadow, a pale, bruised body caught in reeds. Fran noticed the scent when she hurried in, her shadow dipping against the wall, to have her hair brushed before the event. My ministrations had effected a great improvement in it. 'What's that? Oh, it's the stuff poor Roddy gave She-She. I wonder she can bring herself to use it.' Her turquoise skirts rustled disapprovingly.

I had secretly wondered the same myself. Still, it was obviously expensive and it would have been a pity to throw it away. Perhaps Shiona wanted to be reminded of Roddy. Had she loved him, or had it always been Buck as I had often suspected? Was her show of hatred really an inverted love that had never died? What had happened between them? Did anyone know? Did Kate, who was most closely connected with both young men?

'I think that'll do.' I put down the brush and surveyed Fran's satiny crown with justified satisfaction. 'If only you weren't so lazy, you could do the same.'

'There's more to life than a hundred strokes three times a day,' she remarked.

'So for the rest of our lives, I've got to do your hair for you, is that it?'

Fran laughed. 'Naturally, since you're so good at it! You don't mind, do you?'

'Not at present. But we aren't always going to be cheek by jowl. What if we –'

'Marry? Separate?' Her voice altered fractionally. 'That's not very likely.'

'Oh, thank you very much!' I kept my tone light purposely.

'I didn't mean you. You get prettier all the time.'

'Graham's in love with you. We've all got eyes in case you hadn't noticed.'

'Johnnie was in love with Kate. Look where it got them,' she said morosely.

'Kate wasn't in love with him,' I pointed out.

'How do you know I'm not in love with someone else?' Her tone was only half-joking. 'What do you know about me? What can we know of other people but what they show on the surface? I don't take people at their face value anymore, not since – ' Her voice trailed away. She shrugged and got up from the stool in front of the mirror.

Not since Roddy, not since the Stone Maiden, not since Johnnie let himself die. Fran didn't need to specify any event in particular.

'What a fit of the glooms and maybes!' I said mockingly. 'It's a party. Remember?'

'Mother says we can have hide-and-seek. In the dark. So long as we don't wake up Grandfather.' Fran's face was alive again, her eyes mischievous.

'That's better,' I said, approvingly. 'Let's eat, drink, and be merry for tomorrow – '

'We die.'

The sun dipped suddenly below the horizon and the room was plunged into gloom. It wasn't quite the note I'd meant to end on, and if it was a touch macabre, Fran didn't seem to notice. Any more than she seemed to notice the muffled taps from the wainscot.

II

The drawing-room was gay with candlelight when we went downstairs. A white-covered table was spread with cold meats and the result of Ness's baking, interspersed with little jugs and bowls of flowers. The Lammas porridge stood in solitary splendor on the rosewood chest. Shiona was sitting on the tawny velvet sofa, flanked by the two Forbes brothers. Angus stayed with her; Shaun got to his feet and came to meet us. He bent over my hand with exaggerated courtliness and kissed it. The color rose to my face in spite of myself. I noticed Fran looking around the room. Was it Graham she sought or the other man whose existence she had hinted at in my room? Buck? She had said they talked freely about most things but she'd made it sound a brother and sister relationship. Was it – had it been merely camouflage? I couldn't blame her for being attracted to him, not when I reacted as I did to the thought of Buck.

'You didn't hear a word I said,' Shaun complained softly.

'Didn't I?' I started guiltily.

'You know quite well you weren't listening. I don't know that I shouldn't perhaps transfer my unwanted presence to Moira MacDonald. She might appreciate me.'

'Who?'

He indicated a girl who looked vaguely familiar, tallish, young and with red hair. She was wearing a checked gingham dress and talking to one of the shepherds.

'Good heavens! It's "You"!'

'No! It's Moira MacDonald. I'm here. Remember?'

'I didn't mean that.'

'You are in a bemused state, aren't you? Can it be his fault?'

'Whose fault?' I was still pondering over the change in the kitchen maid. Of course, it was just like Aunt Margaret to allow her to dress up and join the guests tonight. The food was all ready so that one could help oneself. A pile of plates had been placed at the end of the buffet.

'Buck's. He's just come in. I seem to recall you spent quite a lot of time with him at Midsummer.'

I turned my head dizzily. Buck was talking to Uncle Rob. I fancied he had lost some of his tan. A hand seemed to clench inside me, constricting breathing, disrupting thought processes. The gap in time since we had last met seemed to have enhanced his dark good looks. He looked up suddenly in mid-sentence and I was submerged in the black shock of his gaze. He went on talking to Uncle without removing his eyes from their contemplation of my face.

Shaun held out a glass to me and I took it. It could have contained hemlock and I'd never have noticed the difference. I sipped and was conscious of neither taste nor enjoyment. Elizabeth Stewart and Graham came in, Elizabeth in a dark-blue velvet dress that emphasized all her fine-drawn fairness.

'Excuse me,' Shaun said. 'I must talk to Elizabeth. Do you mind?'

I shook my head. 'No – no –'

Buck crossed the room. He towered over me, or that was how it felt. 'That's not whiskey, is it?' he asked, smiling.

'Not this time.'

'Good.'

'How did you enjoy London? Did you get what you

156

wanted?' The chatter and laughter merged into a bright blur of sound.

'The silver, you mean? Yes. I did.'

'I wondered if you'd get back for tonight.'

'I tried to find time yesterday to let you know, but the cattle needed bringing down.'

'Oh, yes.'

'How have you filled the time since I saw you?'

'Oh, there was plenty to do.' I told him about my exploits.

'And the riding? You must have progressed.' The dark eyes bored into mine.

'You'll see a big difference.'

'I like your dress.'

'Your mother and Aunt Margaret chose it that time they visited Aunt Bell.' I watched him to see what effect the mention of our mutual relative had on him. His features didn't change noticeably.

A little crowd had gathered around a small, gray-haired woman who sat in the corner. 'Who's she?' I asked, intrigued by the respect with which she was treated.

'That's the spaewife. She'll read all the teacups and tell fortunes.'

'I shan't have mine read. If my future's filled with disaster, I'd rather not know.'

He laughed gently. 'Why should it be?'

'This seems to be a place where things happen.' The words were out before I could stop them. I saw his mouth tighten. His brows drew together in a frown.

'Do you mean anything specific?'

Now was the time to mention the burr under the saddle. My gaze shifted to Shiona, who still sat with Angus. She was wearing a different gown, I noticed. This one was yellow, like primroses. She seemed not to notice me. I watched her put her head back and laugh. She was lovely when she was amused. I found I couldn't bring myself to talk about that near-accident. It must have been my own fault. It must . . .

'Not really.' I could see that he didn't believe it. His eyes had narrowed thoughtfully.

'I told you to take care,' he reminded me.

'Yes, you did. I wondered why afterward.'

'It's the sort of thing you say when you part from someone,' he explained quietly.

'How is Kate?'

'She had a wonderful time. Says it's put her right for the autumn and winter.'

'That's nice.'

'You must let me see your paintings sometime.'

'They aren't particularly good.'

'Let me be the judge of that.' His eyes had changed, become soft and considering, secretly amused. I wondered dreamily who or what he was thinking about. He took my empty glass from me and our fingers touched. Little tremors of excitement ran up my arm like the bubbles in champagne. He went to the buffet table and dipped the silver ladle into the punch bowl. The drink tasted of limes and something warm and burning that ran through my veins like fire. The others in the long room had receded, leaving us on a little island of awareness.

'Why,' I asked him, 'did you scowl at me so horribly that day in Church Street?'

'Did I?'

'You know you did.'

'I suppose I was thinking about your father.'

'And your mother?'

'Yes.'

'It wasn't my fault,' I told him.

'No. It was very unfair of me. Believe me when I say I'm sorry.'

'How did you know it was me? We'd never met.'

'I knew the number of the house. And you did look like Margaret and Fran.'

'I see.' I still disliked the knowledge that Kate had sent him to spy on me.

'I brought a present for you. As you pointed out, it is the custom,' he said.

'I only mentioned it in an academic kind of way.'

'There it is, then.' Buck took a small wrapped parcel from his pocket.

'I'd rather not open it here.'

'Too public for you?'

'A bit.'

'We could go into the garden. I don't suppose we'll be missed.'

I thought Buck was being optimistic in this assertion. Several people would be interested when they saw us leave the room together. Perhaps not Fran and Graham, who were absorbed in conversation in the quietest corner of the room. But almost everyone else.

Buck put a hand under my elbow and we were out in the hall. The front door had been left open because it was mild. The stars blazed and the moon hung, apricot-colored, above the steeple crowns of firs. Somewhere, water slipped by, whispering. The muted sound of revelry floated from lamplit windows. I could see silhouetted figures, the thin film of steam from the punch bowl lying on the panes, blurring reality. The smell of the trees and vegetation was very strong.

I unwrapped the paper to disclose a brooch of turquoise and pearl. I recognized the flower shapes with a thrill of discovery. 'The blue convolvulus.'

'I saw it just before I left London. It seemed appropriate.'

'But it's much too good! One usually exchanges handkerchiefs and ribbons or purses – '

'Aren't I allowed to be different?' His smile was unbearably pleasant.

'Aunt Margaret may not approve,' I said slowly. Having heard that conversation between her and my uncle, I was sure she wouldn't. 'So close to yours and mine,' she had said. But Uncle Rob had been kinder. He might not be displeased.

'I refuse to take it back.'

'Why? Why should you give me something that – that must have been so expensive?' My eyes refused to meet his.

'Because – '

The drawing-room door opened suddenly to reveal hurrying figures. I felt that we must be very conspicuous, standing here in the open doorway.

'So there you are!' Shaun said. His voice was faintly annoyed. My hand closed over the brooch involuntarily. I felt the pin prick my palm painfully. 'We're going to play Hunt the Ladybird. All the girls must separate and hide. Then we look for you all.'

'And *do* remember not to make too much noise,' Aunt Margaret said. 'I don't want Father disturbed.'

'Lady, Lady Lanners,' Fran was singing softly.

> Lady, Lady Lanners
> Tak' yer cloak aboot yer heid,
> An' flee awa' to Flanners.

There was a good deal of stifled amusement. I saw Shiona

just behind Aunt Margaret, her eyes fixed on Buck's face. Angus had hold of her arm in a proprietary way, but I had the conviction she had forgotten him.

'And whichever girl we find must be our partner for the ride.'

'Which ride?' I asked.

'Don't you know?' Shaun was surprised. 'We take our horses down to the loch and ride out into the water. If this place were on the coast, we'd go out into the sea. Right into the breakers – splash!'

'You'll need your cloaks on,' Aunt Margaret said. 'To protect your dresses.'

'And don't be too daring,' Uncle Rob warned. 'Right, lads. Back in here and the girls off to your hiding places.'

The drawing-room door closed on a babel of laughter. Most of the girls went to the stairs and began to mount them, giggling softly as they climbed and objuring one another to be quiet because of the old gentleman in bed. I wanted, suddenly, to be alone, to think of what Buck might have said if he hadn't been interrupted. I realized, a little ashamed, that I was disinclined to talk to my cousins. The brooch still cut into my palm and I knew I wanted to keep it. How carefully he had chosen something that would have more than an ordinary meaning. The prince's morning glory. If ever I went away, I'd have a perpetual reminder of the blue convolvulus, of Maidenstane and Carn Tierlath.

I went toward the kitchen, everyone else having scattered in the other possible directions. It was in darkness, though there was a lamp in the passageway outside that let in a dim glow just inside the doorway and put shadowy glints into the dishes on the dresser and the copper vessels on the shelves. I felt my way around the table and into the recess in the far corner where steps led down to the back door. Crouched at the foot of the steps, I doubted if I could be seen, even dressed as I was, in near white. It was surprising how little I could see in spite of the vague lighting from the passage.

As soon as I had hidden myself, I pinned the brooch to my bodice. It might have been more sensible to have gone up to my room and put it in a drawer until I had decided whether or not to keep it. But it was too late. The hunters were moving about the darkened house and I didn't want the brooch to be dropped or damaged when I was found.

I became aware that someone was coming toward the kitchen, softly and carefully. Crouching still lower, I hid my face in my hands and tried to stifle my breathing. I knew Shaun wanted to find me and I was reluctant to be his partner during the ride to the loch. It wasn't that I didn't like him. I did, very much. But more than that, I wanted Buck to tell me why he had brought me the brooch. Perhaps his feelings for other girls hadn't lasted. With me it could be different, couldn't it? I wondered how many other girls had asked themselves this same question since time began. It didn't make the reflection any less urgent.

The slow, quiet footfalls were in the kitchen now. I became faintly disturbed. I could have expected the hunter to be less stealthy. The was a rustle, a soft intake of breath, the scrape of a foot. I realized, much to my surprise, that whoever it was had no intention of searching the room. Had it been one of the girls, intending perhaps to take refuge here, and changing her mind at the last minute? I stood up and stared in the direction of the doorway, but there was nothing to be seen. Unease settled over me. Inexplicably, the quiet, the feel of the stone flags under my soft slippers became prisonlike. I wanted to escape from my self-imposed isolation.

I was halfway to the front door when Buck came around a corner and confronted me. He stood for a moment, his eyes on the brooch, then he smiled and reached out to grasp my wrist. 'You have me now. For the ride. I thought I'd never find you.'

'I have a present for you, too,' I said.

'Have you, Maggie? There was no need –'

'I couldn't bring it downstairs.'

'Shall we go and fetch it?'

'Yes. From the noise in the drawing room I gather nearly everyone's been found.'

'You gather right.' He laughed and the sound was pleasant.

I went to the staircase, very conscious of him by my side. He let me precede him on the stairs. I could see his shadow following me, tall and broad and somehow purposeful. We passed Moira MacDonald and the shepherd. I fancied they looked at us curiously. Was I being indiscreet in taking Buck upstairs to my room? It hadn't seemed wrong when Buck had suggested it, but those knowing glances put a new interpretation on the matter. Perhaps I was being too sensitive. Everyone, after all, had been given the freedom of the house.

We passed Grandfather's closed door. I remembered his hopes for Charley and me. What would he think if he knew how I felt about the man beside me? I was dangerously close to total involvement. How could I feel like this, knowing or suspecting what I did?

The top floor was dark and quiet. I picked up the candle that burned in a pewter holder on top of the linen chest near the stairs. When I was almost at the landing, I felt a reluctance to go any farther. The ceiling seemed lower than usual as though it were gradually descending to crush me. It must be the effect of the uncertain light.

'You've decided to keep the brooch, then?' Buck asked quietly, bringing me back to the present.

'I put it there for safety, until I had time to think –' The candle wavered and guttered, sending a stream of melted wax into the curved base of the candlestick. It solidified even as I watched, making pallid greasy shapes, peculiarly unpleasant.

'Please keep it,' he urged.

The flickering light showed me the slanted doorway of the steeple room. Something hung against it, swaying in the current of air. I lifted the candlestick higher. The little dancing figure of the corn maiden pirouetted with a horrid gaiety, her throat and breast daubed with scarlet-red drops over the gathered skirt and lacy hem.

My senses repudiated it. Even my voice banished it. 'No,' I said. 'No – no – no –' But the inner core of my being accepted the fact that someone hated me. Only hate could have directed unknown hands to place the corn dolly there, to slash and spatter it with blood. My head was swimming. I felt the candlestick being taken from me, Buck's harsh voice whispering, 'Monster!' I clenched my teeth and forced myself to stand upright while everything inside me willed my subjection to weakness.

Buck went to the door and tore at the string from which the corn maiden was suspended. He pushed the straw puppet into his pocket. I could still see the swaying stalks of her hair and a corner of blotched lace. He set the candlestick on the floor.

'Who?' he asked, but he sounded as if he knew. It hadn't been a question.

'I don't know. It – it happened once before. With the corn mother. Only there was no blood. Not the first time.' My tongue felt thick and woolly.

'And I suppose you told no one.'

'Only Fran. She knew nothing about it. Don't let's talk about it. It was a joke of some kind. A joke –' I felt myself sway. Buck's arms were around me, uncompromisingly hard, reassuringly urgent. I was glad to be there, my body against his, my hands seeking the bulk of his shoulders, touching the crisp hair that curled to the nape of his neck. He was warm, real, concerned for my distress. The memory of the corn maiden receded. 'I missed you,' I said, refusing to think about the paddock and Fleur or the hands aboard the steamer. 'I missed you. All the time you were away – I missed you dreadfully.'

His fingertips traced the hollow of my spine and I shivered. 'I love you,' I said, though I knew I shouldn't. He couldn't love me, not forever. It would all be over one day but I could see only the present. Only his face coming closer. The pressure of his mouth saying what words never could. It was a pity it wouldn't last, that, in my heart of hearts, I knew Shiona had spoken the truth. I was poor Agnes Sampson, my protection against witchcraft long since dead and thrown away. I was in the embrace of the devil. It seemed not to matter.

My arms fell to my sides and my fingertips brushed the spiky hair of the corn maiden. I had said I loved him and already I knew I had made a mistake. But it was easy not to care too much with the blood singing through my veins like some paean of triumph, everything cobwebs and shadows, except him.

The rest of the evening passed in a kind of dream. I refused to let the recurring memory of the corn maiden spoil what remained of it. Fran had called out my name and we had sprung apart guiltily. I thought he had forgotten everything else, just as I did. I leaned over the banister and told her I was getting my cloak as Aunt Margaret had directed. Buck fastened the neck for me because my fingers were trembling. I held up the candle so that he could see his present. It was the picture I thought was best, the Stone Maiden, her feet wreathed with swans, her head turned toward the Warrior. It had been difficult to achieve the texture of stone and the contrast of foliage, feathers and water. He looked at it so long without speaking that I was disappointed. Then I saw the sadness in his face, a kind of anger in his eyes and I knew he thought of Fran and Roddy.

'Perhaps I should have chosen one of the others,' I said.

'No. You shouldn't. I like this one. I like it very much.'

'Really?'

'Of course. I wouldn't have said so otherwise.'

'I'm glad.'

'May I invite myself again in order to collect it?'

'Yes.' I pushed aside the thought of Aunt Margaret's probable displeasure and Shiona's possible, almost certain, antagonism.

'Well, we'd better go down again; otherwise I may decide to stay. All night.'

'To – stay?' My voice shook in spite of all my efforts to control it.

'Was that hope or apprehension?' he asked, and he laughed very softly.

'Both, I suppose. Are you in the habit of staying? All night?' I couldn't help myself.

'You don't really expect an answer to that, do you? What does it matter. The past's the past. This is the present. When one forms a new relationship it has nothing to do with what's gone. How could it?' He was still smiling, but that amusement didn't reach his eyes.

'It couldn't,' I agreed, but I was attacked by a brief fear that he would say this again in the future to a girl who was not myself. Then he bent his head and kissed me, and though it began lightly, the kiss renewed all that mutual necessity to touch, to caress, to keep one's head above the dangerous waters of prurience.

We walked downstairs in close proximity and once again my hand brushed the dried kernels of the corn maiden's hair. 'What will you do with her?' I asked, recoiling.

'Dispose it it, surreptitiously.' He obviously considered her an inanimate object. To me she possessed a kind of life. Or was it death?'

'Is that blood?'

'No. Paint.'

Paint! Fran owned the paints. They were kept in her room. It was next to mine. Fran had moods and attacks of wildness. She was usually sorry afterward, but they existed, undeniably. I remembered how she had stood in the doorway of the kitchen while I remarked on the likeness of the dolly's dress to my new one. Buck had singled me out for his attention tonight. She had hinted she might be in love with some other man than Graham Stewart. Was it Buck? Could she be jealous of me? Had she done this? One could never be sure with Fran. 'What do you know about me?' she had asked. 'What can we know of other people but what they show on the surface?' There was still the unexplained business of the corn mother. Fran was the only person who had known of my revulsion for the creature, apart from Ness. But what possible reason could Ness have for persecuting me? Fear rose in me to be dispelled by the pressure of Buck's fingers around mine.

'You aren't to worry about it. It doesn't matter. Do you hear?'

'Yes. I've already forgotten.' But I hadn't, for all my show of bravery. Matters had progressed since the corn mother had been put there to frighten me. Now there was the threat of violence. The semblance of blood proved that. Who hated me? Who?

Charley and Cathy Forbes were at the foot of the stairs. I had the feeling they had been quarreling. There was that suggestion of strain that follows a disagreement, and Cathy was paler than usual. She smiled, rather forcedly, when she saw Buck and me. 'Shaun's been searching everywhere for you! Where have you been? We've been here for some time.' Her high-pitched voice could be heard for some distance.

'Getting my cloak.'

'I hardly think that can have been all,' Cathy said, enjoying my discomfiture.

'It was all,' I said quietly.

'Cathy – ' Charley muttered uncomfortably. I was sorry for him.

She took no notice of my cousin. 'And Buck with his terrible reputation? He must be getting old. Or disinclined – '

The group of young people in the hall had their heads turned in our direction. I saw Fran's face, alive with interest, Shiona's profile, cold with distaste. It was Cathy and her spite, I told myself, but wasn't it more likely to be for me and my choice of a partner?

'Would you mind?' I said in a low voice. 'Aunt Margaret particularly asked if we'd be careful not to wake up Grandfather.' Cathy's eyes were bright and I saw that she was close to tears. Charley was watching me with the most curious expression. He didn't look at Buck. They were the two suspects for that childhood accident. It wasn't Buck, I told myself, so it could have been Charley. Just at this moment it seemed not so improbable. But he hadn't been on the steamer. That hadn't been Charley. Yet, something about his demeanor suggested a completely different man from the one I had hitherto seen and talked to. Quite suddenly, I knew what they had been discussing. It must be my claim to Maidenstane. Perhaps Cathy had been trying to find out where she and my cousin stood. Their future obviously included the security of a house and an occupation and I was in the way of any settlement. Her present spitefulness bore that out. I became just as sorry for Cathy as I was for Charley.

Cathy turned her back. Charley stayed where he was. Buck took hold of me. His fingers pressed into the flesh of my arm hurtfully and I was aware of the strength of his silent anger. Tomorrow I would certainly be bruised. Like that other time . . .

The heads were all discreetly turned away by the time we reached the door. I heard Fran laugh as if nothing had happened. Graham smiled at me and his eyes were kind. Buck still held my arm as though I were an enemy who must not be allowed to escape. The straw doll still protruded a little from his pocket, and I saw Shiona's eyes widen as he passed close beside her. The corner of white lace was reddened. She must have noticed that too, but she said nothing. Then we were out in the starlight and moonlight and the black frieze of trees swaying. The merciless fingers stopped pressing into my forearm. 'Little bitch!' Buck said harshly. 'Charley should put her over his knee and smack some manners into her. Not that he will. He couldn't hurt a fly. Not big Charley –'

Buck should know my cousin, I thought, as I followed him.

He made it sound the unlikeliest thing in the world that Charley could ever use violence toward another person. So, if Fran were to be believed, that left only Buck, who had just proved he could be cruel in a physical sense, however unwittingly it had been done, and Uncle Rob. But could I believe Fran? I wanted to, but the business of the corn dollies was still unexplained. Fran had the best, almost the only opportunities. She enjoyed frightening people. Her story of the half-dead confirmed that. There was something behind the seemingly friendly aspect of the family at Maidenstane that had its own peculiar horror.

Buck, like all the other young men in the party, had tethered his horse to the long rail provided outside the stables. He flung himself into the saddle, then pulled me up behind him. I put my arms around his waist. Other couples were all doing the same. Angus and Shiona, her hair pale in the dimness, Graham and Fran – what had happened to her scruples about riding? –

even Charley and Cathy, having, I supposed, temporarily resolved their difficulties.

I couldn't see Buck's face, but I knew by the set of his shoulders that he was still angry. I wanted to believe that it was on my behalf. Or had it been that imputation of loss of virility that stung? I thought I could reassure him that he was certainly not lacking in the art of seduction. I forgot everything in the resurgence of physical attraction between him and myself. My arms tightened about him. I laid my cheek against the hardness of his back.

He laughed. 'If that's pandering to my bad temper, I like it.'

'It is.'

'Good.'

The scents and the sounds, the dimly seen lights of the August evening swirled and swung about our heads as the drum of hooves beat faster. The trees parted and the mountains, pale as amethyst glass, shifted in their stony beds. The color was fading from the moon, leaving it bland as milk. There were scattered lights on the water, shivering down through its blackness like golden icicles. There was a magic in riding so close to someone else, in seeing other horses silhouetted, clinging figures and belling skirts and cloaks, tendrils and webs of hair silvered in moonlight like the hair of witches on broomsticks. Agnes Sampson, I reflected. That's who I was tonight. Agnes Sampson with her arms around a devil with burning eyes and cloven feet . . .

We were at the edge of the loch and I pulled up my skirts under the cloak. The white sand was already marked with hoofprints, churned and tossed, its smooth paleness spoiled until the rains came to flatten it again. The horse plowed uneasily, floundered and went into the water. Sure of itself again, it galloped along the bright line of the loch's edge. There were reeds farther out. Reeds that stretched as far as the Maiden's bulk. Roddy in the reeds, caught by his hair. Dark hair like Johnnie's and Buck's. I thought I could see him, floating, drifting, his pale body swollen under the ministrations of that same water that looked so beautiful tonight.

The swans, disturbed by the unaccustomed noise, receded silently into the center of the loch, where they seemed to hang suspended like spirits. Buck took me farther and farther around the perimeter of the loch. We were leaving the others behind. They preferred to splash and scream and throw water

167

at one another in an excess of high spirits. Perhaps the spaewife had foretold good things for each of them, the promise of a warm hearth, a good house and a quiverful of children to lighten their old age.

Buck stopped eventually. The horse made blowing noises. The water lapped almost to its knees, glinting, sending ripples far away into distance. Soon they would reach the swans. Neither of us moved. We could hear each other's hearts beat, I was certain. Then he reached into his pocket and took out the corn maiden. One twist of his wrist and she spun through the air, her arms and legs horribly alive, trying to stop her flight to destruction. She fell into the water some way off, her skirts ballooning, the white light on her throat and breast showing up the dark blotches with an unpleasant clarity.

'You should have put her in the fire!' I said, my voice thick, my heart pounding.

'That's bad luck,' Buck told me. 'The greatest of bad luck.'

'I – I don't want to see her drown.'

'Close your eyes, then.'

For all that I did, she stayed there on my eyes' retinas, the weight of the water pulling at the lace-trimmed gown, dragging her under to be tangled in the reeds. Like Roddy. Poor Roddy Graham, who had died with marks on his body like the ones I had on my arm. The night was suddenly cruel. I shivered. 'Let's go back.'

'Cold?'

'Yes.'

'There are other cures for that complaint.' His voice suggested unnameable pleasures.

'I daresay there are! But I'm tired. I — I feel as if I've been to a funeral.'

'A sailor buried at sea?' His voice was gentle now.

'Something like that.'

'Very well. What you want, you shall have.' He pulled at the reins so that we stood in reverse. I was glad my back was now to the place in the water where the corn maiden had fallen. She had looked so real. So human – so destroyed . . .

The hooves plashed through the shallows, sending up little showers of spray. All the urgency had gone out of the night and something like peace stole in to take its place. Tomorrow I would have to think. Just at the moment there was no need. Neither of us spoke a word until the bulk of Maidenstane rose against the stars and the blue tiles of the steeple glittered under the moon.

There were two letters for me the next morning. The one from Aunt Sarah contained the predictable news that early next year she was to marry Josh Davidson. I found myself wondering if there was, in her feelings for Josh, any of the wild passion I felt for Buck. The other letter was from Jenny. She said she missed me. My account of the house in which I now lived, and the people contained in it, had intrigued her enormously. I had, naturally, made no mention of the attempt to push me over the steamer rail, or the feeling of haunting about my room, the figure in the graveyard that had followed me. James, Jenny told me, had been quiet of late and very engrossed in his work. I thought of James with more than a trace of compassion. To think I had once connected marriage with the wary proximity of two people who, quite cold-bloodedly, decided to set up home together. It could be something quite different. It was warmth, tenderness, being able to laugh at each other, wanting nothing or no one to hurt the object of one's affections. It was using all the senses to appreciate the physical attraction between oneself and the man one loved, and all the sensibilities to understand the occasions when one's partner was sad or unable to communicate his problems. And it ought to mean trust . . .

I forced myself to go on reading Jenny's closely written pages. Did I remember Roger McRae? He was one of the sons of a leading Berwick businessman. They dealt in feeding stuffs for cattle and seed and grain, phosphates to improve soil. In a farming area like that, there would always be a good living for the McRaes. Roger had begun to show an interest and Jenny sounded pleased about this. Her parents and his encouraged the liaison. I was happy for Jenny, though I couldn't feel the same about James. He'd meet someone else. He was bound to. He was only in his twenties, and anyway, I was the wrong sort of person for him. Too imaginative, too unpredictable, too much preoccupied with the fascinating business of kissing and embracing and all that led to. I could never bring myself to do such things with James. We'd be doomed to unhappiness from the start.

'Interesting letter?' Fran asked, pushing aside her porridge bowl. She had stopped being finicky about her meals of late.

'Oh, yes.' I told her about my aunt's prospective marriage

and about Jenny and Roger McRae. Aunt Margaret was interested in the news of Aunt Sarah. 'It looks as if you did the right thing, Maggie.'

'Maggie always does the right thing. She should have been a diplomat,' Fran said, folding her linen napkin and pushing it through the serviette ring.

'Of course I don't,' I answered a little shortly.

'What! When you've got Grandfather eating out of your hand. Not to mention Father! You seem able to manage She-She and me, something no one has ever been able to do up to now. And Mother likes you. Of course you're a diplomat!'

'Cathy doesn't,' I said. 'You forgot her. Neither does Elizabeth.'

'Elizabeth doesn't like anyone Buck's interested in.'

I could feel Aunt Margaret's eye on me. I folded up the pages of Jenny's letter without looking at her. But she said nothing, which surprised me.

'Cathy doesn't matter,' Fran went on.

'Oh, but she does!' I was driven to say with some heat. 'It was quite natural.'

'I heard about it,' Aunt Margaret said with a trace of severity. 'Cathy behaved abominably. I'll be having a few words with that young lady, don't worry.'

'Not on my behalf,' I began uncomfortably.

'Not only on yours. You can save your breath, Maggie. By the way, I wonder what Ness was talking about before you all came down?' She frowned.

'What was that, Mother?' Shiona came into the dining room and took her seat opposite me. 'Sorry I'm late. I was so sleepy this morning.'

'Something about the corn maiden being taken from the kitchen. Now who would want to do that?'

'Taking our luck away!' Fran objected. 'I suppose it was during Hunt the Ladybird. Everyone had the run of the place. The Forbes are inclined to overstep the mark at times. It would be Shaun, you mark my words.'

'You'd be wrong,' Shiona said. 'I wouldn't like him to be accused unjustly. Maggie knows, though being the nice girl she is, she won't say.'

'I don't know.' I remembered, belatedly, the soft footsteps as I hid in the kitchen, the premature departure of the searcher.

'Why, Maggie!' Shiona looked upset. 'Buck had it. You must have seen.'

'He did. But not because he took it. We – we found it to-gether.'

'Where?'

'Hanging above my door.'

'Both of you?' Aunt Margaret queried, her brows raised.

'Yes. It was Hunt the Ladybird. Remember?'

'Well, then. Why didn't you put it back in the kitchen?'

'We couldn't. It was covered with red paint. Buck disposed of it.'

'What a silly trick! I expect he did right,' my aunt said thoughtfully.

'I hope it doesn't lead to trouble. I know we always pretend we take the old superstitions with a grain of salt, but there's a certain unwillingness about breaking the pattern.' Fran looked at me as she spoke and there was calculation in her gaze. I wondered why she didn't mention the previous occasion when I'd accused her of hanging the corn mother in the same place. I experienced a flicker of revulsion as I remembered putting the little figure into a drawer, then finding it empty later.

'Come up with me,' Fran asked. 'Are we painting this morning?'

'I don't think so,' I replied, too quickly. I hadn't forgotten the red splotches on the corn dolly's breast, that vicious slash across the throat. I didn't want to use paint today.

'Come riding with me then,' Shiona begged. 'You've been neglecting me.'

'Have I?'

'You know you have.' There was something vulnerable about her this morning that touched me.

'What about your uncle?' Aunt Margaret interposed. 'He'd rather set his mind on completing the chapter on handfasting today.'

'Oh!' Fran made a face. 'I sometimes think Father would kill anyone who got in the way of his finishing his book!'

'What an unpleasant thing to say,' my aunt said sharply.

'It's very loyal of you, Mother, but you know it's true. He's terribly dedicated – '

'And who's he? The cat's grandfather?'

Fran giggled unrepentantly. 'What are you going to do then, Maggie? You are in demand, aren't you!'

'Would Uncle mind very much if I didn't write today?' I asked slowly. 'I've got a bit of a headache.'

'And the subject of handfasting is such a provocative one,'

Fran said, grinning at me maddeningly. 'Marriage without the ceremony. As if that made any difference!'

'Fran!' Aunt Margaret rebuked. 'Of course there's a difference. There are the children to be considered. There are always the children to be considered.' She was pale now and I sensed that she was thinking of poor Bell's child. Poor, wild, gypsy Bell. My heart plummeted. Then, I knew I had been right because she went on. 'Kate and I will be going to see Bell again in a day or two. But Ness will look after you all.'

'I'll come up with you, Fran. And by the time you've finished breakfast, Shiona, I'll be back. A ride may blow the cobwebs away. Then I could help Uncle Rob later.'

'Good,' Shiona said, smiling her warm, appreciative smile. 'Shall I saddle Fleur for you? It wouldn't be any trouble.'

'I'll be back long before that's necessary. I only want to change into my skirt.'

'Watch yourself, Maggie,' Aunt Margaret said with concern. 'You do look a bit peaky.'

If I was jaded, it was because I hadn't slept well. There had been much to think about. But I had the odd feeling my aunt meant more than she'd said. Was it because of Buck and the now obvious bond between us? Then why didn't she say something more definite?

Fran and I went upstairs in a companionable silence. She didn't walk so badly as she had. Apparently gaining confidence and being happier had worked wonders for her physical state as well as her morale.

She came into my room with me and looked out of the window while I changed into my skirt and blouse and hung up the crimson dress. The banging started behind the wainscot and she looked at me a little shamefacedly. 'I told you a lie,' she said abruptly. 'I do know what that noise is. I've heard it too. I pretended I didn't, because of Charley and you getting preference over him. And then I got to like you and I wished I hadn't started off on the wrong foot.'

'I guessed as much,' I told her calmly. 'Go on, surprise me.'

'It's the water pipes underneath. You are above the bathroom.'

'Is that all?' I began to brush my disarranged hair.

'That's all.'

Then the face at the window had been Ness or Moira after all. I felt oddly cheated, yet there was the relief of knowing. It

172

was always best to know. If only all my queries could be solved so simply.

'Are you cross with me?' Fran asked quietly. 'I deserve it if you are.'

'No. I'm not.' My hair gave off crackling sounds as I went on brushing it.

'But I really had nothing to do with the corn dollies. Honestly, Maggie.'

I looked at her then. I could swear she was telling the truth. Then her own words came back to haunt me. How did one know what went on inside another's mind?

'You do believe me, don't you?' She made it sound important. Again, I was touched.

'Yes. But wouldn't it be better to be honest with one another from now on?'

'It would be, but knowing my own deficiencies, I won't absolutely swear.'

'You sound very cheerful and forgiving,' I said. 'Something's happened, hasn't it?'

'Discerning creature! Don't tell anyone else, though. Especially not Mother.'

'It depends what it is,' I said carefully.

'Well, you know what I said about married people seeing one another?'

'Yes – '

'Well, I do rather like Graham particularly – '

'I thought there was someone else. Someone you preferred.'

'There used to be.' She got up from my bed and began to walk around the room.

'It was Buck, wasn't it?'

'Yes. Everyone falls in love with Buck at some time or other. It's as inevitable as Beltane, or Lammas, or Midsummer. I've grown out of it now. It's a waste of time hankering after the moon when there's something real for the taking. I don't regret it. Buck didn't try to make capital out of it. He couldn't have been kinder, really. It's time Buck was placed out of reach. He needs to be chained up with someone. It won't stop the odd star-struck female cropping up, of course, but it would take away something – hope, I suppose.'

'You were talking about Graham,' I reminded her.

'We rode off like everybody else only there was so much puppy daftness. So we went the other way till we were almost facing the Stone Maiden. There's a little spit of sand there and

173

the moon was shining. And then, I suppose I went a bit crazy – '

'Oh, Fran! You didn't!' I remembered her remarks about handfasting with a sense of foreboding. The Drummond sisters were nothing if not enlightened. Queen Victoria wouldn't have been in the least amused by their forthright views.

'Of course I didn't. I don't always fly when I flap my wings.'

'That's a relief. Well, what did happen during that spell of craziness?'

'It was almost as light as day where we were. The sand's so white and the moon blazing – '

'I know. I saw it.' I still saw it in some special compartment of my mind.

'There's a log on the beach. I was sitting on it, just not thinking much about anything, then all of a sudden I was kicking off my shoe and taking my stocking off. I pulled up my skirt and told Graham to look at my leg – '

My throat felt tight. 'And what then?'

'He'd been watching the lights on the loch. He – he got down on his knees and picked up my foot and – kissed it. Poor little foot, he said, lots of times, and then he was kissing me instead. And I knew he really did love me. He'd seen me as I am and he still wanted me – ' Her voice was filled with wonder.

The tightness in my throat became a pain.

'Aren't you pleased? I wouldn't ever have done it if it hadn't been for you.'

'Wouldn't you?' The words came with difficulty.

'No.'

I knew she spoke the truth. Fran would have become pricklier and thornier, more and more eccentric as time went by. At least this good had come from my advent into the household. Sweetness and bitterness were mingled in my reaction to that realization. I was glad for her, delighted in the thought of her happiness. It was my own love that was precarious, that could recede and grow as spectral as the swans on the loch. She was sure of Graham. I wanted to be as certain of Buck. I thought I was, but there were still questions that had not been answered, might never be. Always questions . . .

'I'm very pleased, Fran darling. So very glad.' I put my arms around her for a moment, then took them away again. She wasn't demonstrative. I wouldn't embarrass her.

'We'll paint tomorrow,' she said, but her thoughts were on other things.

'Tomorrow,' I agreed.

She went out of the room and her carriage was almost straight. Almost, but not quite. I stared after her, then ran down the stairs to look for Shiona. My head really was aching now. I was paid out for my lie at the breakfast table.

12

Shiona wasn't in sight when I went into the dining room. Aunt Margaret was still there, discussing the day's menu with Ness, who looked more like Queen Victoria than ever. Would the queen have looked so severe if her beloved Albert hadn't died so cruelly all those years ago? I fancied she'd have been quite different if he had lived. Just as Kate would have been if Father had reciprocated her love. A band of pain began to tighten around my head, a pain not only for myself.

Ness looked at me curiously as she left the room to get on with her work. Was she only pondering on my likeness to Father and my aunt? Or was it the curious business of the missing corn dolly?

'Is your head aching badly?' Aunt Margaret asked. She was wearing a dark-blue dress that accentuated her fair skin and the color of her large eyes.

'It does rather,' I answered truthfully.

'Wouldn't you be better advised to lie down?'

'I'm sure it'll go away when I'm out in the fresh air. Oh, if anyone comes, I'd better let you know where I'll be. Just in case – '

'Are you expecting someone to call?' The gray-blue eyes studied me. The voice was quiet.

'Yes. Buck may. I've a picture for him.'

'Maggie. There's something I'd better say – '

'Ready, cousin?' Shiona, dressed in riding hat and white

blouse and skirt like mine, came into the room with a rush of vitality and good spirits.

'Where will you be, She-She?' my aunt asked. 'Buck may be calling. Maggie would like him to know where she can be found.'

'Well, we'll go to the paddock first, then perhaps 'round the loch as far as the Maiden.' Shiona's smile was ever so faintly subdued.

'The Maiden?'

'That's right, Mother. Maggie's never been there yet. I said I'd take her some time ago. Today's the day. She can't get into trouble if I'm there, can she! We'll be quite safe. You mustn't worry.'

'I'll give Buck the message.' There was definitely something odd about Aunt Margaret. I was thankful Shiona had come in before there could be any painful disclosures about Buck. I wanted to keep what there was as long as was humanly possible. Once it was gone I could never have it back. It would be like childhood, one moment magically there, then, like the smoke from a fire, dispelled and lost forever.

All the way around to the stables, I thought about what my aunt might have said. That Buck really was Bell's child, adopted by Kate and Johnnie to bolster up a failing marriage? That Aunt Margaret thought it was more than possible that Buck had attacked Roddy and left him to die in the cold waters of the loch? Then why had Buck kept the portrait of his cousin next to his bed? As a kind of hair shirt? A penance?

We saddled our mares in silence; then Shiona said in that soft, considering tone that always roused my acutest affection for her, 'Don't think too badly of me, will you?'

I looked at her, surprised. 'But I've never thought badly of you.'

'I've gone on about Buck, trying to turn you against him. And it's none of my business. I shouldn't have tried to embroil you in what's past. It was wrong of me, I can see that now. Forgive me?' She swung herself up in the saddle and looked down at me from under her hat brim. A tendril of hair escaped from under it – honey-colored hair that stirred and shifted in the warm wind. Seen against the background of moor and trees, she looked more beautiful then ever, her eyes contrite.

'There's nothing to forgive.'

'Truly?'

'Truly.' I mounted the mare and set her in motion. Shiona

176

followed. She began to hum 'Early One Morning' and the little, jerky sound was the music of all disillusion, the essence of deception.

We rode down the long, steep drive with the laurels and rhododendrons pressing closely around the neglected road. Over the lichened wall, I had glimpses of furred tombstones and transient views of Carn Tierlath between firs and beeches. The sun was glittering on the loch, streaking the black water with silver. The swans were all around the Maiden, their plumage shaded with violet and blue. The Warrior was difficult to discern in the morning light. Later, all the grooves and indentations of helmet, armor and physiognomy would be flooded with shadow, accentuating his likeness to a stone giant. Golden fields were offset by white birchwoods, rowans and pines. The hills were a faint, tawny shimmer behind the trees.

Reaching the edge of the loch, I could still see hoof marks in the stretches of sand. The sunlight was hot on the crown of my head and I wished I too had brought a hat. My face felt flushed and my mouth and lips dry. I should be happy, but a weight lay over my spirits, an ominous cloud of doubt that shamed me. Love was trusting, caring . . .

We turned, followed the crescent of sand that curved in the direction of the Stone Maiden. There were other hoofprints here, ending beside the bleached trunk of a tree. This was where Fran had plucked up the courage to lay bare the nightmare that had haunted her since childhood. This could have been the place where Roddy Graham had undressed on the day of his death. I could almost see the neat pile of clothing, the light on his pale flesh, the splash as he entered the shallows. But I couldn't see who was with him, however hard I tried. It wasn't Buck, I told myself over and over again, but my arm still ached where he had grasped it in his anger over Cathy Forbes. Roddy had been bruised, his white flesh marked.

'We can either take the boat,' Shiona said, breaking into my painful thoughts, 'or we can ride the horses through the shallows. I know where they are.'

'Boat?'

She pointed to a barrier of reeds. Through it, I discerned the shape of a little rowing boat, the trailing line of the rope that fastened it to a post just above the waterline.

'We'll ride,' I said, not caring one way or the other. 'But you go first! If I'm to drown, I'll do it in company.'

Shiona laughed. She looked as warm as I did, but there the

resemblance ended. Her expression was amused. Mine was hag-ridden. Agnes Sampson seemed to have crept into my body overnight, her weight hanging heavily around my heart like some satanic millstone. I was possessed by a witch . . .

I watched my cousin ride out into the widening ripples. Her hair hung down her back in a shining ponytail fastened with a black ribbon. She sat the mare effortlessly. I had still not ridden beside Buck. I had sat behind him, but I wanted sud-denly to see him by my side, half-man, half-horse. A centaur or the devil, I had a choice of sorts.

I followed where Shiona went, noting carefully how she swerved left by a large, partly submerged stone, then right again by a patch of yellow iris. Left where the water became clearer and the sand vaguely visible under the surface, then right again by a cluster of rocks. Our boots were wetted, but they would soon dry in this heat.

We came out of the loch through more reeds that stopped at the edge of an apron of glittering sand that climbed to rock and furze and sea pinks to a tangle of bushes and dwarfed trees. Above them reared the blunt head of the Maiden. Something about that bald crown revolted me. Evil had crept up to that windswept plateau, evil with powerful hands and cruel instincts, its eyes fixed on the solitary figure of a child. But Fran hadn't let her dreadful experience spoil her friendship with Buck. She'd been more loyal than I was. Shame began to push out the dark flowering of doubt reawakened. There was always a flatness after wild exhilaration. One couldn't live on the heights forever. There had to be the descent to reality. 'Charley couldn't hurt a fly. Not big Charley.' Buck's own words. I thought they were true. Then who?

My head was aching more than ever. I tethered my mare to a bush and climbed the dusty path after Shiona. My legs moved reluctantly. Every step was an effort. I noted how the bushes grew around little hollows that would have been perfect hiding places for children. Those dark caverns and tunnels had con-cealed all three Drummond children that day and the two Grahams. I wondered just where Roddy and Shiona had been. Even then he must have been attracted to her.

We emerged from the steep climb onto the Maiden's head. A massive bulge of dark rock, patterned with circles of orange lichen. It looked, to my jaundiced eyes, like a disease. I went to the far side of the bulge and stared down. Rocks lay some distance below. A long way for a child to fall. To the right was a hollowed-out ledge, cushioned with heather, about twenty feet down from the lip of the ridge. Swans hung on the black water, drifts of snow and pearl.

A stone rattled and fell over the edge. I sprang back instinctively.

'You are in a nervous state,' Shiona said, her voice infused with laughter. 'I was only going to say there's someone coming along the shore. It's Buck, I think.'

The blood leaped in my veins, wild and high, like Midsummer fire. I turned to look at the mainland. That dark, peculiar grace could only be his. Buck had been given my message and he was coming to look for me. I watched the big horse leave the shore by the fallen log and plunge strongly into the shallows.

'Let's hide,' Shiona went on. 'Like we did when we were children. Why don't we?'

I didn't want to hide, but when her eyes sparkled so with mischief, I could hardly refuse. If I did wonder why Shiona wanted to play tricks on Buck, her apology of this morning seemed to point to more charitable feelings on her side at least. Perhaps she saw that her attitude was going to make it difficult for us to remain friends. Surely that showed that she valued our friendship more than ordinarily? I was overwhelmingly glad.

'All right.'

'Which way do you want to go?' she asked.

'The right, I think.'

'Go on then. He'll think you've been bewitched. Don't scowl so! It's only in fun.'

I hesitated for a moment, then plunged into the labyrinth of bushes. The path dipped and turned, changed from earth into sand and emerged onto a steltered, rocky promontory that led to nowhere and was overhung by part of the Maiden's shoulder. I stood, pressed against a rampart of cracked stone, shaded by the overhang. I felt foolish and a little uneasy. If Buck came upon Shiona and I wasn't with her, how would he react? In anger? They had been enemies of a sort. Was he as detached from her as he would have me believe? I was conscious of a strong unease, an unmistakable sense of danger. Aunt Margaret had been going to tell me something at breakfast time. I should have waited to hear what she said, even if it was that the man I loved was dangerous – had spells of violence for no good reason.

I began to retrace my steps the way I had come. But was it the way? Little tracks ran off to either side, confusingly twisted. I hadn't done mch more than follow my nose downhill, being too preoccupied with my own thoughts. Some of the paths ran over what had seemed to be the main one but which had petered out into a den, the floor of which was of hardpacked earth. I turned back and chose the left-hand track. If I had come down on the right of the plateau, it seemed the best thing to do.

I went higher, seeing little but tangled branches that caught at my hair and clothes and shadowy green recesses that turned and looped and seemed to take me nowhere. Then I became aware of voices. Buck's was hard and raised in anger, Shiona's soft and quiet as though she reasoned with him. I opened my mouth to call out when I heard Shiona cry sharply, 'Don't! Don't, Buck, please! Please – ' Her entreaties ended in a high-pitched scream that was shut off in a silence that appalled me. What in God's name had happened? What had he done?

I ran on. The bushes parted at last to show me the bulge of the Maiden's head. Buck stood there against the sky. He was alone. Still and alone. Shiona had run away, of course. She must have because I couldn't see her anywhere. She had, hadn't she? He heard me because he turned around. There was no expression in his face or his eyes. 'Maggie?' he said in a strange, defeated voice as though he had never expected to see me again. 'Maggie?'

My boots rattled the small pebbles as I went toward him.

'Where's Shiona?' I asked, and then I knew with a black shock of certainty.

He moved like someone in a dream. He was staring down from the edge of the ridge. 'There. She's there – '

'Murderer!' I screamed. 'You murdered her – '

There was animation in his face now, something alive and terrible to see.

'You killed her,' I went on. 'I heard it all, you see. Just as you killed Roddy.'

The words were said and I could never recall them. Even yet I wanted to unsay what should never have been spoken. But they had been justified. As soon as I ran to the rim of the bulge and looked toward the loch I knew that I'd shouted out the truth.

Buck shifted, and more little stones plunged to raise cascades

180

in the water between the fallen rocks.

'Don't come any closer,' I said harshly. 'Don't come near me.'

Out of the corner of my eye I saw Shiona, her body outspread in the hollow of the ledge. The riding hat had come off in the impact of her fall. Her skirts were rumpled, showing the long elegant line of her legs. The swathe of her hair was pale against the heather. Nothing moved, not even her hair. She was dead – dead . . .

I bent down swiftly and picked up a large stone that lay by my feet. I curled my fingers around its sharp edges. I must get away, but he could run faster than I. And already, I had discovered that the little paths were a maze that only the initiated could master.

He moved again and I drew a deep, sobbing breath. 'Stay away!'

'I won't hurt you. I couldn't hurt you.' His voice had softened. I wouldn't let it influence me.

'No? I should have listened. Everyone tried to warn me –'

'You're wrong,' he insisted. His face was gray under the tan.

'Am I? Am I? I trusted you –' But I hadn't. I'd felt everything but that.

'We must get help. For her –'

It was a trick, of course. He'd pretend it was an accident. He'd try to make me believe it so that I'd vouch for his story when we returned. If we got back. . .

'She wouldn't tell me where you were.' He was watching me closely.

'And that made it all right to push her over? Nothing makes that all right! Buck, I heard. She pleaded with you not to do it!'

He made a sudden, unexpected lunge and I shrank away from him. Somehow my hand was raised. It was as though someone else directed my actions. The stone was flying through the air. I cried out as it struck him, as the blood poured from his forehead, staining his white shirt. His legs buckled, and I remember, stupidly, being glad he wasn't at the edge of the drop any longer. His arm came forward as though he tried to reach me, then he fell to his knees, his head hanging almost to the ground like some punch-drunk boxer.

I turned frantically, searching for the path that would take me back to the horses. But the same diversity of tracks faced me. There wasn't time to study them for long. I took the one that was farthest left this time. I mustn't be stranded on the promontory a second time.

Yellow ragwort grew in patches. Thistles caught at my skirt. A blue butterfly flew out of heather. Stonecrop spread in those places where the bushes hadn't taken root. Already my cover was thinning out. I realized that I would soon emerge into the open. Probably on the Maiden's right shoulder.

I turned, panic-stricken. Another path ran downward into a thickness of shadows. I plunged into this, then, realizing that my labored breathing and hurrying footsteps would give away my position just as surely as being seen, I went on more slowly, tiptoeing now in an excess of caution. The sunlight struck through gaps in the interlaced branches, scattering gold on the rough track. I could see the end of the tunnel of green. Perhaps I was nearing the beach where Fleur was tethered. I'd taken note of the landmarks between the island and the shore. I was almost sure I could remember the way through the shallows.

I stopped suddenly and shrank back in a rank-smelling recess that opened up most opportunely to one side. A shadow lay across the mouth of the tunnel. Someone moved cautiously and I saw boots – long black boots that were spattered with dust and damp sand. There were strong thighs encased in breeches, the lower half of a shirt that was blood-spattered as the corn maiden's dress had been.

I crouched, frozen. If he set foot on this path, I should never be able to unlock my muscles. Buck stood quite still. He was listening for telltale sounds of movement, his eyes would be searching for a glimpse of me. Even if he bent his head to stare into this green dimness, he might see my white blouse or the pallor of my face and hands. I waited for an eternity of eternities.

The boots shifted slowly. 'Maggie?' Buck said tentatively. 'Maggie?' Then the darkness was gone from the round of sunlight. The footsteps receded. He had gone to the right. I would give him a minute or two, then take the path to the left. He called my name a few more times. His voice still had the power to move me to a useless regret. One idiotic part of me wanted to answer. But he was what everyone thought him. I had to get away from the Maiden. I would have to tell someone what he had done, even if the words choked me. He couldn't really be blamed if his illness – for that was what it must be – was inherited from Bell. But he would be shut up

182

for his own good. How Kate would suffer, feeling as she did about incarceration. She'd lost her lover, one of her adopted sons, her husband. Now Buck . . .

More than two minutes had passed. I came out of the recess with infinite care, my head lowered as the roof of branches descended sharply. The sunlight entered the shady tunnel. Just outside the opening I saw the marks of his boots in the dust. Again there was that foolish urge to follow him and his strong, glowering darkness. I had today no protection against witchcraft and enchantment. Shiona was dead, I reminded myself brutally. It was my business to tell my uncle and aunt. I had loved Shiona too.

I looked out of the hole into full daylight. The sun struck my eyes painfully. I saw no sign of Buck. Straightening my body, I went in the opposite direction. Out in the open, I was terribly conscious of my vulnerability. He had only to retrace his steps and he'd see me. My back was toward him. I would never know. With a little choked cry, I began to run.

The path looped to the right. I looked over my shoulder as I turned the bend. Still no sign of him, but I had made more noise than I'd intended. Even as I debated, he could be on his way back. I tripped and stumbled. This was rougher than any of those other tracks. But I was going in the direction of the loch. I had glimpses of water through the twisted branches and the patch of iris that marked the shallows.

I could hear Buck. He had dispensed with caution now that he knew where I was. The clatter of his boots sounded much too close. 'Please don't let him catch me,' one part of my mind was saying while the other whispered something very different.

I burst out into the open at last. The sand dragged at my feet, slowing my progress. Fleur raised her head some distance away. Water plantain held out pink flowers toward the sky like an offering.

'Maggie! We must talk. Please, Maggie – ' We must talk, Maggie. I must convince you you never heard what you did. I must persuade you that it was all a dreadful mistake. If I use my arms and my lips and my voice. I can talk you into anything, Maggie . . .

I shut my ears to the devil's voice. My boots dug holes out of the loose sand. The swans floated close to the shore, near enough for me to see the patches of black and orange around their beaks and eyes. Beyond them, the curled yellow flowers of the iris were speared on their sharp leaves. Farther away still, the curve of the white beach where the log, dwarfed by distance now, lay in shade. My eyes followed the sweep of fields and hedges, the gold and purple hills, the steep slope where the houses nestled, almost lost in their ramparts of trees and shrubs. I could even see the tiny, leaning shapes of the tombstones in between.

My fingers snatched at Fleur's rein, fumbled and wasted a few precious seconds. I almost threw myself upon her, pulling and dragging at the bit so that she leaped into motion. My knees dug themselves into her sides. Startled, she flounced and pranced through the water plantain and into the loch. I could hear the thud of Buck's boots not far behind.

'It's not what you think. Listen, Maggie –'

Again, that treacherous, half-pleasurable urge to acquiesce. Rebellion began to drain out of me, then I heard the splash of Buck's mount entering the water and the instinct for survival flared up as strongly as ever. I had a start, small though it was, and I thought I was capable of following Shiona's instructions about the negotiation of the shallows. There was the cluster of rocks. I went left there, didn't I? Doubt crept into my thoughts. If I started wrongly, I would end up in disaster. But the maze of paths had confused me. Left and right were merged into a pattern of fear that caught at the tentacles of my mind as it sought for reassurance. I had to do something so I went left. The water deepened perceptibly and I knew I had made a mistake. Then the ground rose again and I had nothing worse than wet boots and a dripping skirt hem.

I tried to remember the next landmark. Was that the right word when one rode through loch water? I didn't think it could be. The only thing I could see was the patch of iris. That must be my objective. I forced poor Fleur in the direction of the tall, spearlike leaves.

'Maggie! Don't be a fool! It gets deep there. Maggie, do wait!' Buck shouted.

I took no notice of him. I'd expected him to do something like this. Pretending I was riding into danger so that I'd slow down! Then he would catch up with me. Would he treat me as he'd treated poor Roddy? Would he hold me under the water until I drowned? Everyone would think I'd missed the way in my distress over Shiona's fatal 'accident'. Buck would be able to return with his tale of having found both girls tragically dead. And there'd be no proof otherwise – none at all.

184

I glanced over my shoulder. Oh, God! He was only a few yards away, his face all distorted and encrusted with dried blood, his shirt torn and spattered with rusty red. Like the color of the curtains in that strange hotel in Edinburgh. I remembered how Shiona had come in to stay with me as I lay sleepless, how she had lent me the turquoise dress, how willingly she had accepted me. I hardened my heart against Buck. James might not have stirred my blood, but he was a good man. I'd never have been required to fly for my life from him. He would have been kind. Shaun was half in love with me. I knew that without being told. A little while and it could be more than half. Only there might not be even a little while . . .

Fleur gave a sudden, violent lurch that threw me off balance. My feet came out of the stirrups and I slid sideways, my skirt ballooning around me, reminding me of my umbrella outspread in the sea that dreadful day on the steamer trip. Too late I knew that the yellow iris had not come next. There had been the patch of shallow water first. I would have reached that if I had gone straight on. I floundered desperately, my boots and the weight of my skirt pulling at me, dragging me down as the corn maiden had been – was it only last night? I saw again that parabola of flying arms and legs. She hadn't wanted to die either. I remembered how she had struck the loch's surface, the terrible, human frailty she exuded. To me she hadn't been merely an object . . .

Water blinded me and poured into my mouth. I struggled upward to break the surface, the sun glittering on the drops that coursed over my face. Fleur was some distance away, swimming strongly, her head turned toward land. I screamed out her name but she took no notice. She was close to the iris now. I saw her climb out onto the shallow loch bed and shake herself, then I sank again.

Buck was shouting something, but I didn't hear him. My ears were full of water and my chest was all tight and painful. I was a poor swimmer. I made myself move my arms and kick out my booted legs, but my skirt impeded my attempts. Real fear began to fill me. I turned my face toward the shore. It seemed miles away, though I knew it wasn't far. I shook my head to get rid of the water in my ears. There was splashing quite close to me and I realized it must be Buck. I forced my arms to perform the necessary motions, but there were weights on my limbs. Each minute that passed made it more difficult to remain afloat. With a despairing cry, I slid below the surface of the loch. The water was very cold. Uncle Rob had told me how cold it was. Roddy had drowned in this, poor, poor Roddy . . .

Something huge and black loomed beside me. My hands touched chill, human flesh. My heart stopped beating – or that was how it seemed. They had found Roddy, hadn't they? There was a stone in the graveyard. Kate put flowers on the mound that covered what was left of him. So this wasn't Roddy.

Arms reached out and fastened around me. Dead men couldn't catch at the living. Only Fran's beastly half-dead had tried to do that. I could see them coming down to the shore, advancing toward the villagers who hadn't been able to get into the boats that were to take them from Clach Mhiceil – like walking sponges.

I screamed and went on screaming. I fought with the thing that held me. Something hit me very hard. Harder than anything since the earth rose up to meet me after I fell from the merry-go-round. Briefly there were stars . . .

I was on the tawny velvet sofa when I came around. The first thing I saw was the window, the trees pressed close against it, giving the effect of water. Watery, shadowy depths, the loch. All the horror of that struggle came back to me. Even worse was the memory of Shiona.

I pushed at the blanket that covered my body.

'Now, we don't want to be indecent, do we!'

I turned my head. Fran was sitting beside me, seeming oddly mature. There was wariness in her eyes.

'Indecent?' I muttered. 'Why should I be that?'

'You took a swim with all your clothes on. Buck had a dreadful job to get you to stop fighting off his efforts to rescue you.'

'Rescue me? Is that what he said?' My voice hardened.

'Yes. Wasn't it true?' Her face whitened. She looked quite old.

I said nothing for a while. Then I asked, 'And what about Shiona?'

'She-She? She'll be all right. She was luckier than I. Her legs didn't break. She's very badly bruised; but Doctor Forbes said she'd fallen well – whatever that means. She let herself relax, apparently, instead of stiffening herself against impact as most of us do in like circumstances. And, of course, she was fortunate in going no farther than the ledge, which is quite thickly covered. She bounced.'

'You mean she isn't dead?'

'No. She isn't. Haven't you been listening? I've just finished telling you that She-She's very much alive. She won't be able to move for a few days, well, not without it hurting. But nothing's spoiled. She didn't even get her face scratched. So, stop looking so worried! Maggie. You aren't crying, are you?'

'I'm so glad.'

'I thought you would be.' Her voice was very gentle.

'I was going for help.'

'We know. Buck told us. Apparently you misunderstood what happened. You thought – Well, it wasn't true, you know – '

'You believe him?'

'Oh, not only him! She-She says it was her own fault. She took a step backward, forgetting where she was – '

'She's forgotten! It wasn't like that. Truly, it wasn't.'

'Maggie,' Fran said carefully. 'You mustn't stir up trouble where it doesn't exist. You've had a dreadful experience – '

'And I'm deranged as a result!' I finished sharply. 'Everyone mistrusts my head. There's nothing the matter with it. I'm quite compos mentis.'

'I'm sure you are.'

'Shiona's trying to protect someone.'

'Why don't you say Buck? That's still his name. He wants to see you, by the way.'

'I don't want to see him.'

'You sound as if you mean that.'

'Oh, I do.'

'Charley's shepherd saw him trying to fish you out of the loch. He was on his way from the village. It was when he came out of the trees that he saw you both. He shouted that he was coming and Buck had to – render you unconscious is, I suppose, the best way to describe how he overcame your opposition. Does your chin hurt?'

The wild hope that Buck really meant to rescue me was dispelled. Only the advent of the shepherd had saved me. I lived again that terrible moment when I had sunk, had reached out to touch his cold, wet body, chilled and sodden with immersion. He'd meant to drown me so that I couldn't tell anyone that Shiona's fall wasn't an accident. 'Don't! Don't, Buck, please! Please – ' I would hear her cry until my dying day.

'Does it, Maggie love?' Fran persisted.

'Does what?'

'You just aren't listening to anything. Your chin. Does it hurt?'

I lifted my head and touched it tentatively. 'Yes. Yes, it does.'

'Won't you see Buck?'

'No. It's not only what happened today –'

'What you *think* happened,' Fran corrected. 'Shiona says differently. No one will believe you. You realize that, don't you? Your head's so stuffed with the past, snippets of things that happened ages ago and haven't been properly explained –'

'I still don't want to see Buck.'

'You're making a dreadful mistake.'

'I see I'm being coerced into agreeing with something that's false. When I see Shiona and hear from her own lips that she wasn't harmed, then I'll believe it, and not before.'

'That won't be for some days. She's been shocked. Doctor Forbes wants her left strictly alone.'

'Very well. I'll wait until it's all right. Then I'll speak to her about it.'

'He's waiting –'

'He can wait forever as far as I'm concerned.' My voice was high.

'You're upset. Maybe he should come back later. Tomorrow –'

'Never.'

Maggie. Don't be hasty –'

'Oh, leave me alone, will you! I want to be left by myself. For a long time.' I closed my eyes. They burned in my head like hot pebbles. Somehow Buck had convinced the Drummonds that nothing had been his fault. But how had he convinced Shiona? I must leave Maidenstane. I wanted Charley to have the estate. He could marry his Cathy. His troubles would be over and he could look forward to a good future, doing what he most wanted. Fran would marry Graham Stewart now. She'd make a good wife, her unexpectedness being the quality that would bring freshness and sparkle to their life together. Angus was devoted to Shiona. But she could have any man she wanted. She didn't have to take Angus if she didn't love him. It was I who had to go away. A job needn't present too many problems. I could always become a governess with my convent training – or a companion like Miss McNab.

Perhaps I'd be luckier than she had been in her choice of an employer. Could I endure a Mrs. Leitch for the rest of my life? My soul shrank from the thought.

They said that people who had awful things happen to them often forgot what immediately preceded the accident or attack. That was obviously what had happened to Shiona. The dark memory had been blotted out by some safety mechanism in the mind. If she still had some feeling for Buck, she would put the best interpretation on the event afterward. 'Early One Morning' – she had been thinking about him. He had been cruel to her once. He could be so again, and not only to Shiona.

Aunt Margaret came in, obviously sent by Fran, for she had the same look of guarded pity. 'We shouldn't have had you if it wasn't for Buck,' she said.

'No.' I swallowed the lump of rock that was lodged in my throat.

'He was very brave.'

'She-She's all right. That's good.' I didn't want to think of him or talk about him.

'Yes. There's a way 'round the back of the ledge. Bruce and Buck were able to get her down without too much difficulty.'

'Bruce?'

'The shepherd.'

'Oh, yes.' The conversation was becoming unreal. I had a picture of Shiona in Buck's arms, being held in front of him on the ride back through the shallows. Was that when he had told her she'd stepped backward? 'Don't, Buck, please – '

'I must get up and do something,' I said, pushing myself up. 'I'd be much better occupied. Truly, Aunt Margaret.'

'Fran told you you mustn't go to She-She. Not yet.'

'Yes, she did say something of the sort.'

'I don't know if I should let you.'

'Please – '

'Look, I'm going into the morning room. Come and keep me company. There's some hot soup Ness kept simmering. We'll take a tray. Slip into this house robe. Your slippers are there, just by your feet. Read or write a letter to your friend. Something undemanding. There's no reason why we shouldn't have a nice peaceful time together.'

Nice! Peaceful! Poor Aunt Margaret. She'd be horrified if she knew what was going on in my mind. She wanted me with her, though, as she'd have welcomed a daughter.

I got up, feeling weak and languid and let her fasten the

house robe around me. My hair was still damp. I shivered as it touched my neck and bare shoulder. She made me take her arm and we walked to the room at the end of the passage. A fire of logs burned in the grate and the air of the room smelled pleasant. I drank the bowl of soup I was given obediently. My jaw was stiff and still painful. I refused anything else.

'I'll look in on She-She,' my aunt said when we'd finished. 'Just help yourself to a book or to writing paper. Jenny sounds a nice girl. Why don't you write and tell her how pleased you are about – what was his name?'

'Roger.'

'Roger. That's right. I'll be back in a minute. I've some sugared almonds. I'll bring them with me. Nice things to suck when it's difficult to chew.' Everything she said reminded me of Buck. If I couldn't chew it was because he'd used violence to reduce me to unconsciousness.

I rose, desperately, and went to the desk. I opened the drawer in which the sheets of thick, creamy paper lay, the fat towers of envelopes tied with narrow ribbons. I took out two pieces of paper and an envelope and laid them on the desk top. Just as I was about to move back to the armchair, I remembered the photograph. The small drawer slid open to reveal the dark gypsy face that was so like Buck's. I stood motionless, staring down at it, stamping it on my mind indelibly. There was bad blood in him. It wasn't his fault, but the realization didn't improve anything. Buck was a man to keep away from. Inconstant, violent and who knew what else –

'Maggie, dear – ' My aunt's voice, so close to my ear, startled me.

'I was getting the paper. Whose – whose picture is this?'

'That?' She looked over my shoulder. 'That's Kate's mother. Buck's having a miniature painted for her and this is to be delivered to the artist when Rob goes to Perth later in the month. It's to be a Christmas present. Mrs. Buchanan was very shy about being photographed, and Buck thought the miniature would be a more durable remembrance of his grandmother than one or two pieces of pasteboard with a limited lifetime.'

'Oh. Do you – do you have any pictures of Aunt Bell?' My hands were shaking.

'Strangely enough we did until very recently. She fancied – you know how people, when they get older, like to relive their youth – seeing herself again. So I took it on one of our last visits along with' – her tone became guarded – 'a picture of someone else.'

Someone else. She'd never say who the someone else was. 'Close to yours and mine.' If Bell's child wasn't Buck it must have been Roddy. It wasn't at all improbable that Johnnie Graham's brother had married a relative of Kate's. All the families in the neighborhood were interrelated. Roddy. Was there a conspiracy between the Drummonds and Grahams to conceal the sad fact of Bell's child? Had Shiona once shielded Roddy as she had shielded Buck today? How confusing it all was. I thought I should never get to the bottom of the mystery. I still didn't want to see Buck, but I couldn't help the little flicker of relief that came with the knowledge that this pictured face wasn't Bell's.

I pushed in the drawer, but all the time I was writing to Jenny I saw Mrs. Buchanan's strong, sensual features and the wildness of her hair.

13

Everyone was very kind to me during the next few days while Shiona was recovering. I still refused to see Buck. Whatever Shiona said now, I knew I had heard her entreaties, her cry of pain and shock, the dreadful silence that ensued.

It began to rain, heavy, soulless rain that hardly stopped. The Forbes boys called with fruit and flowers and were typically lively. Cathy didn't come with them and I thought I knew why.

I went up, as usual, to read to Grandfather. He was looking better and more cheerful. 'Charley doesn't love me,' I told him. 'And I don't love him. It's hard for him to be set aside. He wants to marry but he doesn't know what he has to offer. You must get Graham Stewart to break the entail. In your heart of hearts, you know it's the fair thing to do.'

'And what of you?'

'Let time take care of that.'

'You won't go away?'

'Not yet,' I said, but I wondered how long I would be able to keep my promise. Looking out of my bedroom window at night to see the upper windows of Carn Tierlath alight had been a subtle torment ever since the day at the Maiden.

I read to him by candlelight because of the rain.

I helped Uncle Rob with his notes and manuscript. My handwriting was not quite so regular and I wondered if he'd noticed. I sewed for Aunt Margaret and gardened with Fran, but there was a great emptiness in me that nothing seemed to fill.

It was a week before I saw Shiona. I was glad I was the first person she asked for. The emptiness was flooded with gladness as I stood in the doorway of the room with the white paint and the dark, junglelike wallpaper where leaves and stems climbed to the plaster fresco. I had forgotten how odd and secretive this bedchamber was. Roddy's perfume clung to everything.

Shiona sat up against piled pillowcases, a little pale, but smiling. There was no sunlight to make golden patches in her brown eyes, accentuating their beauty. Her hair was loose, cascading over the cambric-covered shoulders. There were narrow yellow ribbons threaded through the bodice of her nightgown. I could see blue veins in her arms and on the backs of those strong hands that had pulled me from Fleur the day of the burr under the saddle.

'Faithful Maggie,' she said softly. 'I couldn't bear any of the others. Only you.'

My eyes stung painfully.

'Come in. I'm not going to eat you. Well, not immediately.' She laughed and I laughed with her. I don't think it convinced either of us, that slightly hysterical amusement. The smell of the scent suddenly sickened me. Roddy's scent . . .

'We've both had a bad time, haven't we?' The rain made mourning noises against the pane. A beech leaf fluttered against it and stuck to the glass.

'You more than me,' I said huskily. 'I was all right days ago.'

'But to be nearly drowned! How unpleasant for you.' She smiled and my heart contracted. I could so easily never have seen her again.

'How much do you remember about that day?' I asked, seemingly casual.

'Hardly anything, strangely enough.' She shivered. 'I can't think how I could have been so careless. Familiarity breeding contempt, I expect. Mother and Father dinned it into us to be careful after poor Fran – '

'Not so much of the poor Fran,' I said, with an attempt at lightness.

'No?' Honey-colored eyebrows rose delicately.

'Graham's going to be your brother-in-law. Only for goodness sake keep it to yourself. She hasn't said anything to anyone else yet.'

'And what about you?' Her eyes challenged mine.

'Me?'

'You know what I mean.'

'There's nothing to tell. There won't be. Not ever.'

She stared down at the counterpane, her eyes lost in shadow. The rain made more noise than ever. 'Poor Maggie. You too – '

I said nothing. The minutes stretched out into years. There was a curious, distorted pleasure in my own misery.

'Has the corn been cut yet?' she asked.

'Not yet.'

'They always choose the bonniest girl to cut the last sheaf. Then there's supper in the barn, with beer and barley bread and cheese. Tam the fiddler comes and there's mouth music. Ness roasts a yearling lamb and makes dumplings. And the last man to complete his harvest is sent a straw dog.'

'Whatever for?'

'It's a deadly insult. Charley's never had it yet.' She sounded pleased.

'Charley's a good farmer.'

'Shaun'll give you a snood and a bunch of ribbons.'

'Will he?'

'You don't sound very interested?'

'It'll be lovely. I'm sure it will.' My voice, for all my efforts, was flat.

'I could kill him for hurting you!' she said violently. 'I did warn you – '

'Yes. You warned me. I should have listened.' It wasn't Shaun she meant. There was no need to say Buck's name. It hung in the air like a cloud.

'I'll be up soon. Then we can go out again. As we used to – ' Her tone softened.

'Yes. It'll be just the same.' But it wouldn't. It wouldn't –

'Have you been out on Fleur since?'

'No,' I said abruptly. 'No, I haven't.'

'We'll go together,' she said happily. 'I'll tell Doctor Forbes I'm better.'

'We'll have to wait until the rain stops.'

'Yes. There's Fran calling. You'd better go.'

'Do you want to see her?'

'No. You'll come back though, won't you?' She looked tired now and her eyes were bruised. I was concerned for her.

'Of course.'

I came out of her room quiet and sad. The smell of the perfume followed me like a ghost – a dog at my heels.

'Shaun's in the garden,' Fran told me when I came downstairs. 'He wants to have a word with you.'

'Why didn't he come in?' I asked, surprised.

'He's only got a minute, and if you once go into someone else's house, it can be difficult getting away.'

'I suppose so. Where is he?'

'By the stable.'

'All right.'

I opened the front door and stepped outside. The rain had stopped temporarily, but the gravel was soaked and the flower beds washed flat. The roses hung, sodden and moldering, their beauty spoiled. They echoed my inner bleakness.

The stable door was open. There was no sign of Shaun, but I supposed him to be inside. I ran across the cobbled forecourt, lifting my skirts away from the deep puddles that collected in the hollows.

'Shaun? I know you're there.' I peered into the musty dimness. The rain had started again, little spiteful stabs against the rounded stones, patters on the roof. A horse stirred sleepily. A mouse rustled the straw. The atmosphere should have been peaceful, but it was inexplicably charged with electricity.

'Shaun?' I saw him now, standing against the wall at the far end of the building. He seemed to have thickened and broadened, to have changed from boy to man with a startling suddenness.

I went forward. My heart was pounding my rib cage like a hammer. I think I'd known all the time that it wasn't Shaun. I turned to run away, but Buck snatched out at my hands and held me fast.

'You must listen to me, Maggie. It's not fair to refuse.'

I could see the shape of his face now, his compressed lips, the shadowy eye spaces. The smell of rain and sheep and fresh air lay on his clothes. The weak core of my nature melted and

194

responded to him. I wanted to lie against him, to be made to feel that I was a woman. But the part that remembered Shiona's words made me want to push him away. So I stood, still and cold, saying nothing, waiting, with the rain quickening on the court and the shingles, the cobwebs swaying between the uprights of the stalls.

My fingers melted into his fingers, but my eyes refused to soften to his. My lips were soldered together, giving him neither harshness nor encouragement. I could feel the planes of my face rigid and unmoving as marble and as cold. At last, the pressure of his hands relaxed. He gave a queer, choked sound and pushed past me like an automaton. The rain was gushing down, but he seemed not to notice. I watched him step out into the deluge, his figure huge and dark against the shining oblong of the aperture. He was gone, his footsteps drowned in rushing water.

Then I cried.

I hid the convolvulus brooch at the bottom of a drawer. I would have to return it, of course, but for the present, it was something that had been his. That last meeting in the stable had shown me that his feelings toward me were, perhaps, deeper than I'd suspected. Not that the realization was any surety that he'd never change. Better to learn to do without him now. When I left this house, I'd leave the brooch of turquoise and pearl to be given back to him. Fran would take it.

Everyone was very kind nowadays. Grandfather must have spoken to Charley, for Cathy came to see me. She apologized for her behavior on the night of Lammas and brought me a satin-covered box full of extravagant sweetmeats.

Graham came with his sister Elizabeth. She was still quiet and restrained and both of us seemed to have a kind of kinship. We both had wanted the same man and neither of us was to have him. People must have talked of my refusal to see him, just as Bruce, the shepherd, must have spoken about the accident and near-drowning at the loch.

Aunt Margaret hovered near me as if she must keep Shiona and me out of mischief. She said we must take one of the stable hands with us if we went riding in the future. We did this regularly until the day she went to see Aunt Bell. The trap had no sooner gone than Shiona said, 'Don't let's take the boy today. I want to be free.'

195

I opened my lips to say all the proper things. All the constricting things. Then I closed them again. I felt as rebellious as Shiona. I had developed into an accomplished rider. What could possibly happen to us? The rains had stopped at last, leaving the hills and valley burnished, jewel-bright, everything blue and gold and tawny.

I had expected Shiona to choose the moor for our ride, but she said it was a long time since we'd been down the village track. This took us past the beach with the log, the shallows and the Maiden. 'Do you really want to revisit it?' I asked.

'We live here,' she answered. 'We can't spirit away the local landmarks because one or two unpleasant things happened there. Anyway, I'm fond of the Maiden. There's a queer kind of magic about it and the Warrior –'

'Black magic.'

'Perhaps.'

I said nothing else to dissuade her. We rode toward a vista of golden hills and silver birch, against which the black crests of pines made shadowy blotches and the firs were stroked in like dark feathers. The swans came out of the distance, blindingly white against the blurred water. The sky was heavy, but the sunlight invited. All the way to the shore I watched the clouds deepen and crowd, bloated and bruised, over the mountains. 'The rain isn't finished,' I said.

'I hope there's a storm,' Shiona replied. Her eyes were odd and bright as though she had a fever. Her face was flushed and her movements jerky. Something about her filled me with unease. I began to wish we had taken the stableboy with us. Shiona had been quite ill, after all.

'Shall we go over to the Maiden?' she suggested when we reached the shallows.

'Is there any shelter?'

'Oh, yes. There's a cave down on the far shore, the rocky one. It'll be quite spectacular if the storm breaks while we're there. It happened once when I was with Roddy and Buck –'

'Were you very fond of Roddy?' I asked carefully.

'He doted on me.' She hadn't really answered my question. There was, too, a note of derision in her voice that I'd heard before. 'And that's where Rizzio groveled on the floor, hanging onto the queen's skirts,' she had told me at Holyrood, with just that inflection of scorn. It didn't take much imagination to know that this was how Roddy had felt about Shiona. Beautiful women were often unkind toward the men who were besotted about them. She had accused Buck of cruelty, but I had the sudden, traitorous thought that it was she, and not Buck, who had been the guilty one.

I followed her as I had always done, but for the first time, I went unwillingly. We splashed through the shallows. The big rock, the patch of iris, the shallow water, the group of rocks. I knew the way well enough now. I'd seen it often enough in my dreams. Shiona led the way, tall and strong as an Amazon. Beautiful, a goddess . . .

I watched her hands tether her mare to a bush, strong, supple fingers busy, her wrists capable. I wished I hadn't asked her about Roddy. Her answer had opened up tunnels and canals of conjecture that I knew I couldn't negotiate safely.

The maze of paths sprawled and twisted like hollow snakes. One felt swallowed, eaten up, as one bent down inside them, the overhanging branches holding one prisoner. The livid clouds cast them into dangerous shade. The maze gave way to the patches of stonecrop and heather, the spikes of thistles. We were on the left shoulder of the Maiden. I recognized it from the previous visit. This must be the way to the ledge where Shiona had fallen. As I went forward, I saw the scratched track scrape around the lower part of the bulge that was the head.

Looking back, I saw that Shiona was sitting on the heather, staring ahead at the Warrior and the dark strokes of the Sun Stones. The Troth Stone was a little apart, above the well. Her eyes seemed suddenly empty as though she saw nothing but a chasm. I could think of nothing to say that would comfort her. At that moment, I was sure she was unaware of my presence.

I skirted the base of the head and found a path that looped around to the summit. Climbing, I could see the sky, sullen and plum-colored, the sun obscured behind thick layers of cloud. We would be drenched on the way home. I hoped there wouldn't be lightning. Horses were nervous in thunderstorms and it could be unpleasant riding through water. Tension began to build up in me.

The plateau opened up, littered with loose stones. I remembered Buck kneeling at my feet, his head cut, his arms reaching out for me. The yearning for him hadn't lessened. If anything, it had grown, filling me with a vast, restless pain. I stopped where I was, conscious of a sense of change. The sky was different and the air fresher. And I was no longer alone. There was a child building a little cairn of stones, a girl in a long robe and cummerbund, her head wrapped turban-wise in a towel.

Even as I watched, I saw another taller figure, also robed, the head obscured under a kind of flowered shawl. This anonymous creature leaned forward and thrust with all its might, and the child vanished in a shower of dust and stones, the dying remnants of a scream.

The figure turned slowly, and I saw the eyes caught briefly in a gleam of sunshine, the wind-torn fragment of hair that escaped from under the shadow of the shawl. And I thought in that moment that my heart was broken.

There was nothing in front of me but the grape-blue mounds of the storm clouds. But I still retreated from the ridge, my hands shaking uncontrollably. I turned to look for some path to safety. Shiona was there, the emptiness of her gaze replaced by something I recognized.

'You know,' she said without surprise. 'Was it *temps perdu*?'
I nodded.
'Your face is the color of ashes,' she remarked calmly.
'Is it?'
'I wish you hadn't found out.'
'I – I think I began to know when you said what you did about Roddy.'

The thunder growled then, deep and menacing, and the Warrior seemed to shift ever so slightly as the legend said he must one day. Only not today . . .

'Oh? What did I say? Something perfectly innocuous, wasn't it?'

'I don't remember the exact words but you told me he was weak and foolish, that he groveled for his favors. That he lied for you –'

'Good gracious! You are mad! Everyone wondered – ' Her laughter pierced me.

'Not me. You She-She.' I'd never called her that before. But now I saw her as everyone else did, the jungle creature, the tiger that had tasted human flesh and wanted more.

She smiled and her peaty eyes weren't warm and lazy now. They were intent as a cat's on a mouse it has come upon unexpectedly.

'You overheard me say I was repelled by the corn mother. I suspected poor Fran –'

'Poor Fran!' The brown eyes flashed dangerously.

'So you tried to scare me with both corn dollies. Because

Buck had let you see how he felt about your treatment of poor Roddy. Because he preferred me.'

'Poor Roddy! What do you know about any of it! He shouldn't have said what he did. He was going to tell everyone that he and I hadn't been together after all on the day Fran fell – '

'Was pushed,' I pointed out harshly. 'I know. I saw – '

'Who's going to believe you? *Temps perdu!* No one will take any notice.'

'So. Roddy's lie was on his conscience. And once he told, Aunt Margaret's and Uncle Rob's fear would come out in the open. They'd know that you had enough of your mother's blood in you to be dangerous. As she is – '

'Mother? What are you talking about?' Her face was as pale as mine.

'Don't you know?'

'I know what you're trying to say, but it's all lies. You know nothing about me. My parents are Rob and Margaret Drummond. They always have been.' Her voice changed, became hard and ugly. 'You're just saying that because I succeeded in turning you against Buck, aren't you! Why should you have him when I couldn't! Why! Why!'

'You never liked being thwarted, did you, She-She?' All the bravery was draining out of me. That day on the steamer. Shiona had put on her deep-hooded cloak so that even if I caught a glimpse of her, I'd only see someone dressed in black. No wonder the hem of her gown had been marked. I'd struggled hard enough. She'd stepped behind the lifeboat. She was there all the time I talked to Buck and Uncle Rob. She was as strong as a man . . .

Roddy. He had told her he intended to tell the truth about the day of Fran's accident. Perhaps he had been influenced by the suspicion that had been attached to Buck and Charley. Buck most of all.

I thought of the evening in the barn with the rain falling and I wondered if Buck would ever forgive me. I would beg for forgiveness. If he loved me, he would overlook that betrayal . . .

'Well, Maggie, dear. What are we going to do about you?' The sky was shedding a peculiar blue light over everything. The thunder growled harder than ever and rain began to spot the bald, shiny surface of the Maiden's head. That blueness had been lightning. I felt suddenly vulnerable and exposed. Afraid too of Shiona.

'We should get into shelter,' I said. The rain began to fall more heavily.

'And carry on this most interesting conversation, I suppose. Or pretend it never took place?'

'It was only between ourselves. No one else knows.'

'Except that you'll feel free to run after Buck again,' she pointed out, not making any move to go. Even in the rain she never lost her attraction. The water was molding the white blouse to her body, flattening the honey-colored hair.

'We've both said too much, haven't we?' I observed.

'Yes, Maggie. We have.'

I shivered in my wet clothes, watching her all the while. The next flash illuminated her pale, set face and showed me her eyes, darkened into active hatred. All that had been sweet and pleasant between us seemed doubly lost. I wished, futilely, that Josh Davidson had never existed. If he hadn't refused to marry Aunt Sarah so long as I was an encumbrance, none of this would have happened. But it would, inevitably, have happened to someone else.

Somewhere behind Shiona, there was a small furtive sound. She spun around sharply and I took my opportunity to run for the nearest opening. I was only halfway down the rocky path when she caught me. Her hands tore at my shoulders, ripping the white stuff of my blouse, scoring hot grooves down my flesh.

'Don't, please –' A hot panic rose up in me.

'Save your breath,' she advised harshly.

I twisted in her grasp, facing her in the pouring rain. She raised her fingers to my face and I flung myself sideways to slip on the wet rock.

'Stop it, She-She! Or, by God, I won't be responsible for what I do.' It must be a hallucination but it sounded like Buck's voice. Shiona's face turned away slowly. I got up onto my knees and stared through the rain curtain. He materialized out of grayness almost as though the farewell in the barn had never quite finished. 'It's no good, is it?' he asked softly. 'You can't run forever, She-She, or pull the wool over everyone's eyes indefinitely. Give up now –'

She screamed something I didn't properly hear. One minute she was there, the next there was only the opening to one of those tunnels, sheeted over with rain. There wasn't even the sound of her flight because the sky spat thunder, thunder that seemed to have no end to it, that flung the universe about to let it fall around my ears.

Buck's arms were reaching out for me, but this time I didn't try to evade them. He held me close against him, shutting out the chill of the day, muffling the sound of the wind. I felt his body stiffen and his arms slacken. 'Oh, God!' he whispered. 'God –'

I drew away from him slowly. Shiona was above us now, quite visible beyond the trenched tunnels of green. She wasn't running, only moving slowly and inexorably, her skirt clinging to her knees, her white profile empty.

'Shiona!' I cried, forgetting Buck, conscious only of her deep unhappiness. 'Come back!' The sense of evil that always hung about the summit had never been so strong. Perhaps her actions were not of her own doing. There were ancient influences that could still affect, centuries later, shadows and mists of wickedness that hung like a dark miasma. I felt them now.

She heard me. Her head turned and I saw her eyes, curiously blank and uncaring at first, then quickening into fear. She began to run. I fancied I heard her sobbing, and my emotions turned to pity.

My legs moved of their own volition, dragging against the force of falling water, my heart pumping hurtfully as I followed her. The gray slabs near the summit gleamed, their smooth surface marred by the orange pox of lichen. It was like a disease from which one would never recover, that would eat into one – like leprosy.

I emerged, tired and drained of feeling, on the rock-strewn platform. But there was only the sky, filled with torn cloud, and the stony face of the Warrior staring down at what I knew must lie on the shore below.

Dr. Forbes had given me something to make me sleep, but I still saw her in my dreams, half in and half out of the water, her hair caught in weeds. She was no longer beautiful because half her face had been crushed by the fall. I dreamed of the Sun Stones, furred with spongy moss, walking down to the loch to take away those who were not in the safety of the boats, and the Troth Stone shouted things I didn't want to hear from the round hole of its mouth.

Buck was there when I came downstairs and Aunt Margaret left us alone in the morning room. I could see the rose garden from the window, and I remembered the flower festival and the first ray of the sun on the largest stone, the sky flushed with dawn.

He didn't touch me and I was glad. There were things to say first, questions to be answered. I had to tell him I was sorry. That was most important.

'I still don't understand,' I said, not taking my eyes from the drenched roses, 'about Shiona's first fall. Those things she cried out –'

'She meant you to find us struggling. We both heard you coming. That's when she made it sound as if I were attacking her. But she overreached herself. I think she really forgot she was so close to the edge. The whole scene would have lost its impact if you hadn't felt she was truly in danger. It was just what I said. An accident. Though, even then, she was lucky. It would have been a vastly different matter if she'd gone all the way to the rocks –'

'Like Fran. Why did she do it? She–She –'

'Push Fran? She wanted to be king of the castle, only the rest of us chose Fran because she was the smallest. I wish now we hadn't. I've never stopped wishing it. We'd all separated and you know what the maze is like. Roddy let himself and She-She out. He'd have said black was white if she'd asked him. She probably made it sound quite innocent, an unavoidable accident, only she'd get into terrible trouble from Rob if he knew. He hadn't realized how the rest of us would be suspected, not until it was too late. He might even have thought it was worth it to have She-She grateful to him for something. She took everything that was decent in Roddy. She spoiled him as a person. I couldn't forgive her for that. No matter how much she once meant –'

She'd meant a great deal to me too. Had it all been a façade, that instant friendliness? Had she feigned indisposition the day I'd waited in Edinburgh Station because it pleased her to have her unknown cousin imagine herself to be stranded in a strange city? Those red curtains. Did she guess at my imaginative streak when she described them as she had? I should never know and that was what hurt so much. I wanted there to have been something I could hold on to, to offset the rest. It must have been Shiona in the graveyard, dressed in her black cloak, following me. She'd put the burr under the saddle when I went to fetch her handkerchief.

'You're wearing my brooch,' Buck said. 'Does that mean what I hope?'

I came away from the window. The crimson dress made me look paler, but the convolvulus brooch was lovely against the dark-red material. My fingertips touched the turquoise and pearl briefly. 'I – I hate myself for doubting you. I'm so very sorry, Buck. It would serve me right if you never wanted to see me again. If you hadn't come to the Maiden just at that moment – ' I shuddered. 'Why did you?'

'Aunt Margaret had been worried about She-She's behavior for some time. She'd noticed things you hadn't. And knowing she was Bell's child, she'd always feared she might go the same way. She told me she was sure She-She would disregard the matter of taking the stable hand along while she was out of the way, and she asked me to keep an eye on you both – for your sake. So I did – '

'You saved my live. Twice – three times if you count the wheel – '

'Because – because it happens to be the thing most precious to me.'

Our eyes met, and pain and disappointment faded and were drowned in the truth and warmth of that regard.

'I want you so much,' I told him. 'How I want you – '

Then he was holding me in his arms.

'Why,' I asked him when we were apart, 'why did you come to Berwick?'

'I was going to London – on antique business – and your grandfather asked me to stop at Berwick on the way back. He'd grieved considerably over your father and that long estrangement. He was curious to know what sort of granddaughter he had – if you were the kind of girl who'd want to settle here. Are you?'

'You know I am.'

'Kate wouldn't expect you to share the house with her. She'd go to Hampstead. She always planned to if and when I brought home a wife. You are going to marry me, aren't you?'

The future was suddenly flooded with life and light and beauty. A time of roses, of fire, boats on the loch in the shapes of birds and Viking ships, flowers on the water, horses in the shallows, the swans drifting.

'I'll marry you,' I said. Then there was no more to say.

*

It was November. The woods smoked, black and orange, behind the dark pearl of the loch. There was a purple fuzz on the birches. The sun lay on the stubble fields and the larches were tipped with flame. The air was intensely cold, but it tasted of pleasant things, like the first bite into a crisp apple.

Buck and I rode into a tunnel of beeches, all gray and orange, and fringed with the ghosts of willow herb. Black water and tawny sedge, the white birchwoods, the loch in shadow, pools of green velvet where the sun shone. There could be no deeper happiness than this. Unless it was the content of lying in the dark, our hands touching, our bodies remembering passion.

We had been married for a month. I'd worn the magnolia dress and Buck's brooch, and Fran had attended me. She and Graham would be next, then Charley and Cathy. The entail had been broken, and Maidenstane was no longer mine. Elizabeth had met a doctor in Perth and would soon become his wife. The two Forbes boys were in Edinburgh, at the Royal College of Surgeons. They were not so gay and wild as they had been. Their father approved the change, but I was a little sorry for them. Angus put flowers on She-She's grave. No one, apart from the Drummonds and the Grahams, had known her other face.

The pale, dead grass reminded me of my last sight of her. The watery outlines of distant mountains accentuated that shiver of the heart and senses. The brown face of bracken torn by the wind was the very color of her eyes; the glinting savagery of the Leny falls held the same peaty effect. She had loved me a little, hadn't she?

The hills, gray velvet powdered with gold dust, held their secrets as Shiona had kept hers. It couldn't matter too much, for I was beloved. I really was . . .

We came into Callander. The painted MacGregor on the inn sign was redly ferocious in the sunlight. He seemed to watch, with approval, the postal barrow that trundled along the quiet street and was covered with his own tartan. The barrow took up its position. It must be waiting for the coach which would bring letters from the North, from Inverness and Perth, and disgorge its passengers to be fed hastily on ale and oatmeal bread and pigeon pie. The picture of Queen Victoria would frown over the meat and whiskey, the oranges and preserved fruit.

Buck went into the shop which was the object of our visit, and I waited, on Fleur, thinking about our prospective visit to

Berwick in the spring. We were going when the fair was in town. I wanted to hear the hurdy-gurdies, see the dark gypsy faces, the circling horses and swans. Kate was to come from London in the summer for two or three weeks.

The sound of the approaching coach broke into my dreamy reflections. People appeared in doorways and in the square. I saw the horses first, all black, their nostrils ejecting clouds of steam in the sharp air, then the dark bulk of the conveyance, the roof passengers wrapped in cloaks and huddled in plaids.

The door opened and a woman began to descend. Her loud, bullying voice carried to where I waited under a linden tree, a voice that was familiar. 'Get a move on, McNab! You must find us a place and order the meal. I have to go into this shop. And make sure we have the best table. I shall complain, never fear, if you neglect in your duties.'

Mrs. Leitch! I had almost forgotten her, but the train journey came back to my mind, her ungraciousness, her abandonment of me at Waverley, her hardness and lack of feeling.

Miss McNab climbed down and stood on the cobbles. She looked older and tireder than when I last saw her. I fancied there was a shade of desperation in the curve of her back, the set of her mouth. She began to hurry toward the doorway of the inn and I was stricken with pity. Dismounting swiftly from Fleur, I looped her rein over the post and began to hurry after the companion.

'Miss McNab! Miss McNab! Just a minute!'

She slowed and stopped, looking over her shoulder in a worried fashion that made me more sorry for her than ever. She didn't recognize me, obviously, for my hair was up and my face shaded by the brim of the riding hat.

'Miss McNab,' I said gently. 'Do you remember me? Maggie Stewart?'

She frowned briefly, then her face lightened into a smile. 'Why yes! The young lady in our charge on the train from Berwick. It was wrong of us to leave you and your uncle not there – '

'Not you. We know who it was, don't we?'

She paled a little. 'Oh, dear! I ought to be in there, doing something about luncheon – '

'Let her wait for once. Only, of course, it's you who'll suffer.' A wonderful idea had come to me and I laughed out loud. 'Why not let her wait forever, Miss McNab?'

'If only I could.' She bit her lip and her brown eyes misted over for a moment.

'You could. I'm not Miss Stewart any longer. I'm Mrs. Graham. Mrs. Buchanan Graham. My husband's in there. How would you like to work for us instead? We need – will be needing – a nanny. We intend to have lots of children and I'll never be able to manage alone. I feel we'll get along very well together. Do you think you could tear yourself away from Mrs. Leitch? You could help me in other ways until the babies make their appearance. What do you think? If you make up your mind quickly, Buck, that's my husband, could lift down your boxes before Mrs. Leitch comes back. If you'd rather just disappear? It would be such fun, wouldn't it?'

Her poor face crumpled, then straightened out again. It looked so different that I was amazed. Then she grinned as she'd done when we parted at Waverley. 'I'll come to work for you, Mrs. Graham. I'd go to work for the Devil to be rid of her –'

'That won't be necessary.'

Buck was looking around the square. He saw me and began to come toward us, carrying a parcel, which I took from him, my words of explanation tumbling out in a spate. 'So you see why you have to hurry, don't you? Miss McNab will show you which luggage is hers.'

'There isn't much time. Only one bag.' Her eyes pleaded.

He stood there for a minute, staring at us both, then he burst out laughing. 'Why, you unscrupulous little minx! I didn't think you had it in you. But I'm glad you have.' He held out his arm and Miss McNab took it gratefully.

It was the work of two seconds to remove the portmanteau and to guide Miss McNab into the hotel, from the windows of which we were able to enjoy all of Mrs. Leitch's frenzied disbelief. We laughed until I thought we should be sick. Long after the coach had resumed its journey, my sides ached with renewed hysteria.

Buck was utterly charming to our new nurse over luncheon. I did wonder what he would say when I explained Miss McNab's future duties. I gave him a sidelong look and caught his eyes on mine, no longer amused, but filled with something more than affection. Much, much more. Perhaps it was the effect of the wine or the sight of the wild, flaunting hedges beyond the houses, the silver water and black trees, but sud-

206

denly, there was no one else in the world, only Buck and I saying nothing – and everything.

There would be children, of course. And perhaps one day I might find out where Prince Charlie's silver was hidden. There was still *temps perdu.*

ROMANTIC SUSPENSE FROM CORONET

DOROTHY EDEN

☐	00320 0	The Bird in the Chimney	60p
☐	01923 9	Whistle for the Crows	65p
☐	10768 5	Listen to Danger	60p
☐	12778 3	The Pretty Ones	60p

ELIZABETH PETERS

☐	19678 5	Borrower of the Night	40p
☐	19677 7	The Jackal's Head	40p
☐	19934 2	Shadows in the Moonlight	60p

PHYLLIS WHITNEY

☐	12503 9	The Winter People	60p
☐	19861 3	Columbella	60p
☐	15713 1	Seven Tears for Apollo	60p

All these books are available at your local bookshop or newsagent, or can be ordered direct from the publisher. Just tick the titles you want and fill in the form below.

Prices and availability subject to change without notice.

CORONET BOOKS, P.O. Box 11, Falmouth, Cornwall.

Please send cheque or postal order, and allow the following for postage and packing:

U.K. – One book 22p plus 10p per copy for each additional book ordered, up to a maximum of 82p.

B.F.P.O. and EIRE – 22p for the first book plus 10p per copy for the next 6 books, thereafter 4p per book.

OTHER OVERSEAS CUSTOMERS – 30p for the first book and 10p per copy for each additional book.

Name ....

Address ....

....